HACKNEY LIBRARY SERVICES

Please return this book to any library in Hackney, on or before the
last date stamped. Fines may be charged if it is late. Avoid fines by
renewing the book (subject to it NOT being reserved).

Call th[...]

People who a[...] ed

15

03/06/18		

⊖ Hackney

SATANS AND SHAITANS

OBINNA UDENWE

JACARANDA
LONDON

First published in this edition in Great Britain 2014 by
Jacaranda Books Art Music Ltd
5 Achilles Road
London NW6 1DZ

www.jacarandabooksartmusic.co.uk

A CIP catalogue record for this book is available from the British Library

ISBN: 978 1 909762 05 3
eISBN: 978 1 909762 11 4

Typeset in the UK by James Nunn in Sabon 12pt/16pt

Printed and bound in Great Britain by CPI Group (UK) Ltd,
Croydon, CR0 4YY

MIX
Paper from
responsible sources
FSC® C020471

…because you force us to listen to your stories –
and we laugh
Ifunanya Anastecia Udenwe

... And tell of matters of life and death
How he can't wait to burst into flames
Taking his countrymen along with him.

Blind Bartimaeus
Funminiyi Omojola

PROLOGUE

In the year 2009 AD God looked down to the earth and saw Satan's plot to put evil in the heart of men. The evil was to come in the form of terrorism. And the war, having started in the Middle East, was meandering like river courses down through Asia, America, Africa, everywhere. God looked the other way. After all, was it not His world? Had He not the power and prerogative to allow the Satan He had trampled on to mess around a little?

Satan, having completed the weaving of his plots, and knowing that he would not regain his freedom until man rejected him, blew his plots out from his mouth, in the form of hot air of deceit. Some men who were the followers of Jesus Christ inhaled the air – and, filled with the quest for power, fame and wealth, embraced it with utmost magnanimity.

That same year, *Shaitan* whispered into the hearts of a few men who were the followers of the teachings of the Prophet Muhammad, peace be upon him:

… do you not want power, fame and wealth? I will provide for you the means… reject Christianity. Fight the Government…

And a marriage was woven between the souls of these men. And they derailed from the ways of the great holy prophets.

And evil was born.

SECTION ONE

MISSING

Then I saw an angel coming down from heaven,
holding in his hand the key to the bottomless pit and
a great chain. And he seized the dragon, that ancient
serpent, who is the devil and Satan, and bound him
for a thousand years, and threw him into the pit, and
shut it and sealed it over him, so that he might not
deceive the nations any longer, until the thousand
years were ended. After that he must be released for
a little while.

Revelation 20:1–3
The Holy Bible

ONE

The house where the girl lived was quiet. All the maids were calm. The two security men, one of whom doubled as the gateman, were silent. They sat on the cushions in the large sitting room. Their eyes showed fear. The gateman was worried; he had his hands on his head the whole time. He was not sitting like the others but stood in the corner of the room, just beside the entrance. The gateman was of average height and dark in complexion, with eyes that bulged as if about to jump out of their sockets. He had a little potbelly that looked like a beehive. He wore a uniform with a badge saying *Towers Security*. His boots looked larger than his feet and the sleeves of his shirt were longer than his arms. The oldest woman among them sat on the edge of the leather sofa, just beside the telephone on a side stool. Her name was Miss Spencer, and her left hand was on top of the phone while the other hand flipped through the large book on her lap. The other maids occasionally stared at one another. Miss Spencer picked up the receiver and dialled the number of the divisional police office. She turned on the speaker of the phone and a thick male voice said, 'Hello.'

Miss Spencer did not know how to begin. She took a deep breath. 'Good morning, Sir. Is that the police?'

The silence in the room surpassed that of a graveyard. The strain in Miss Spencer's eyes showed that she had not slept. There were no sounds from the television in Adeline's room and no muffled noise of pages turning from her frequent novel reading binges. This new silence, a product of Adeline's absence, unnerved her. They had phoned all of the Chubas' friends but got negative responses. Miss Spencer had to make another call, a very difficult one – she needed to call Evangelist Chris Chuba. The entrance of a stern-looking man with a cleanly shaved head, wearing a starched black uniform, interrupted her.

'I am Officer Leonard Omelu, the DPO, Ishieke Police Division. Our station received a call to come to this household—'

'Yes, I called. My name is Miss Spencer. I work for the Chuba family. I have a report to make – our mistress is missing.'

'Mistress?'

'Yes, Sir. The Evangelist's daughter, Adeline, is missing.'

'The Evangelist's daughter?'

Miss Spencer sighed impatiently. 'Yes.'

'When did you see her last?'

'We haven't seen her since…' she looked at the others in the room. They all looked away, avoiding her eyes. 'Since yesterday afternoon.'

There was a pause.

'What about the Evangelist?'

'He is not in the country now, Sir.'

'And the girl's mother?'

'Madam travelled with the Evangelist.'

There was a brief pause.

'Chris Chuba's daughter? *Hmmn?* My God.'

Miss Spencer said nothing. She was sure that the police officer could hear the sound of her heart beating heavily, as if a talking drum was sounding inside it. She wiped some sweat off her brow.

'I want to call my *oga*,' she announced.

'*Heey! Heey!*' one of the maids cried.

'God! We are dead!' the gateman said.

Miss Spencer looked sternly at the staff around her. 'Please be quiet… the line is ringing.'

The humming of the air-conditioner could now be heard as silence enveloped the room. As soon as the thick masculine voice of the Evangelist said hello, Miss Spencer placed the phone on loudspeaker.

'Sir… Sir… good morning, Sir.'

'Miss Spencer… Ah, good of you to have called. Is everything all right? You rarely call me when I travel—'

'Sir. Please… Sir… there is trouble—'

'What's happened, Spencer?'

'Adeline, Sir. Our Adeline is missing... We have not seen Adeline since yesterday afternoon—'

'Are you drunk, Spencer?'

'No, Sir. But—'

'Are you sick?'

'No, *oga*.'

'Then where is Adeline? Where is my daughter?'

'Adeline... we haven't seen her since yesterday.'

'Jesus! Jesus!'

'Sir, we have called everyone. We don't know where she is—'

'When did Adeline leave the house? When, Spencer?' the Evangelist yelled at the woman.

'Sir—'

'Spencer? Spencer? My God. Spencer?'

The Evangelist fell silent until Miss Spencer feared he was no longer on the line. 'Sir,' she began tentatively, 'we have the DPO here.'

'Put him on the line!' the Evangelist snapped. Miss Spencer passed the phone to Officer Leonard, watching as the man tried to speak but was prevented by the screaming voice of Evangelist Chuba barking demands on the other end of the line. Suddenly the screaming stopped, and Leonard returned the phone to her, realizing Chuba had hung up.

TWO

Miss Spencer was the only one who saw Adeline leave when it was drizzling in the late afternoon of the previous day. Adeline had told her she was going out with Donaldo, her boyfriend. Donaldo had not come into the house, and Miss Spencer had not seen him. She hadn't seen his Volkswagen Bug either. Perhaps he'd parked outside the gate, she'd thought. Miss Spencer remembered that her mistress was sulking when she left. And there was neither laughter nor smiles as she ran out of the house, into the compound and down the gravelled drive that led to the gate a few metres away.

'Tell no one I have left. I will be back in a jiffy. Before you even know I'm gone, I'll be back,' Adeline had told her, and hugged the elderly woman. Now, if the young girl's life was in danger, her own life was in danger too. Miss Spencer was the only one who knew when Adeline had left and where she'd said she was going. But how could she break her promise and tell the others? It would

17

also amount to doom for her if their master found out about the secrets they kept.

As Leonard walked up to one of his officers, who was waiting to speak to him, the door opened and a very handsome young man walked in and went straight to Miss Spencer. They hugged and he whispered in her ear, then sat down on one of the cushions close to the entrance.

'What is it, officer?' Leonard asked.

'We want to search the girl's room, Sir.'

'Go ahead,' he consented, then looking in Miss Spencer's direction he asked, 'It's not locked?'

'It's open. Please, don't disorganize the room.' Miss Spencer was sitting on a stool, the other maids clustered around her. What they did not know was that very early in the morning before calling the police, Miss Spencer had gone into Adeline's room and removed everything – all the portraits and drawings and artworks made by Donaldo, who was avoiding eye contact with the others. He was crying.

Leonard called over Officer Jubril, a tall man whose dark complexion showed that he was Hausa, while the other policemen, about seven of them, busied themselves combing the house.

'Listen up, I want you all to co-operate with us. Help us and we will find your Adeline for you. All right?' His eyes wandered to a framed photo that hung neatly on the wall.

He pointed at the photograph. 'Is that Adeline?'

'Yes,' about three people responded at the same time.

He walked up to one of the girls. 'When did you last see Adeline?'

'Ha, *oga*, master. I did not see her for the whole of yesterday,' the maid replied.

'Why?' He was looking at her mouth.

'Because I went on errands very early in the morning after I returned from morning mass. I did not come back till evening. When I asked about my madam, Miss Spencer here' – she pointed at her – 'told me she was not yet back.'

Leonard straightened his crisp shirt and asked, 'What is your name?'

'Michelle Ugbala, Sir.'

Leonard saw the crucifix around the young woman's neck.

'You are Catholic?'

Miss Spencer made a sound between her lips, unimpressed by the laborious questioning. Leonard looked briefly in her direction before turning back to Michelle and signalling her to answer.

'Yes,' Michelle replied, 'a devout Catholic. I don't miss my mass, Sir.'

'I see.'

There was another young woman sitting close to Michelle. Leonard looked at her and asked, 'What is your name?'

'Demola.'

'When did you last see Adeline?'

'I saw her in the afternoon, yesterday. I gave her cold tea. My small madam loves cold tea, a lot.'

'Where was she then?'

'In her room.'

'At what time?'

'I don't know!' She folded her hands to hide their trembling. 'It was before lunch was ready.'

'Did she eat lunch? And when does she normally eat?'

'1.30. But the lunch would be ready before 12 – in case small madam was hungry.'

'And you saw her eat?'

'No, Sir. I was doing my laundry.'

'But you saw her when she left the house?'

'No, Sir—'

'By the way, what are you to Adeline?'

'I am her nurse, Sir.'

The officer paused at hearing that. He wondered how many young Nigerian girls had resident nurses. He watched the faces of all the people gathered in the room. He needed to be a little tough, he thought.

'You are Yoruba?'

'Yes, Sir.'

'Which state are you from?'

'Oyo State, Sir.' She was sweating. Officer Jubril recorded that.

'How far is Oyo from Ebonyi State?'

'I don't know exactly, but very far, Sir.'

'If you tell us lies and we find out, we might lock you up and deal with you, young woman. Can you imagine how long it will take your people to come and save you from Oyo?'

The nurse was breathing very hard, looking at Miss Spencer and at Donaldo. 'Sir, please. I didn't see her leave the house. Please.'

'I think you are intimidating my girls, Mr Leonard,' Miss Spencer said. She was ignored.

Officer Leonard stared at another maid before asking, 'What is your name?'

'*Oga*, my name na Ngozi.' Her pidgin was thick. Ngozi wore a flowered shirt and a black skirt. Leonard noticed that the collar of her shirt was dirty.

'Where did she say she was going to when she left?'

'Me I no see her leave, *oga*. But I dey when she chop for afternoon. Na me comot the plates. I no see small madam again.'

'You are supposed to be Miss Adeline's maid?'

'Yes, *oga*.'

'That is enough,' Miss Spencer interjected. She was not about to let the maids be bullied – there was far too much at stake.

Leonard looked at her, then addressed the room. 'I have noticed that you people were not attending to your job of taking care of Adeline, *abi*?' He sat down on a stool close to the gateman, Moses.

Upstairs, the officers searched Adeline's room and her closet, but saw nothing except old clothes. They pulled out all the clothes, searched the drawers, under the bed, the mattress, stripped the bedlinen and searched the shelves.

They were looking for clues, any clue at all. Another officer scanned through a collection of photographs, removing several of Adeline with different people.

Evangelist Chuba lowered himself onto one of the plush leather chairs that decorated the room of the Canadian hotel suite where he was staying with his wife. Since he had ended the call with the officer in Nigeria, tears were rolling down her cheeks and she was asking him lots of questions, but he ignored her.

After a moment, he stood and walked into his own adjoining room and locked the door. He needed to make another call to Nigeria. This one his wife must not hear. His heart was heavy and in anticipation he waited with dread for the line to connect.

'Hello.' The voice on the end of the line was sombre.

'I think it is done.'

'When?' the voice asked.

'I got a call from my household. I called the police too. They are right now in my house questioning my staff.'

'Good. See you soon.'

Chuba was angry. *Is it good that my daughter is gone?* He put down the phone and took a deep breath, turning back towards the room where his distraught wife awaited him.

Leonard turned to the tall lanky man whose shirt bore the badge *Towers Security*, and said, 'So, you are the gateman?'

'Yes, Sir. My name is Moses, Sir. Moses Ukpai.'

'You are with Towers Security?'

'Yes. I did not see Adeline leave, Sir—'

'Did I ask you?' Leonard stood and stared at the gateman, contemplating something. He licked his lips and smiled. 'What is your job here, Moses?' The DPO's eyes caught Donaldo's for the third time. He was struck by the young man's good looks. Donaldo looked away. Nervously Miss Spencer listened.

Moses answered, 'I watch over the gate. My duty is to open and close it, Sir. I also work as a security man, but with this other man...' he pointed at his colleague. 'I was inside the room reading for my GCE exams, Sir. You see, Sir, here in this compound, people don't come in often, so we sometimes leave the small gate open. And we are not afraid of anything. We have not had any trouble before, Sir.'

It had occurred to the DPO as he entered the compound that it did not receive many visitors. Its serenity was striking.

'Does Adeline always leave the compound?'

'*Haa!* No, Sir. She has no need to leave. She has no need for friends. Not at all, Sir.'

The DPO was amused at the idea that she had no need for friends.

'How many people visit her in a month?'

'None.'

'In a month? I need an estimate.' At his side Officer Jubril was still taking notes.

'Sir, if anyone is visiting, it must be to see the Chief

and big madam when they are around. No one has visited Adeline before.' The gateman exchanged glances with Miss Spencer.

'I see. This is a kind of prison, *hmmn*?' No one answered. 'Who is this young man?' he asked, looking at Donaldo.

Before Donaldo could answer, Miss Spencer spoke up. 'He is Chief Amechi's son, a very close family friend.'

'Chief Donald Amechi?'

'Yes.'

Leonard knew who Chief Donald Amechi was. He was one of the most influential politicians in Nigeria.

'Young man, any idea about Adeline's whereabouts?' he asked, focusing his gaze on Donaldo.

Donaldo unfolded his hands and smoothed his hair.

'I do not know, Sir. I heard about her disappearance. I was called and that's why I am here.' The officer was intrigued by his chocolate coloured face, his straight pointed nose and long hair. He deduced that the young man had mixed-racial parentage. He wondered how one person could possess so much beauty.

'Who called you?'

'Miss Spencer.'

Leonard turned to Miss Spencer.

'Why did you call him, Miss Spencer?'

'Like I told you,' she replied, coldly, 'the two families are close. I called to know if she had gone to the Island where the Amechi family live. I guess he is here because he felt concerned.'

'Hmm,' Leonard considered this for a moment, before once again addressing Donaldo, 'so, Donald —'

'Donaldo! My father is Donald.'

'OK, Donaldo, what's your relationship like?'

'With Adeline? Cordial, just cordial. She doesn't have friends that I know of.'

'When was the last time you saw Adeline?'

Donaldo said nothing.

'Think. Think. You must remember.'

'Easter.'

The maids looked at each other. The security man exchanged a glance with the gateman. Officer Leonard scratched at his bushy hair. He stood up and tucked his shirt tightly into his black trousers. He looked at all of them.

'There are possibilities that she was kidnapped from this place since none of you saw her leave. And if so, Moses, I will have you beaten to a pulp, and thrown behind bars. And you, the security man, I will make you a warder inside Kpirikpiri prison at Abakaliki.'

'Sir?'

'*Shhee.*' Leonard placed a finger on his lips. 'Kpirikpiri prison is not far from here. Should I remind you that it is the notorious prison where General Yar'adua died?,' Leonard put both hands inside his trouser pockets.'Think about it. All of you. Have a wonderful day.'

When his boss had finished speaking Jubril grimaced and added, 'I advise that none of you should leave this compound. Nothing should be removed from here.

25

Especially anything that belongs to Adeline. And don't fail to contact us immediately if there is any information.'

Officer Leonard gave Miss Spencer his personal phone number.

'What about journalists?' she asked. 'We don't want them coming here—'

'Journalists?'

'Yes, officer. Our *oga* is an important person. As soon as the news gets out they will invade this place. That… that… will be disastrous.'

Leonard thought about it. What the woman said was true. 'Don't worry about that. We will post an officer at the gate.'

He joined his men who had already climbed into a worn out police van. They sped off, causing dust to rise from the gravel drive into the sunny morning sky.

That morning, a very tall, slim man with broad shoulders lay on a mat in front of a mosque located inside the Centre for Islamic Knowledge. Beside him were the book of Hadith and a Qur'an. His eyes were closed and in his mind roamed thoughts – very strong thoughts – that if said aloud would send shivers down the spine of his followers, his soldiers. The war had begun; the weapons that he had stockpiled were so numerous and so sophisticated that not even those of the Nigerian army could outdo them. He knew that he had power and fame in his hands. He smiled to himself. Everything was possible – all he needed was to believe. No, he smiled to himself; all he needed was to make the five thousand foot soldiers who were loyal to him believe that this war was in the name of Allah. They did not need any incentives. The money his friends in the South had brought to be used to lure the youths into the war had not even been spent. He had simply diverted the money into his Nigerian account.

Just a while longer, he thought, just a while longer and power, fame and fortune would be his. No one needed to know his true motivation, not even his friends in the South, and especially not his soldiers.

He smiled again. Then a young man came to him.

'*As-salamu 'alaykum*, Sheikh.'

He startled. Who dared to disturb his meditations? He sat up and his face brightened.

'Oh, it is you, Musa.' He smiled. '*Salam.*'

'Yes, Sheikh, it is me.' The young man bowed a little.

'Please sit.'

'I cannot sit beside my Sheikh.'

'Your Sheikh understands that you do him great honour. I know that your loyalty stretches to the shores of India.'

The young man sat down. 'My journey was successful. I have come to do the will of the Almighty.'

The Sheikh smiled broadly. He took the two hands of the young man into his and said, 'You do not know… you do not have any idea what great work you are about to do. What you are bound to gain when you complete the task before you, Musa. Listen to me, brother, in Sunnah al-Tirmidhi it is narrated that the least reward for the people of heaven is eighty thousand servants and seventy-two wives, over which stands a dome of pearls, aquamarines and rubies.'

The young man's face radiated happiness.

'I am made bold by your words, my Sheikh.'

Later that morning, Evangelist Chris Chuba rang the Governor of Ebonyi State, where the town of Ishieke was situated. His wife had started packing, even though her husband had not informed his staff to get his jet ready. The Evangelist had locked his room again. When the Governor answered, the Evangelist greeted him. 'Peace and love, brother.'

'Peace and love, Evangelist.'

'It seems... that it is done.'

'The solemn offer?'

'Yes.'

'Have you heard from the men sent to do the will of the Sacred Order?'

'No, Your Excellency. But I have received a call from my family. The girl is gone,' Chris Chuba reported with a heavy feeling in his stomach.

He heard the Governor take a deep breath.

'This must be hard for you, brother.'

'Very hard... what do I do? We cannot be sure. The mobiles of the men sent to perform the task are not connecting.'

'We have to take necessary steps nonetheless, Evangelist. The police have been informed, right?'

'Yes, Your Excellency.'

'Then I will call the State Commissioner of Police and ask him to personally take charge.'

The Evangelist rubbed his eyes. He yawned, out of hunger and exhaustion.

'That must be done, Your Excellency.'

'You must not grieve too much. Everything will be all right, Evangelist.'

'Peace and Love, brother.'

'Peace and love, Evangelist.'

The Ebonyi State Governor ordered the Commissioner of Police to take charge of the case. The Commissioner deployed four armed policemen at the gate of the Chubas' residence and ordered that no journalist should be allowed to get into the compound.

THREE

A swift wind swept up dust from the ground. It rattled the aluminium roofs. Children played about in the compound of the Centre for Islamic Knowledge. Some *Almajiri* walked in carrying plastic plates. They were talking excitedly. Sheikh Mohammed Seko sat on a mat in front of the mosque, with Abouzeid, his deputy, and one other man. Some children were reciting *anasheed*.

> Allah is the greatest
> Allah is the greatest
> There is no God except Allah
> Allah is the greatest
> Allah is the greatest
> Glory be to Allah…

The Sheikh recalled when he was an *Almajiri*. It was a long time ago. They were sweet and bitter memories.

The Nigerian Government had reneged on their truce with Jama'atul al-Mujahideen Jihad. They'd paid the terrorist organization to cease fire, and when they did, the army had clamped down on the terrorists' base in Yobe and shot everyone. Everyone. Then, they set the place ablaze. The terrorists' contact in the South had given them orders to resume operations.

'Abouzeid, we have orders to resume attacks as soon as we can.'

'Good. I have been itching for war.'

'At their end, our friends in the South are tightening up some huge bolts in Government. Big changes are coming, changes that will benefit our mission.'

Abouzeid sat up straight. He was curious. 'What is their plan, my Sheikh?'

'*Insha' Allah*, the House of Representatives will move a motion to impeach the President. We must increase our operations so that the whole world will see that the President is weak. *Kajiko!* That is why the new attack is important. We have a new order to attack in the heart of Government. We will strike right in the seat of power.'

Sheikh Seko wore a white turban, a *quftan* and a *gibba*. His *masbaha* of nintey-nine beads was in his hands. He had been through it twice, and was fingering it for a third time. A big Qur'an sat beside him. Some young men carrying Kalashnikovs loitered about. Abouzeid was dressed in a long gown and his head was covered with a red and white *kufiyya*. His face looked so young and handsome. The other man with them had just joined them from Yobe. He was the second in command there and had not been at the camp during the attack.

A very dark man in his fifties approached them and the Sheikh motioned him to join them on the mat. The man, who spoke fluent English and seemed highly educated, said, 'All the Southerners in Yobe and Maiduguri have been evacuated. The Southerners are fools. They are foreigners in a land, yet they build industries, petrol stations, big hotels, and mansions. Now they will have to carry them on their heads. They cannot go to their churches again because we have bombed almost all of them.'

'*Alhamdulillah!* That is the goal. That is the objective of Jama'atul al-Mujahideen Jihad! May Allah guide our paths!'

'He is with us.'

'Now, listen everyone. The explosive is ready. It was finished yesterday in Abuja. The boys are ready to move back to the university from the flat. Our *Ustaz* said that the fortunate one must leave for Abuja in a couple of days.'

Abouzeid's eyes lit up in excitement. 'Who is it this time?'

Sheikh Seko paused before replying. 'I do not want to bother you with this. It is better you do not know till the job is completed.' But he did not name the person because he did not trust anyone. Not even Abouzeid. The first *intifada* in Kano had failed because they had trusted someone too deeply.

Abouzeid looked at the man sitting beside him. The man's eyes glowed with radiance. Abouzeid knew then

32

that he must be the martyr. It must be him. Otherwise why did the Sheikh permit him to share their discussions?

'Where is the target, my Sheikh?'

'The target is a place they call Shoprite.'

Abouzeid had seen one of the massive shopping malls in Lagos when he'd travelled to every state around the country to meet some of their men who were working on establishing their bases there. Their mujahideen were scattered in most states in Southern Nigeria as sleepers – waiting for a signal to carry out attacks. Abouzeid was jubilant. He smiled wryly. 'Those who falsely claim to follow Isa son of Maryam will surely bleed this time.'

'Yes. We will be triumphant.'

Abouzeid stood to allow the two men to talk alone. The martyr must be briefed and guided by the Sheikh. When he left, the Sheikh looked the older man in the eyes and said, 'In the Holy Book of the Qur'an it says "fight in the cause of Allah and know that Allah is hearing and knowing".'

Evangelist Chris Chuba and his wife returned to Nigeria from Canada, and the church sent a convoy to pick them up from the airport. The Evangelist was a celebrity, but the difference between him and other celebrities in Nigeria was that anywhere in the world his name was mentioned, men trembled in adoration. He was handsome, tall and huge. He walked like he was Jesus of Nazareth. He was so rich that money made him stink and people just kept on donating to his church. Every month his network of church branches all over the world remitted many thousands of dollars to his treasury.

When the Evangelist and his wife entered their large compound, Mrs Chuba could not wait for the jeep to stop before she rushed into the house. She ran straight to her daughter's room, followed by devoted churchwomen singing hymns. The church pastors had admonished everyone to stay awake and pray against the great temptation Satan was bringing into the folds of the Christian faith. The superintendents had told the congregation that if Adeline was not found, it could seriously hinder further development of their church.

At the door, the women were turned back by a guard who stood outside Adeline's room. Mrs Chuba held her daughter's clothes and wailed. She cried till all the tears in her eyes were exhausted. Her husband could hear her cry but chose to ignore her. He had watched his wife while they were on the plane and in the vehicle and had seen how she had wanted so much to cry. He thought it would do her good.

The police were combing the town and its suburbs without luck. Chris Chuba had finally asked the police to place pictures of Adeline in the media and a substantial reward was announced for anyone who knew her whereabouts or had information that could lead to her location, but no one seemed to know the girl in the pictures. In town, people gossiped. They had often heard about the Evangelist's beautiful daughter, but very few had ever seen her face.

It was less than two days since the case had been reported and Officer Leonard was already so preoccupied with the investigation that he had abandoned all other tasks. He went home late and rose for work very early.

Leonard was not a tall man. This made him self-conscious – as if to compensate, he was known for his aggressiveness and the harsh way he spoke to his men. He was also thorough and took his job seriously. Leonard had studied Geology at university but joined the police force because there were no other jobs on offer when he graduated. By the time he left Police Training College he had fallen in love with the job and he became so dedicated to his work that in a few years he had risen through the ranks to become a District Police Officer. His black uniform was always starched and ironed by his wife, a banker. He shaved his head every Wednesday and Saturday. The fact that he had no child contributed to his devotion to work – for whenever he thought about his misfortune, he would throw all his mental and physical energy into his role to escape the worries of a childless man, a man whose wife was operated on a year after their marriage to remove a large tumour from her stomach.

Five men climbed down from the police Hilux van. Two were from the State Security Service, another two were from the Criminal Investigation Department of the police headquarters, and Leonard was the fifth. He had insisted that he was going to lead the investigation since Adeline's disappearance had happened in his jurisdiction. The Evangelist saw them from the balcony of his room but wanted them to wait. DPO Leonard took a walk round the compound after he was informed that the Evangelist was busy but would join them shortly. He studied the garden – there were cycads and canna lilies everywhere. Fig trees were planted close to the wall and bougainvillea lined the walls near the gate. By the pool, he saw some Queen of Philippines orchids and several guava trees. He came back just as his men were entering the house.

'Good to see you, officers.' The Evangelist shook hands with them. He wore a very white, sparkling robe and was holding a King James Bible. It was the evening of the day he had returned to the country. Leonard looked intently at the Evangelist, who had taken a seat, noticing that he looked tired but also that he seemed too handsome to be human. *No wonder people worship him and tremble when he preaches*, he thought. Chuba looked more angelic and attractive than his photographs suggested.

'How was your trip, Sir?'

'Fine, thank you. Do sit down, please. Which one of you is Officer Leonard?'

Leonard remained standing. 'I am, Sir.'

The Evangelist was quiet for a long time, then asked,

'What is going on? I need to know how far you have got with the investigation.'

'You see, Sir, it's not been as easy as you might think. This case is far more difficult than we had envisaged.' He coughed. The clock in the room ticked. He spotted a large framed photo of the Evangelist with his daughter on the wall just beside the clock. 'Sir, we thought that by now the abductors… that is, if Adeline was abducted… the abductors would have made a demand. They would have asked for a ransom, owing to who her father is and all. This is the third day of her disappearance. So, Sir, we are keeping our eyes and ears open.'

One of the men, a CID officer with a protruding stomach, cleared his throat and said, 'Sir, so far, we have interrogated your two security men. We picked them up yesterday evening. They were released this afternoon. But we are keeping them under surveillance.'

The Evangelist sighed. 'Those men. Those men. You cannot believe how much I pay those two.'

'Sir, your security men were thoroughly interrogated, but so far we couldn't find out anything from them. We will also be watching their every move.'

'So this is all there is to it since my daughter went missing on Monday?'

The men were silent.

'This is rubbish!'

Chuba rose and walked away without saying another word.

FOUR

Leonard and Jubril entered the Chubas' large sitting room in a hurry. Chris Chuba had seen them drive in and came down to receive them. It had been less than fifteen minutes since Leonard had called him to say that they had a good lead.

Two young men dressed in tight fitting polo shirts were also in the room. Yesterday, Leonard had seen about six bodyguards in the compound but none in the sitting room.

'Sir, we would like Madam to be present,' he said.

'Sampson! Get Madam,' Chuba commanded one of his guards, who in turn signalled to his colleague, who rushed upstairs.

'My wife's been crying. This has really broken her.' Chuba paused. 'I too have not been myself since I heard the news.'

Miss Spencer entered with the nurse and the maids. They stood beside the door leading to the dining room.

'It's all right, Sir, we are making some progress. We

have questioned all your house staff,' Leonard said, with a sweeping glance at those gathered in the room, 'and it seems none of them knows much about your daughter's possible whereabouts.'

The Evangelist looked at Miss Spencer sceptically.

Leonard continued. 'This is the fourth day, but still no one has called for a ransom. We are still thinking that this is not a kidnapping. Now tell us, Sir, we need to know more about your daughter. Her friends, or any one close to her that she could have visited.'

One of the maids tried to speak but Chuba broke in, silencing her. Miss Spencer had warned them that it would cause them a big problem if they told anyone about Adeline's relationship with Donaldo. It would make the Evangelist very angry. He had always preached against waywardness, and Adeline was taught to believe in no other person but Jesus Christ, her parents and Miss Spencer.

'See, officer, my daughter rarely left this house… she has everything here. Everything.'

'Are you sure, Sir?'

'Oh, don't be ridiculous. Of course I am. For heaven's sake, the girl in question is my daughter. I know her too well. I brought her up in the ways of our Lord.'

Mrs Chuba came down, followed by the bodyguard. She looked bedraggled, dressed in a brown nightgown with her hair dishevelled and her eyes swollen and red. She sat beside her husband.

Officer Leonard dipped his hand into his pocket and brought out a letter that Jubril had found in Adeline's room, assuming it to be written by the girl herself. It seemed she had copied it out and then sent the original, leaving the draft inside one of her novels.

'Sir, is this your daughter's handwriting?' He handed the piece of paper to Chuba who looked at it carefully, but was not sure. He gave it to his wife who was sitting quietly on the sofa clutching Adeline's picture, but she was not sure either. She handed it over to Miss Spencer.

Miss Spencer knew that it was Adeline's handwriting. '*Uhmn*. I don't think so.'

'What do you mean you don't think so, Spencer?' the Evangelist barked.

'I can't be sure, Sir.' She was worried about what the letter said.

'Then give it back to your boss to read,' Leonard ordered. Chuba read it. It was a love letter but addressed to no one.

'Sir, do you think your daughter has a boyfriend?'

Chuba was enraged. 'Listen to me, Mr Man! My daughter has no boyfriend. Someone must have kidnapped my daughter!' He was furious and embarrassed by the letter.

'What about the letter?'

'It could be she was just writing a story. This letter isn't addressed to anyone.' He looked at Miss Spencer, then at his wife and then back at the letter.

'Sir? I would appreciate it if information is not hidden from us.' Leonard looked at all the people gathered in the room. 'If she was kidnapped as you think, her abductors would have made demands by now. I sense something fishy. We cannot pinpoint it because I sense conspiracy. High level conspiracy.'

'What if Adeline was abducted by ritual killers? It happens in this country. We... we need to keep every option on the table.'

'Eh!' Mrs Chuba screamed in anguish at her husband's words.

'Sir, that is a possibility. But we also know that ritual killers abduct people in the streets. With the information we have from your staff, it seems that Adeline didn't leave this house to go anywhere.'

'It is clear now that she did.'

'We will find out soon. But ritual killers don't wake up, take their bath and walk into a wealthy man's house, risking all the security,' Leonard looked pointedly at Moses and the other security man and went on, '... and kidnap his daughter. There is more to this than meets the eye, Sir.'

Leonard sensed that he was going to get nothing further from the household and, sighing, made a move to leave. 'Please, do keep us informed. This will be an extensive investigation, but we cannot investigate thoroughly if information is withheld.' He shook hands with the Evangelist and as he reached to retrieve the letter, Chuba tore it into shreds.

Leonard was dumbfounded. 'Sir, you have just destroyed evidence that could have led us to her. With all due respect, you are obstructing the police from carrying out an investigation that could save your daughter. I can get you arrested for this.' He was angry, but even he recognized the emptiness of his threat. He turned and beckoned to Jubril. They walked away. The whole house was quiet.

When the policemen left, Chuba exploded. 'Rubbish! Rubbish! I can't have the police thinking that my daughter is wayward just because they have a mere letter. In a matter of seconds, the media would be broadcasting it on air.' He turned to his staff standing before him. 'And now, I need a detailed report on who has been coming here and the number of times Adeline has left the house. Where she went to and why.' With that he headed upstairs to take a shower.

Sampson and the other bodyguard left the sitting room and went outside.

'Get me a glass of cold water,' Mrs Chuba demanded once the Evangelist was gone. All the maids rushed out at once. Moses left with the other security man. Miss Spencer came close to her madam. Hugging her, Mrs Chuba sobbed.

'Now, Spencer, tell me about her. Tell me about my daughter.'

Miss Spencer was in her room, weeping bitterly. Donaldo called her often and she was happy when he called. When everyone had gone to bed, she would bring out Adeline's portrait and stare at it till her sobs could be heard from upstairs.

That night, Mrs Chuba sat on her wide matrimonial bed. She had just finished saying her rosary. She had been a Catholic before she married the Evangelist, but her husband hated the rosary, so she only said it when she was in trouble and he was not around.

The door opened silently and she hid the rosary under her pillow. Her husband entered carrying his Bible.

'Woman, I think I have told you to stop crying. All will be fine.' He sat on the bed beside her.

'When? The letter the policemen found, it worries me. Was Adeline seeing someone?'

'You are her mother.'

She stared at her husband with disdain. 'Oh, Chris. You break my heart with your words.' She began to cry. The Evangelist ignored her. 'Nwuzo wrote to someone saying that we never cared for her, that we love evangelical work more than we love her. That... that we placed her in the care of maids and forgot—'

'Her name is Adeline. Stop calling her Nwuzo. I have been telling you this for close to nineteen years now.'

'What happened to my daughter?' She stared with rheumy eyes at her husband. 'That letter... it worries me. We caused this. If we had stayed here more. Cared more for Nwuzo... Perhaps travelled with her—'

'Please! You are making me feel guilty. She is not dead yet. And her name is Adeline! Stop calling her that local name of yours!' Chuba stood up angrily and undid his nightrobe.

'How sure are we that she isn't dead? It's your fault.

Has it ever occurred to you that she might have committed suicide, drowned or something? Has it?'

'My fault? My fault? Oh, don't make me mad tonight!'

He paced around the bedroom, scratching his head. He tried to take his mind off the letter and what his wife had said. They had both thought they had given their daughter abundant care, protection and love. But now they knew how wrong they were. *If we could have a second chance*, he thought, *we would make things right*. But something deeper than that was bothering him.

Finally, he lay down on the bed and allowed his mind to drift away, back into the past.

Evangelist Chris Chuba recalled how Chief Donald Amechi had approached him one evening, just as the sun was setting. He had been sitting in the gazebo, watching *asha* birds weave their nests on the branches of gmelina trees, his King James Bible lying beside him. The Chief, a tall striking man, came into the garden and walked straight to where he was sitting. They shook hands firmly, locked their fingers and gently released them while making a clicking sound with the thumb and the forefinger.

The Chief stared him straight in the eyes. Chuba looked away, fearing the bad news the visitor bore.

'The sacrifice is being delayed—'

The Evangelist interrupted. 'I know. Do you think it is easy?'

'I know it is not easy. You are listed in *Forbes* as

the wealthiest God's messenger alive. You command respect. Your fame stretches to the horizon. All these gifts were bestowed on you by the Sacred Order of the Universal Forces. What you possess in fame, fortune and success, surpasses that of the President of the United States. There is no country in the world where hundreds of thousands of people of various religions do not lie at your feet to receive your miracles and wonders… all this, the Sacred Order did for you. What does the Order ask in return?' Amechi came close to him to emphasize his point. He whispered but his voice was still deep and rich. 'A sacrifice, but not a yearly sacrifice like small occult groups request. The Order requests a solemn sacrifice every seven years from you. Seven years, Evangelist. Seven years. This is another seventh year. Is it too much to ask? That you give your daughter, is it too much to ask?'

Tears came to the Evangelist's eyes. 'My Lord, it is but a little sacrifice.' His heart disagreed with him. 'But my heart is heavy. She is the only one that I have.' He looked at the tree before him, at the birds flying freely into the air, calling to each other. Oh, how he wanted to be as free as those birds, but his soul had been sold years ago and in return he had what only a handful of men had had, since the creation of the world.

Chief Amechi spoke again. 'Brother. What will be, will be. Wait no longer or you will dance to the music. That is the message from the Universal Temple. My duty is to deliver it, brother.' He smiled and turned to leave.

Evangelist Chuba stared at his friend as he walked away. Whenever he brought messages of this kind, the Chief never exchanged pleasantries or discussed other business.

FIVE

Ever since Adeline had gone missing, days had turned into nights in Donaldo's life. He'd stopped eating and when he managed to take anything, he ate only a little. He talked to no one, not even to Madam Vero, the housekeeper.

Madam Vero was worried. She had no idea what was wrong with him. He was hiding so many things from her – including the beautiful girl he had once mentioned to her. Indeed, she did not even know that this beautiful girl was the Chubas' missing daughter.

Donaldo had not dreamt of Adeline since she disappeared, though he desperately wanted to. He missed her like a mother would miss a dead infant. He felt her all around him. Always. But then, Adeline's lovely face began to vanish from his memory, confused with other, darker images. Yet, at other times, it would be so clear and defined that he would almost go mad. Donaldo would feel Adeline's presence and fear would grip him and constrict his breathing.

Donaldo was in his room, filled with pain and loss and fear, when three jeeps sped into the compound and parked in front of his father's mansion. Six bodyguards – hefty men, openly carrying pistols – jumped out of the front and rear jeeps. A thickset man got out of the passenger side of the middle vehicle and opened the rear door – Chris Chuba emerged clutching a Bible by his side.

Donaldo's father, Chief Donald Amechi, came out of the house to meet the Evangelist. They didn't exchange greetings but hurried into the Chief's library and locked the door behind them.

'Peace and love, brother.'

'It is an honour to have you.' Chief Amechi held his friend's hand. 'You are overwhelmed, my friend.'

'You have no idea, Donald.'

The Chief released the Evangelist's hand, walked round his imposing desk and sat down on his swivel chair. 'Sit. Sit,' he said.

Chuba sat, placing his Bible on the desk. The Chief looked at the Bible and said nothing.

'I am confused, Donald. I should have heard something by now.'

'Me too. Now I have news about the men sent to do the will of the Sacred Order.'

Chuba's heart began to beat fast as soon as he heard this. He leaned forward, his arms on the desk.

Chief Donald Amechi said, 'They are dead. The men are all dead.'

'Oh my God.'

'Yes.'

'Assassinated?'

'No. They were involved in an accident along the Enugu–Abakaliki expressway. A trailer carrying cement hit their vehicle and they overturned into a ditch. I got the news this morning.'

'And Adeline?' Chuba asked.

Chief Amechi shook his head. 'There was no sign of her. It seems this occurred before they were able to carry out the assignment.'

Evangelist Chris Chuba's world came crumbling down. He stood. He began to sweat. His suit added to his discomfort.

'Turn on the air-conditioner. Please.'

The Chief stood and turned on the machine. The Evangelist began to pace about the room, saying repeatedly, 'Oh my God'.

'It means that your daughter is alive. Somewhere.'

There was a mixture of relief and sadness in the Evangelist's heart. He didn't know whether to laugh or cry. He quickly sat down again. He wiped his forehead with his arm, using the sleeve of his jacket.

'Chief Donald… help me. Help your friend. What do I do now?'

The Chief stammered. 'I – I am as confused as you are. The men died on their way. Yet Adeline is missing. So where is she? I have asked myself this question a million times, Chris. Where is she? I do not know what to tell you. Honestly, I do not know.'

'God!' Chris Chuba inhaled deeply. The tears in his eyes stung him. He knew that a great punishment, a great painful chastisement, awaited him in just a few days if the sacrifice wasn't performed.

'Chris. You must find her—'

Chuba stood in frustration. 'How do I do that? Tell me, how do I do that?'

'What are the police doing?'

'Nothing. They are a bunch of idiots... ignorant, unintelligent fools.'

The Chief was silent. Chuba's right foot tapped the tiled floor repeatedly.

'The Nigerian Police are fools. Fools!'

'Calm down, Chris. Please, sit.'

After a minute, Chuba sat back down.

'I have an idea. We will need to send for a private investigator.'

'A private investigator? From where? What will he do that the police haven't done?'

'We will send for one from outside Nigeria. I know of a man in Ghana called Kwame. He is very good. Trained in the US. Very, very good, Chris. We must act fast, whatever it costs to get this man here in a few days we must do it. Otherwise, *eeh*,' the Chief shook his head in defeat, 'otherwise, your head is on the line. Not just your head, Chris, you will be shamed.'

That same morning, inside a large fenced compound, a 1988 Toyota Corolla was parked in front of a large building. A big man with fine combed bushy hair and a clean shaven face was standing beside the Sheikh, who was looking through the driver's open window. Musa was behind the wheel of the Toyota. Occasionally a gentle breeze blew and made them shiver.

'Do you understand all Shedrack said, Musa?' the Sheikh asked.

'Yes, my Sheikh.' The young man's heart was pounding like a pestle against a mortar.

'Tell me what he said.'

'He said, Sir, that when... when I drive into the university... my university... that I should find my way to the library and drive very fast into the building. He said that as soon as the car hits the building I should touch this wire, the red one to this black one connected to the device.' Musa indicated to the wires as he talked. 'Then all will be done.'

'It is finished.' The Sheikh beamed with joy. The dashboard of the car had been unscrewed the day before and the powerful Improvised Explosive Device built by Shedrack Obong had been carefully planted inside.

'Shedrack,' the Sheikh called, 'this will work?'

'*Haba*, Sheikh, after our training in Yemen, I have consolidated my knowledge with further research. I am an engineer, and our brothers sent me for special technical training.' He looked into the eyes of the Sheikh and said, 'I know a lot that you do not know. It is my duty to build and plant this. I won't fail.'

The Sheikh took both of Shedrack's hands. 'If this

succeeds, *insha'Allah*, I will reward you beyond your imagination, Shedrack.'

Musa smiled as he listened, but just then the Sheikh saw Musa's mouth quiver.

'You are scared, brother?'

The young man shook his head. He was just twenty-one years old.

The Sheikh walked round and sat in the front passenger seat. He placed his hand on Musa's leg reassuringly and said, 'Have no fear, brother. You are blessed. What you have chosen to do is a great duty. Listen, Musa, it is said: "And we will most certainly try you with somewhat of fear and hunger and loss of property and lives and fruits and give good news to the patient." We belong to Allah and to Him we shall surely return. So rejoice.'

Musa turned and looked with pride at the Sheikh.

'Thank you for finding me worthy to do my duty.'

'Thank you, brother,' the Sheikh replied and got out of the car.

'We meet in paradise.' The engine revved and the young man drove off.

The Sheikh smiled to himself – at times even he was surprised at the ease with which he lied in the name of his faith. By quoting the appropriate chapters and verses, he could bend the will and heart of the soldiers to do his bidding. He had never been so happy. Now he must stay close to his transistor radio and wait.

'Shedrack!' he called to the man who was now heading

towards the building. 'Great news awaits us today! Great news!'

That afternoon, Donaldo Amechi received a long letter from Ogiji, a friend of his who had just moved to Germany. Donaldo had convinced his father to include Ogiji's name among the people he was sending to Europe for training in rice milling, so he could better himself, as his family lacked contacts.

He sat on a rocking chair at the back of the mansion. Madam Vero was gathering firewood. He read the letter slowly and then dropped it on his lap. Ogiji said that he had grown big with beard and the training was going well.

Donaldo went upstairs with the letter without saying a word to Madam Vero. Stealthily, he took his bath and then drove away. It was the second time he had left the Island since Adeline's disappearance.

The sun was already setting when he stopped at the outskirts of Ishieke. He drank palm wine with Mr Ogiji, his friend's father, and some elders, sitting on the exposed roots of an *oji* tree. Mr Ogiji was always happy to see him as he could never forget how Donaldo had helped to send his poor son abroad.

Then Donaldo drove to the café. The same café where he first met Adeline. He could not eat what he ordered, so he drove home. Donaldo lay on his bed, and as the fear and worry began to creep over him again, he remembered how it all began.

SECTION II

A RECIPE FOR MURDER

To show your feelings is to risk opposing your humanity.

Felice Leonardo Buscaglia

SIX

Donaldo Amechi and Adeline Chuba stared at each other across the café till he started to feel shy. It was the first time a woman had looked at him like that. Donaldo folded his unfinished copy of *Vanguard* and made for the door. As he approached it, he looked at the mirrors in front of him and saw the reflection of her face still staring at him. The doorman opened the door before he reached it.

'*Nee anya*, look out!' an old man yelled as they almost collided. Donaldo stepped out of the café and stood for a moment before heading for his car. His mind was full of the beautiful face and those eyes that stared so piercingly at him. He had never seen that face before.

It was breezy as he jumped inside the car and sped off. During the short drive to the Island he kept thinking of the girl's face and slender body.

He had watched as she came in with an older woman, and she had stared continuously at him without blinking an eyelid. *That face must be drawn immediately,*

57

he thought as he accelerated, as if the image would disappear if he went too slowly.

As he approached the driveway to the Island, he slowed down, whistling to himself. Only his left hand held the wheel, while the right hand made an imaginary drawing in the air. Children playing on the Island field waved as he passed. He honked gleefully.

Williams Island was located in the small town of Ishieke, some kilometres from Abakaliki. It was not a large island, and only thirteen families lived on it, in rambling, old fashioned mansions, the kind with long passages and balconies. It had a small cafeteria operated by one of the families, a sports court, and at the far eastern end a small golf course that was rarely used, except occasionally when his father, Chief Donald Amechi, and his associates held meetings in one of the halls and played golf afterwards. There were two public pools and a nursery school at the northern end.

The beauty of the Island was enhanced by the beach that nearly surrounded it, separated only by the Mile 50 road that led to the town on its northern side. At the climax of some rainy seasons, it became a complete island when the river overflowed its banks and rushed towards the inside of the Island, cutting it off.

There was a large expanse of forested virgin land and swampy fields near to the Ishieke River, where the Islanders cultivated rice, one of the major agricultural products of the Abakaliki people.

Madam Vero was like a mother to Donaldo. She had been of tremendous help to him since the death of his mother when he was six. She loved him like her own son but Donaldo had never loved anyone, because he did not know what love was.

Donaldo's father had no time for anything on earth except football and politics. The little spare time he had, he devoted to rice farming and his business empire.

'Donaldo, you're not eating your food,' Madam Vero said as she entered the dining room. The woman was in her early fifties. She had worked for the Chief for fifteen years, ever since the death of his wife. She was employed to take care of Donaldo and the old mansion. She had a family in Ishieke town, and she visited them every weekend.

She placed a cup of homemade juice on the table for Donaldo and sat down on one of the chairs.

'*O gunu?* What's wrong?' she asked in Izzi dialect.

Izzi was the main clan in the Ishieke area and one of the three clans in Abakaliki. Ishieke used to be a small quiet community, but it grew quickly thanks to the foresight of Chief Nwiboko Obodo, a notorious and wealthy warrant chief during colonial rule. He attracted many great men to Ishieke and the stories of his exploits abounded until he was hanged by the state. The rapid development of Ishieke was also due to the early arrival of the missionaries. They settled there and fought for dominance with the Chief, building the Mile Four Hospital and the Leprosy Centre.

'I met a beautiful girl today,' Donaldo said and smiled broadly.

'Oh my God!' Madam Vero gave him a hug. 'That's good, *nwam*, my son.' She sat down beside him. 'Where?' she asked, her face brightening.

'I won't tell you.'

'Donaldo! You need to open up more to people—'

'I know. But I am a grown man. I can't tell you everything I do.'

'Listen, I have always longed for the day you would start going out with people, even with the opposite sex. You are always alone. Sometimes I wonder if it's some fear—'

'Fear?' Donaldo interrupted. '*Ahah,* no, no, not at all. I enjoy concentrating on my art. For my future, for Mum and for you. Dad says women have killed many great men. He says that women are the problems of the world, you know that.'

Madam Vero's face furrowed. 'When you mix with people, especially with women, it will enhance your art. It will bring out the real person in you... make you brighter, cheerful, more focused. *Inugo?*'

'Yes... maybe you are right.' He gulped down the juice.

'So, Donaldo, who is she? Is she someone I know?'

'*Ah*, no. How can you know her? No. Never mind... Ma.' He walked to his room. He could see the girl's face clearly now and was determined to paint it.

Donaldo did not tell Madam Vero anything more

about the girl he'd met at the café, like so many other things he kept hidden – perhaps he would never tell her. But she was more than happy that for once he had spoken confidentially and intimately with her. No matter how briefly.

She was pleased the girl was beautiful; at least he could see beauty in things. It gave her joy that Donaldo had laughed after so many years of solitude. She couldn't remember the last time she'd heard him laugh. Occasionally, if she teased him, he would smile, but then, as if recollecting himself, he would walk away.

Later that evening, Donaldo and Madam Vero sat in the dining room as usual; the young man appeared to be thinking about something. Madam Vero had learnt not to disturb him at such times.

'He will be coming back tomorrow,' Donaldo told her as she served their dinner.

'Your father?'

'Yes. He is in England, visiting his old football club.'

'A footballer is always a footballer.' She laughed, but he did not. What his father did, and where he went, was not his concern.

As they ate, she enquired, 'Tell me about the girl you met.'

'Please. I am eating. You made the rules, remember: "Do not talk while you eat." '

She smiled.

When he finished eating, he went to his room and

fantasized about the girl at the café. He saw her face, the innocence in it. There was something in that face that seemed to beckon to him.

The next day Donaldo drove to town in search of her, but came back without any luck. It was raining when he drove back to the Island. As he pulled up in front of the mansion, a maid came out with an umbrella to help him inside. He was dressed in a suit and wearing a silver necklace, but no tie. The priest at the Island chapel said ties were badges of slavery.

From the sitting room, he called his friend Ogiji on his mobile phone. The temptation to discuss the girl with him was strong, but then again he wanted to keep the memories to himself. He did not dare to share her with anyone. How could God make one person so beautiful? She was an angel in human form.

SEVEN

The harmattan blew the trees this way and that, their branches swirling in all directions, and dried leaves fell in abundance to form a thick bed beneath the trees. *Asha* birds and pigeons roosted in their nests and on branches, flapping their wings once in a while to shake off the cold. A group of men was gathered in a large room at the golf club on Williams Island, seated around a very long table. White papers and files were scattered in front of them. They deliberated quietly about issues that would change the history of Nigeria forever, while outside the wind gained momentum.

'Sheikh Mohammed Seko, Allah will bless you for this great honour you are about to bestow upon Islam,' Alhaji Abu Rabiu Mukhtar said. The other men in the room, about sixteen of them, were calm, their cruel eyes studying the face of the young Sheikh who was about to be entrusted with a tremendous power – the power to command death.

Chief Donald Amechi said in a rich baritone, 'Sheikh

Mohammed Seko, thank God the *madrasa* has been expanded to a bigger institution. It will serve as a cover for our operations. For the young men who are preparing to do the will of Allah—'

A voice cut in rudely, taking them all by surprise. 'The will of Allah? Your words are *haraam*! Allah can never be happy with this! Islam does not support this—' Alhaji Umar Hassan spoke up for the umpteenth time, waving his hands in the air. The Chief cut him off.

'Alhaji, be quiet in my presence! This is the fifth time we have called a meeting. You attended every one of them. You even contributed some of the ideas—'

'Yes. Yes, I did. But that was at the beginning when it was to expand the *madrasa* to propagate Islam in Nigeria, and to try to Islamize Northern Nigeria. Did I ever know that we would be sitting here today, planning terrorism? *Haba!* Islam forbids terrorism. The Holy Book forbids terrorism.' The Alhaji folded the thick paper in front of him. On top of the paper, in bold print, were the words *Jama'atul al-Mujahideen Jihad* – 'A Group of Youths Striving for Holy War'.

'Alhaji! Alhaji!' Evangelist Chris Chuba called out. 'Do you say the Holy Qur'an does not support jihad? Do you? Have you read the Holy Book well? Does it not say: "Fight those who do not believe in Allah…"? What we do is provide you, our brothers, with support. We all benefit as brothers.'

'Evangelist, do you believe in Allah yourself? This is not jihad to promote Islam. What you plan is evil.

Terrorism against the Nigerian state to gain power! Jihad is different from terrorism.' The Alhaji was frantic. He was sweating profusely. His small eyes roamed from one man to another. What was revealed in those eyes was fear. Great fear.

He continued, 'Jihad means to "strive or to struggle". Striving against oneself for holiness, to become a better person. Striving against the *Shaitan*. Striving to teach people the correct doctrine of Islam. To defend the religion from external attacks from hostile or violent people. Terrorism is deliberate killing. To kill is "*qitaal*", not jihad.' He reshuffled the papers before him. 'Do you not know that I know your hearts? Evangelist Chuba, you are not a Muslim, so do not challenge me over the Holy Book. In the Qur'an it says: "There shall be no compulsion in the acceptance of the religion of Islam." So, Mr Evangelist, the Almighty does not teach war against governments and against other religions. Sir, people should be free to choose the religion they like. But anyone who follows Islam has gained a great deal. If you compel people, do you think they will worship Allah with all their hearts?'

'Be calm, Alhaji!' Professor Saturday Effiong shouted. 'We are the owners of Nigeria. We cannot burn down the house we built. No. This is not terrorism against Nigeria.' His pockmarked face looked at the others and they nodded their heads like lizards, with the exception of Alhaji Umar Hassan. 'Listen, Alhaji Umar. This is a win-win game. If we start Jama'atul al-Mujahideen

Jihad we help the North with their quest for Islamic states. We Southerners... we oust the President and put in a better man, a man who is a member of this Sacred Order.' Professor Effiong sat back. He was a professor of Medicine at the University of Calabar, and had served as a Minister of Health. His influence in South-South Nigeria knew no bounds – it was like water overflowing its banks in an ocean, encroaching dry lands.

There was silence.

He continued, 'And everyone benefits.'

Every man in that room except one belonged to the Sacred Order of the Universal Forces – a secret organization with its headquarters in the Netherlands and branches in almost every country in the world. Members of the Sacred Order were men of power and wealth, ranging from politicians to business moguls, religious leaders to academics, security chiefs, sportsmen and media executives. In Nigeria, Chief Donald Amechi was the Sacred Lord, the most senior member of the Order in the country. As such he was responsible for communicating the rules, orders and decisions to all the members below him – a position so powerful he could institute events that could lead to the impeachment of the President of the Federal Republic of Nigeria.

Members of the Sacred Order occupied twenty-two out of the thirty-six state governorship positions in the country. The only man in the meeting who was not a member of the Universal Order was Sheikh Mohammed

Seko, who was now being entrusted with the authority to lead an evil war.

Alhaji Umar Hassan was silent. His right foot was tapping the terrazzo floor in a steady rhythm. His long garment made of *safari* material was soaked with sweat even though rain had cooled the air and the air-conditioner was on.

Sheikh Mohammed Seko spoke up slowly, his heavy voice wrapped in a sharp but slurred Northern Nigerian accent. 'Alhaji Hassan, I am disappointed. I did not think it would be you who would stand in the way of the progress of Islam. Our forefathers dreamt of this opportunity. Today, it is presented to us, at last. Are you scared because of where it has come from? Because it has come from our brothers from the South?' The young Sheikh touched his white turban. 'I am your *ibn*, because you are as old as my father. But you are not worthy to call me "son". The words that come from your mouth make me ashamed to refer to you as *Ustaz*, master.'

Sheikh Mohammed Seko was a tall man; he had to stoop to enter any room. He wore a long *quftan* that stretched almost to his feet and, if he had removed his turban, they would have seen his bushy hair, covered with grey. His moustache and long beard were grey too, though he was still young. Hair sprouted from his ears in a startling way. He held his prayer *masbaha* of ninety-nine beads in his right hand and hadn't stopped fingering the beads since the meeting began.

He looked at Alhaji Umar Hassan and said, 'Islam

is the religion of the world. And we must strive to bring it to greater prominence, *insha'Allah*. Our Holy Book says, "Oh you who believe! What is your excuse when you decline to go forth in Allah's way? Are you contented with this world's life instead of the hereafter?" To do the will of Allah and his messengers is a sign of a true Muslim, Alhaji.'

Some of the men around the table took a deep breath. They knew then that the young Islamic scholar was not someone to be challenged in the affairs of Islam. They feared that in those cool, darting eyes were lodged dreadful deeds of terror, waiting for the final opportunity to be unleashed, like an atomic bomb waiting to explode. Some of them also feared that a bomb, when it explodes, does not wait for its owner to escape before it performs the duties for which it is made.

Chief Donald Amechi spoke up. 'Sheikh Seko, a week from today, Sheikh Kabiru Ibrahim here and Alhaji Damba Tambuwal will contact you. You will receive twenty million naira. You know what to do with it. Evangelist Chuba will commence a West African evangelist mission in two weeks' time. He will travel along the Trans-Saharan highway on his way back to Nigeria, through the Jibya border. He will hold his final crusade in Katsina State. With him will be the arms that are being held in Mali.'

'How will he transport them to us?'

'Do not worry. Not even the American Marines if they are on the border will bat an eye as his entourage passes

through. He is a renowned man of God. Very renowned.'
The Chief put emphasis on 'very' to convince the young
man that the European arms they had purchased with
millions of dollars through the rebels in Mali would
arrive safely in their hands in Northern Nigeria.

'*Alhamdulillah!*'

'You know what to do with the weapons?'

The Sheikh nodded. He was a man of few words.
Asking him such a question was like testing his
capabilities. Looking at the men gathered around
the room, he smiled to himself. He could see endless
opportunities – wealth, fame and power were within
his grasp after his training in Yemen, Pakistan and the
United States of America.

The men sat in silence. Most of them were glancing
nervously at the many documents before them, re-
reading them because they were not permitted to leave
the meeting with any papers, except the Sheikh, who
had been writing on a small pad the names and phone
numbers of the contacts he was to make after the
meeting.

During a break for some members of the group
to make calls and others to use the restroom, Chief
Amechi asked the Northerners to talk to Alhaji Umar
Hassan. They took him out to the passage that led to
the restroom.

'Alhaji, *haba*, Alhaji. Why?' asked Alhaji Damba
Tambuwal.

'*Hmmn*. Alhaji Tambuwal, when the endowment was

set up for the *madrasa*, this was not the plan—'

'But this is a good plan.'

'It is not. This is not Islam. This is not the teaching of the Prophet Muhammad, peace be upon him. Listen, the Southerners want to use us. If Jama'atul al-Mujahideen Jihad succeeds, there will be a great crisis in the North, in Katsina. People will be massacred, in Yobe, Maiduguri, everywhere. Look, I suspect deceit.'

'What deceit?' Alhaji Musa Donga asked. He was a Governor in one of the states Umar Hassan had mentioned. 'My state is becoming filled with Christians. With infidels and *mushriks*! With this new force, we will outwit them, and win the next election.'

'Yes. That is it.' Alhaji Umar was becoming more nervous. 'That is it. We may win the Northern states. But what of the Presidency? The President is a Northerner. If the war starts in the North, the whole country and the world will blame Islam, they will call us bad names. They will say we are evil. Then a Southerner will win the election, even if he is a weakling. He is bound to win. And if the terrorism continues, the more people are killed, the more hatred there will be for the North. I bet you, no Northerner will ever rule Nigeria again. Who will vote for him?'

One of the men laughed at Alhaji Umar's words.

'You talk like a kid, Umar. Yes. You fail to realize that if this starts as planned it will grow to be an international force, recognized by more established terrorist organizations in the Middle East. No one can

70

stand in our way. We will rule Nigeria forever, *shekena*!'

Alhaji Umar Hassan stared at the ceiling. 'No. I cannot be part of this. What you say is *haram'aleik*, a sin upon you, my friend.' With that he walked away and out of the clubhouse. Chief Donald Amechi was talking with the Evangelist and a few others. They watched as Alhaji Umar Hassan left the building, slamming the door behind him.

Chief Amechi allowed a smile to cross his lips. But it was the kind of smile that a man would give you if he caught you on top of his wife yet said nothing. If someone gave you that kind of smile, it meant that he was not finished with you yet. It meant that he would not take action against you right now. But you would be afraid. You would have to watch your back always.

EIGHT

Alhaji Umar Hassan had not been himself since the last meeting where preparations were concluded for the terrorist attacks. There was nothing he could do to dissuade his friends from the task they had chosen. His brothers and friends from the North were all in support of the operation, and heavy arms were arriving in Nigeria from Chad and Mali. There was only one man who had the power to talk to the Sacred Lord and maybe change his mind. Alhaji Umar Hassan took a flight to Abuja.

Dr Bode Clark was sitting in his palatial sitting room with his family when Alhaji Hassan entered. They shook hands as was the tradition of the Sacred Order. Dr Clark dismissed his wife and two children, after the visitor had exchanged long greetings with the woman of the house.

On the wall hung a framed photograph of the Tais – the Committee of Supreme Lords ruling in all the countries where the Sacred Order operated. They took decisions for the Sacred Order as it concerned each of their members and in other matters. It was the duty of the Sacred Lord in each country to pass on these decisions and messages to other members under him. There were other pictures of Dr Clark in academic gowns, standing with academics from universities in Nigeria and the West, receiving honorary doctorates. Alhaji Umar Hassan drank from the glass of mango juice he had been offered, while Dr Clark sipped from his glass of Hennessy.

Alhaji Umar put his glass down on the table and sat next to Dr Clark on the sofa. He cleared his throat so that the spirits of his ancestors would listen, as he conversed with the only man who had the power to convince Chief Donald Amechi to cancel his plans.

'I bring bad news, brother.'

Dr Clark looked at him and moved closer. He said, 'I know why you have come.' The Alhaji was not surprised; he knew that the Chief must have briefed his host. 'I am sorry I was not present during the last meeting. My firm is building a fertilizer plant in Zimbabwe. I was away.'

'Sir, you are the only one who can stop this—'

'And tell me, Alhaji, why must I do that?'

Alhaji Umar Hassan shifted anxiously. Inside his socks, his feet sweated. 'Islam does not support terrorism, Dr Clark. What is being planned will consolidate the Sacred Order's powers in Nigeria. We will gain greater control over the Government. But we will destroy the holy religion of Islam in Nigeria. Forever.'

Dr Clark frowned and did not answer for some time.

Eventually he replied, 'Why come to me? I am not the Sacred Lord.'

'But you are the richest man in Africa, with a global business empire. We are lucky you belong to this organization. And Chief Amechi is your friend. He listens to you.'

'You go against the decision of the Brotherhood, my friend. Our actions have been approved by the Tais.'

'I want to save my religion, Sir.'

'Does the holy war not happen in the United States, the most liberal country in the world? Are there not attacks in Afghanistan, Pakistan and Palestine? In Africa, are you blind to what is happening in Somalia, Mali? Even in Kenya? Do you not know that these events are all a creation of people's ideas? People who seek power. People like us.' He came closer to the Alhaji. 'The young men who are to benefit from this, do they not have a reward in paradise? If they die in this war, do they not have seventy-two virgins awaiting them in paradise? You cannot take the decision for these men, my brother.'

Alhaji Umar Hassan looked at him with pity. 'Sir, Islam does not support terrorism or suicide bombings. My Lord says: "And do not kill yourselves. Indeed, Allah is to you ever merciful. And whoever does that in aggression and injustice then we will drive him into a fire. And that for Allah is easy." There is no mention of seventy-two virgins for a killer in the Holy Qur'an. That is Western Islamophobia. The Qur'an condemns the killing of innocent souls whether Muslim or Christian.

74

Islam rebukes forceful conversion. I know you may not understand the Holy Book, but I tell you, Sir, nowhere does it encourage terrorism and the murder of innocent people.'

There was hope in his eyes that his superior may be agreeing with him.

'I… I don't know what to say, Alhaji.'

'Dr Clark, if we continue with this plan we will benefit as individuals, but our people will suffer. Think about Yorubas, Itsekiris, Ijaws, Igbos. Think about all the hundreds of different ethnic men and women and children residing in the North. When this starts, they will suffer. But my people will suffer more. If I bring war to my house, my enemy will suffer, but I suffer more because I will lose my belongings and my people too. That is what will happen.'

There was a long silence. The muffled sound of a football match could be heard from a television in one of the inner rooms. Dr Clark stood and moved to another chair. He finished his drink and sat back against the cushion.

'What you ask for, my friend, is difficult. Very difficult.'

NINE

Thursday, 11th February 2010

In Katsina State, close to the Jibya border separating Nigeria and the Republic of Niger, Kafurzan, a town of approximately three thousand inhabitants, stood proudly like a fat woman on a stool. It had produced several Northern leaders and Islamic scholars. Along its borders with Jibya, a small river ran on its way to other towns. It was the only river in the area and during the intense harmattan people would troop to it with carts and donkeys to fetch water and do their laundry. The river never dried up; in the extreme heat it shrank, but there was always enough water to serve the inhabitants.

It was in this town that the Centre for Islamic Knowledge had been built. The Centre served the educational needs of the town alongside the elementary and secondary schools. The walls were high and inside the compound was a long mosque with modern aluminium windows. There were also hostels with hundreds of rooms. The tutors lived in some of the rooms but most of the rooms were empty. The hostels had been built for a special purpose, which was now approaching.

The expanse of land where the Centre was built had only a few trees, and brown sand covered the ground. During hot weather, it scorched the feet of the students and worshippers who walked barefoot into the compound to attend the mosque. There were two blocks that served as classrooms, with mats on which the kids sat to recite from prayer books and the works of great Islamic poets. There were several long halls that were locked up, but no one wondered why they were locked.

Sheikh Mohammed Seko had established the Centre originally as a *madrasa*, a traditional elementary school which taught reading, writing and the Holy Qur'an. People wondered why the elementary school should be bigger than most of the secondary schools in the state and how this man, whose intelligence matched his impressive physical stature, had got the funds to build such an institution. In no time the *madrasa* had expanded and become the Centre for Islamic Knowledge.

When Mohammed Seko was a child, his father had sent him to an Islamic school in Kano, where he lived with his uncle, who was the *Ustaz*. His uncle was a cleric who had studied in Al-Azhar University in Cairo and in King Abdulaziz University in Saudi Arabia before returning to work in the civil service as an Islamic scholar. In the afternoons, after their recitations in the school, Mohammed and over thirty other children would be handed a plastic plate each and they would move from street to street begging for alms. This practice, called *Almajiri*, 'the servant of God', was to instil humility in these young scholars. Mohammed abhorred this practice as he grew up under his uncle's instruction, but it was a custom that stretched back through uncountable years, passed on through generations. When his uncle died, and after Mohammed had studied religion and Islamic history at the University of Zaria, he returned to Kano to train as a cleric and took over the running of the school.

He rose quickly through the ranks. Soon after he became a Sheikh, Christians and Muslims clashed in Kano and many Igbo traders were massacred. The school was burnt down. An organization which he had never heard of before instituted an endowment and sent him to Afghanistan and Syria for special training on warfare, and gave him support to build his own school. His mystery benefactor was the radical Sheikh Kabiru Ibrahim, who had watched him silently for months as he called on hundreds of jobless youths who were *Almajiri* to take arms against the Christians – Mohammed Seko had preached that it was an individual responsibility of every Muslim in Kano to cleanse the town of infidels. He was already a very ambitious man who sought to set himself up as an indispensable authority in the Islamic world in Nigeria, by any means possible.

That day, Sheikh Mohammed Seko sat in the mosque saying his morning prayers. He lifted his head to see a young man approach. He was as tall as himself and his beard was very long. A dagger was sheathed at his waist. The Sheikh could see a bulge inside the young man's shirt where his pistol was hidden.

'*As-salamu 'alaykum!*' the young man called in cheerful greeting.

'Ah! '*Alaykum salam!*' Sheikh Seko responded. 'Please sit. You have returned. *Alhamdulillah! Yayade?*' One would expect that they would hug each other, after five years of separation, but their hearts were jubilant.

'*Lafia! Lafia! Lafia!* I am very fine. I arrived about twenty minutes ago and I've been walking round the whole place. The classrooms, the halls, the quarters. This place is great. All praises go to Allah!'

'*Masha'Allah*, brother.' Sheikh Seko spread out his hands, his prayer beads dangling. 'Look what Allah has brought. Praised be His name!'

The young man sat down next to the Sheikh. 'When I received your letter, explaining all this, I could not believe what I was reading.'

'Have you ever had cause to doubt me, since our days in Kano and Zaria? We are the fortunate ones. We have education. Now, we are about to have power in our hands, Abouzeid.'

'Now, what I do for others in Mali and Chad, I can do here, for my people. I am blessed to see this day. You were in Afghanistan and Syria?'

'Yes. And other countries too.'

The Sheikh looked up to the aluminium roof and clasped his hands together in prayer. 'May Allah be praised. Now, you see why I insisted you obey the words of Sheikh Kabiru Ibrahim. He is the *Ustaz*. May the all-knowing Allah guide his path.'

Abouzeid opened his palms and raised them to his face.

A hot wind came through the open windows and ruffled the men's *quftans*. It carried dust too. The Sheikh rubbed his eyes. Beams of sunlight filtered into the mosque through the windows and the door.

'How is Mali? How is the camp?'

'*Hmmn*. Brother, it has been difficult. But we do the work of the Creator. Who are we to complain? We are making progress. Significant progress. That is why I am glad that this is here now. The camp and recruitment into the Jama'atul. Tell me, now that I am here, what is the plan?'

The Sheikh recrossed his legs and straightened out his *quftan* before answering. 'Soon after you left for Mali at Sheikh Ibrahim's command, he took me to the South, a town close to Abakaliki. There I met the most influential men in this country and learnt that whoever becomes the President or State Governor or any position of power is not made by God. Oh no, rather it is certain men who dictate what happens. Yorubas, Igbos, even some of our brothers here in the North. Very wealthy men. They belong to a society, but they have interests in our affairs.'

Abouzeid was uncomfortable. He was trained not to trust the infidels. 'This, all we have here, your journey to meet our brothers in Afghanistan and Syria, and mine to Mali, you mean to tell me this was not from one of us. The endowment was not from friends of Sheikh Ibrahim?'

'They came from his friends. But his friends who are infidels—'

'Then by Allah, I am not happy about this. Infidels do not know the ways of the Prophet, peace be upon him. Do they know the ways of Islam?' His voice was raised, and some men sitting at the far side of the mosque looked in his direction but said nothing. Sheikh Seko noticed three young men carrying Kalashnikovs as they walked past the open door. He knew they had come with Abouzeid.

'Listen, brother, the Centre, where is it? Is it not on our land? Can the infidels come here to take it away or demolish it? No, brother. Put your mind at rest, I pray you. I have met them once. Their plan is to equip us to start an *intifada. Hmmn?* Then we cause trouble and their men will gain control of the Northern states. That is their goal.' The Sheikh's face became more serious. 'Brother, what do we gain? We need to flush Northern Nigeria free of infidels. So we will start what we did in Kano, which failed that time. But now, we use the arms they will supply to wage war against them. Against their own people.'

The wind outside raised dustwhirls and hurled them into the sky.

Abouzeid sat in silence for a long time, contemplating the words of his friend. 'Where will the arms come from?' he finally asked.

Sheikh Seko looked him hard in the eyes. 'That is why you have been summoned. You must journey to Kano tomorrow to meet Sheikh Kabiru Ibrahim.' He lowered his voice. 'Our friends have purchased weapons worth millions of dollars and soon they will be transported to Mali. You are to ensure that when they get there you take charge until one of their group comes to transport the arms to Nigeria.'

'How will that be possible? Interpol are everywhere. The Nigerian Government is strengthening security.'

'Abouzeid, you still do not realize that the men behind us are strong not just in this country but all over the world. Have you heard of Evangelist Chris Chuba?'

'Yes. Yes. I hate him—'

'Do not. Bury your hatred. He will be the one that will contact you in Mali. He will transport the arms with you to Nigeria.'

Abouzeid's mouth fell open in shock. 'How are we going to be able to carry out wide reaching attacks in Nigeria? Nigeria is more organized than Mali and Chad and Somalia.'

'Be calm, brother. One step at a time. Do your part, I will do mine and they will surely do theirs. Soon, we will begin.' The Sheikh stood up and his long *quftan* swept the floor. 'Abouzeid, I have a goal. We get the money, the arms and start the war against the Government and the Christians. Then, if we are efficient, bigger organizations abroad will seek us out and we will say goodbye to the infidels and their aims. I know their plans, but they do not know mine. I made friends in the countries I visited. Let your heart be at rest, *eh*.'

It was then that the ingenuity of his long time friend dawned on Abouzeid. He smiled and said, 'I met an Ijaw man in Mali. He is a Muslim and one of us. He once told me, "It is easy to give a monkey some water to drink, but difficult to collect back your cup." It is true.'

TEN

'If my parents were around, you know I wouldn't be going to church with you.'

'But they are not around, so today you're going to come. Besides it is Sunday, you need to worship God.'

'All right then.'

'It is a special Sunday, Adeline. It is Valentine's Day.'

Miss Spencer smiled. She recalled when she was a young girl in Cameroon and how she would receive cards and flowers from boys on Valentine's Day.

'I am almost ready,' Adeline told her.

Adeline Chuba was eighteen. From a distance her straight face could make her pass for a boy. Her large eyes were as slanted as those of a cat and her neck was smooth and elegant; a mere glance at it could set a man's heart on fire. She had long legs like a gazelle, skin that was chocolate-brown and small but firm breasts. Miss Spencer always told her she was as beautiful as her father and as pretty as her mother. 'If your dad were a woman, people would faint just looking at him,' she would tell her.

Her father had once told her she had his pointed nose and his curved mouth. At primary school, a classmate of hers had tried to be her boyfriend. She had refused because her father had said that befriending a boy made one go to hell – that Jesus hated a relationship between a young boy and a girl, especially if the boy tried to kiss the girl's mouth. 'Your lips belong to Jesus alone. Only he has the licence to kiss them,' Adeline's father had told her the day she turned twelve. Adeline had noticed that when her father's friends visited they would gawk at her, even the pastors, and if she left the compound with Miss Spencer, people would stare at her and praise her for her beauty.

Adeline loved the attention she received, especially from men. She enjoyed watching the pastors who were supposed to be holy men fawn over her. They fantasized about her, she was sure. But an experience at the hands of her uncle, Simon, when she was twelve always made her shudder.

Miss Spencer had travelled to Cameroon, so she was sent to Anambra to stay with her uncle, who had just divorced his wife. Throughout the time she was with him, she was uncomfortable – her uncle couldn't stop staring at her. She had to stop wearing a nightgown around the house and wore loose trousers and shirts instead because he would stare at her breasts, which had already started to develop, and at her buttocks and hips.

One night, her uncle attempted the unthinkable – as

she slept, convalescing after a bout of malaria, she felt someone lift her bedcover. She was dreaming. Adeline felt the person's hands on her breasts and her stomach. She thought it might be Jesus, and then her hands sought the person's head. The head was bald. *But Jesus had long hair*, she thought. Adeline forced her eyes open. She screamed.

Her uncle jumped up and hurried out of the room. She still had a week left to spend with him but they rarely talked to each other for the rest of her stay. She locked her room at night and wedged the door with a table and anything else she could find.

Miss Spencer's outfit was made of *Ankara* material tailored to suit her plump figure and she wore a headscarf in the same fabric. She held a Catholic missal under her arm and a King James Bible in her hand.

'Do you have the slightest idea that we are running late, Adeline?'

'I'm ready now.' Adeline buckled her shoes, picked up her missal and glanced at the mirror once again to check her reflection. She also had a novel in her hand called *Envy* by Sandra Brown. Adeline was an avid reader who never went anywhere without a book to read.

'Why are you wearing a special dress?' Miss Spencer asked.

'Because I am in a happy mood... and you say today is Valentine's Day. Maybe I will receive a most fabulous blessing from God.' They laughed and their laughter walked down the stairs with them, leading the way.

St Mary's Church in town was full to the brim. Adeline and Miss Spencer walked through the large car park and sat on a bench under a spreading *ukpa* tree, watching as luxurious, flashy cars arrived and parked. Men in rich Sunday outfits emerged from the cars.

'Do you notice anything special?' Adeline asked.

'Yes, I think you've forgotten—'

'Of course! The Islanders are coming for the special thanksgiving service. I remember now.'

It was a special mass at the big church in town as the Islanders were celebrating the Rice Festival, an annual event celebrated by all the thirteen wealthy families that occupied the Island. Rice was harvested during the dry seasons, especially in November. It would be parboiled and sun-dried between December and February, and around this time the Islanders would celebrate the bounteous festival. They walked to the entrance, but the crowd was so big that they had to shuffle to avoid jostling each other. Adeline held Miss Spencer's hand as if she was her security from people's stares.

Just before they stepped into the church, a very expensive fragrance caught Adeline's nostrils. Instinctively, she turned in the direction of the scent.

And behold, she saw the face again. It was the same face that had stared at her at the café.

Blood surged through her veins and made her heart beat faster. Her eyes itched and the hairs on the back of her neck stood on end. She started to perspire and felt she was losing control.

'Please, young lady, move.' An older woman nudged her and Miss Spencer pulled at her hand. They found a pew on the left side of the church where women sat. She looked round and the young man smiled at her. She watched as he walked to the men's side. Miss Spencer knelt down and said a short prayer. When she arose, she asked, 'Adeline, what happened?'

'I... I'm all right.'

'*In nomine patris, et filii, et spiritus sancti...*'

The hoarse words of the priest coming through the loudspeaker caught them unawares and Adeline was startled. They stood and made the sign of the cross almost at the same time.

'Amen!' the congregation chorused in unison.

'His voice is bad,' Adeline commented.

'Please, can we talk later?' Miss Spencer pinched her as the words of the priest came again.

'*Dominus vobiscum.*'

'*Et cum spiritu tuo*,' Miss Spencer responded, trying to concentrate. She folded her hands on her chest and looked towards the altar with ecstasy.

Donaldo sat quietly as the choir sang the offertory hymns from the Catholic hymnbook.

From the time he sat down, he replayed in his mind what had happened at the church entrance. There was no doubt that it was the same face he had seen twelve days earlier. *She likes me*, he thought.

Then a hefty man approached and tapped him on the

shoulder. 'Hello, Donaldo. Time for the thanksgiving procession.' He was one of his father's bodyguards. Donaldo stood and buttoned up his suit.

'Where is the Chief?'

As they went outside, Donaldo in front and the guard following, he turned to his right and saw her. The face that had so haunted his soul. Their eyes met again.

'Son? Stand with me.' The Chief held Donaldo's hand. Donaldo hated how his father treated him – as if he was a small boy. Together they entered the church, processed down the aisle to the altar, and lined up in front of the priest. All the Islanders and their guests carried bags of rice, yam tubers, bunches of plantain and even goats. Some carried crates of eggs, chickens and baskets of fruit. A little girl had a blossoming hibiscus, which she handed to the priest. The altar boys collected the gifts and the worshippers knelt down as the priest prayed and sprinkled holy water on their heads and clothes, before returning to their seats.

The priest began to sing a traditional gospel song and the congregation joined in. He danced as he did so. The gifts were many, which was one of the reasons why the priest and most Catholic priests in Nigeria looked forward to every Sunday. The faith Nigerians had in the church was so strong that the country had been pronounced one of the strongholds of the Mother Church in recent times – financially, spiritually and socially. People donated everything they had to the priests, even to the detriment of their starving families. Families sent their loved sons to become priests, and to become a Catholic priest in Nigeria was an express road to wealth, nobility and respect. The continual ordination of young Nigerians supplied the Mother Church with enough manpower to send to other countries that were losing their faith. Countries such as the United States.

'*Ite, missa est!*'

'*Deo gratias!*' The congregation waved their hands in jubilation to the heavens as the mass ended. They waited as the clergy and the servers marched round the altar and into the sacristy, before rising to leave, discussing the service in twos and threes. Some genuflected and made the sign of the cross as they left the church. Miss Spencer and Adeline followed suit.

Outside, Adeline wanted to see him again and craned her neck searching for him in every direction. When he'd walked down the aisle with his father, he had glanced at her and flashed a quick smile. She had been overjoyed.

Donaldo had put on his sunglasses. The blooming umbrella trees helped create pleasant shelter from the sun that had just begun to shine. Donaldo walked about looking for her. He was not going to make any mistakes this time. He remembered what Madam Vero always said, and at that moment she came up to him.

'Donaldo! What are you looking for?' Madam Vero asked.

'I saw her. The girl I told you about.'

'*Igwarom*, you did not tell me about her.'

'Ma. She is here... I saw her.'

'Then go after her,' Madam Vero encouraged him. At that instant Donaldo turned towards the gate and saw her walking with the same woman he had seen her with inside. He could only see her back now. Adeline's hips were so inviting. He wondered if anyone else had noticed them.

Someone tapped his shoulder and he turned. It was the same guard who had called him outside for the procession.

'What are you looking for?'

'There is this girl—'

'A girl? *Chineke*. What are you waiting for? Go after her,' he said.

'Chike,' Donaldo replied in desperation, 'the Chief might need me. I want you to follow her. I want to know where she lives.'

'Okay, Donaldo, anything you say.' Chike was surprised to see him in such a happy mood. Everyone in the Chief's household knew that the young man did not care about women. Chike slapped Donaldo on the shoulders jokingly. 'Where is the lucky girl?'

Donaldo strained his neck to point at the two women, who were almost at the gate where a black Mercedes was waiting to collect them.

'Donaldo, her back is gorgeous!'

'Follow her. I will give you money.'

Without wasting time, Chike ran to the car and sped off, hooting noisily.

There were endless green forests on either side of the road that led to the biggest mansion on the Island. Donaldo walked down the road awaiting the return of the bodyguard. A strange feeling of anxiety encompassed him and his heart yearned.

As he walked to the mansion, his hands in the pockets of his plain trousers, a voice called and he turned around.

Donaldo called in response, 'Hey, Ogiji!'

'Happy Sunday, my man.'

Donaldo walked back to his friend and stretched out his hand.

Ogiji said, 'Hope you are fine? I am hungry after church.'

'Hunger? Forget it… you hunger for food, I hunger for more.'

'The girl you talked about on the phone the other night?'

'Yes.'

'Let's go then, let's go and find her in town today… Just bring your car.' Ogiji loved Donaldo's car. But that was not the only thing he loved about his friend. Donaldo always gave him money, more money than Ogiji's father made working at Chief Amechi's rice mill. Donaldo had also bought him his mobile phone.

'No. No need for that. I saw her today,' Donaldo said. Ogiji's mouth fell open. Birds flew across the road, singing, but their song was lost at the sound of Chike's car approaching. It stopped and Donaldo rushed to open the door.

'Where does she live?' he demanded.

'Hey, calm down.'

Donaldo wasn't laughing. A lot of things weighed heavily in his heart.

'What do you mean, "calm down"?'

'Listen. I think I know where she lives.'

Donaldo's eyes lit up. 'Serious? If you come with good news, I will buy everyone drinks at the restaurant.'

'*Ozugbo nu*. I come with good news.' Chike was surprised at the young man's behaviour. It was the first time Donaldo had really talked to him in the two years he had worked for the Chief.

They headed over to Donaldo's favourite restaurant where Donaldo ordered tea, bread and boiled eggs and Ogiji chose *fufu* and *esusa* soup. Chike just drank beer after beer, while smoking his Benson and Hedges.

While they waited for their food Donaldo enquired, 'How did it go?'

'All right. I followed them down to the market and waited as they shopped. Later they were driven to a large compound, the Chuba residence. When I saw them drive in I came back here. I am sure that is where they live.'

'Wait,' Ogiji added. 'How sure are you they live there? Just like they stopped at the market, they might have gone to say "Happy Sunday" to some friends. Today is Valentine's Day, after all.'

'Good point,' Donaldo agreed.

'That is where they live, I am sure. The men at the gate lowered their heads in greeting as the young lady passed. Donaldo, I think she is the daughter or a relative of your dad's friend, Evangelist Chuba.'

Ogiji noticed that Donaldo looked unsettled at this information.

'The address is 12 Obashi Crescent,' Chike told him. Donaldo borrowed a pen and wrote down the address on a label he tore from a can of milk. Then he reached inside his pocket and gave Chike some money.

ELEVEN

Monday, 15th February 2010

There was a little drizzle that morning. Chief Donald Amechi was sure that it would make the harmattan worse. He sat in front of the small hall at the golf course, waiting for his guests who had been picked up from the airport in Enugu.

When he saw the cars driving towards the building, he walked inside and sat down on the chair at the far end of the long table. There were two bulky manila envelopes before him.

Two men walked in. Dr Bode Clark was dressed in a suit and his stomach protruded from his shirt. Alhaji Abu Rabiu Mukhtar was dressed in an overflowing *babariga* that he kept gathering up and placing on his shoulders, only for the folds of material to fall, and he would collect them again and place them back – that was the beauty of the *babariga*. The hem swept the floor as he walked.

They bowed before Chief Amechi.

'Peace and love, brothers.'

'Peace and love, our lord.'

The men sat down.

'Dr Clark, you are everywhere these days.'

'We are investing in everything possible. The President has been good to my business. When my companies develop new products he bans the importation of competing foreign goods or increases import duties on them.'

'That is how it is supposed to be,' Alhaji Mukhtar said.

'I have to leave for a World Economic Forum round table meeting later today,' Dr Clark explained.

'Then I will be brief.' The Chief opened the envelope before him and brought out some sheets of paper. He gave each of them some of the sheets.

'These are the changes we need to make in the President's cabinet.'

Dr Clark studied the names.

'The Director General of the Nigerian Port Authority?' Dr Clark's eyebrows furrowed. The man in question was Alhaji Umar Hassan. But they needed to put in another member of the Sacred Order that they could trust.

'Yes. We need carte blanche cover on our imports. The President must announce the removal of the man in one week.'

'So Alhaji Umar Hassan must go?' he asked.

'Yes, I don't trust him. You said he came to you to complain about JMJ. He may kick us in the balls… kick us so hard that recovery may be difficult.'

Dr Clark took a deep breath and read the other names from the list. 'The Minister of Information. The Minister of Defence. The Special Security Advisor to the President. The Inspector General of Police.'

Chief Donald Amechi nodded.

Alhaji Mukhtar was uneasy. 'The Information Minister and the Inspector General are from the South. Why do we need to put in Northerners? These positions are currently occupied by Southerners whom we can control.'

'*Haaa*, Alhaji. You can never control a man when you do not know the direction he faces when he sleeps—'

'Unless you threaten his life and family,' Dr Clark added.

'Yes. Yes. But we don't need to. When JMJ starts we need Nigerians to see that the North is in control of the sensitive positions. A Northerner is currently the Security Advisor, but we will remove him and put in our own man, a member of this Order who is also a Northerner. We'll put in a Northerner as Information Minister. A Northerner is currently the Minister of Defence, but we'll remove him and put in our man. As for the Director General of the Port Authority, a member of the Order, whether from the North or South, should take over the position.'

There was silence as each man studied the documents before him.

'We can do this. Can't we, Alhaji?' Dr Clark asked.

The Alhaji hesitated. 'We can,' he responded.

'Alhaji,' the Chief said reassuringly, 'your friend is the President. You have his ears. Work with Dr Clark on this. We want these changes to happen in one week. Two weeks at most. Do not hesitate to drop the hint that I know about these changes. The President owes me some favours.'

'Yes, Chief.'

'What means do we use?' Dr Clark asked.

'The means are outlined. We have some information on these men already. When the President is presented with this information, he will do as we say.'

Dr Clark, in a hurry to go, said, 'Leave that to me, my lord. I am not the wealthiest African for nothing. I control the economy of Nigeria too.'

'He should also know that the presidential election is next year. He wants to run for a second term. He understands what must be done in the South. I own most of the Governors.'

'We will drop these hints to him,' Alhaji Mukhtar said.

Chief Amechi stood up. 'Very well then.'

'Peace and love to you, Sir.'

He led them to their cars, each holding a thick envelope in their hands.

Before Chief Donald Amechi travelled to England as a teenager, he was called Nwiphuru, an Ikwo name which means 'child of a thief'. There were many reasons why people were given such a name, just like there were many reasons why at that time people were named Nwuzor, 'child born on the road', or Nwite, 'child of a pot', or Nwewo, 'child of a frog'. People were named according to the circumstances surrounding their birth.

Donald Amechi was born in the season when some criminal organizations from the nearby Izzi clan were terrorizing the Ikwo people. His father was wealthy because he was one of the few at that time with a Western education. His father worked with Norwegians in a small agricultural research centre. He boasted about his education before his people and caused a lot of trouble. He was well feared because murder ran in his blood. 'Don't fight him,' people would say. 'Remember, his father once killed a man and hoisted his skull on a tree at his compound.'

When the Norwegians were leaving, they offered to take his son Nwiphuru with them. He was a brilliant boy – and at the age of nine he already knew how to bud oranges. At the age of seventeen, his gift for football took him to England for a teen tournament, where he was spotted by a club that signed him up. He played for them until he was eighteen before relocating to Spain. At twenty-two he returned to England and played for Leicester City, and after four years he transferred to Italy to play in the Italian League.

When Donald returned to Nigeria, no one from his clan would give him their daughter's hand because of his father's reputation, so he travelled back to England. Soon after, he sustained a major injury and his doctor said he would never play football again. He worked as a TV football analyst for two years before coming back to Nigeria as a national hero with his young Italian wife, whom he had met in England. However, despite all his success Donald could not deny the bloodlust that ran through his veins, nor the origins of his name, and he soon became an influential member of the Sacred Order, rising swiftly through the ranks, until he took on the role of Sacred Lord.

The evergreen trees swirled in different directions. The wind sent electrifying waves through people's nerves. Donaldo drove steadily, only swerving occasionally to dodge the potholes that characterized the roads leading to the outskirts of the town from Mile 50.

The car windows were down and raindrops splashed him. He needed to think. He wondered what he was going to say when he got to his destination. He became nervous.

As he drove into Obashi Crescent, he slowed, passing No. 15, and kept going. On a rectangular sign attached to the fence was the inscription 'No.12'. From his car, he saw hibiscus and some Queen-of-the-night flowers that had overgrown and spread their branches along the security wires on top of the fence. It appealed to his artist's eye.

He got out of his car and pressed the buzzer by the gate. The bell chimed several times before someone peeped through a small opening in the gate. Several seconds elapsed before the guard opened it. He might not have opened it at all had he not seen a Volkswagen Bug parked by the man who was standing at the gate. The gateman carried an umbrella. Donaldo tried to enter but the gateman blocked him so he could not pass.

'Who are you?' the gateman asked, looking at Donaldo from head to toe.

'I wish to see the young lady who lives here.'

'What's the person's name? I mean the person you are looking for?'

'Sir, sincerely, I do not know her name.' Donaldo gave a boyish smile. The gateman looked at him and pushed the gate, trying to close it.

'Wait, please. She is tall, black, with black hair,' he explained, brushing off some water from his own hair.

'Oh. You want to see my madam. No, people don't see her like that. Just leave.' He began to push at the gate again.

'Wait, Sir—' The gate slammed instantly against Donaldo. By now he was wet all over. There was a sudden flash of lightning, followed by a roar of thunder. *Why is it raining in February?* he thought. Then he remembered that in the car he had a thick pad of paper that he used for his outdoor sketches. He grabbed it and used it for an umbrella. Then he pressed the bell again and again until the gate opened. The gateman came out with an older, tough looking man. He became more nervous. *What do I do now?* his mind sang.

'This is the boy,' the gateman said.

'I am the security here. You have been disturbing us with the bell. Who are you?' The older man wore a khaki security uniform with a logo saying *Towers Security*. He had protruding eyeballs and broad shoulders with a lean body and a flat stomach. His bushy eyebrows almost stretched into his eyes.

Donaldo hated telling people he was the son of Chief Donald Amechi, but he knew that without the name he would not gain entry to the compound.

'I am Donaldo Amechi, I live at Williams Island.'

The two men exchanged glances. 'So you are the Chief's son?' the gateman asked, surprised.

'Yes, Sir. Sir, *biko*, could you permit me to see her?' The two men looked at each other again and ushered him in. They took him to the porch and offered him a seat. The security man went inside and called Miss Spencer, who emerged a few minutes later wearing a sweater. Her feet were encased in black socks and Dunlop slippers.

Miss Spencer's heart skipped on seeing the handsome boy stood before her.

'Good morning, young man.' She eyed him cautiously. 'Can we help you?'

Donaldo faced her. 'Good morning Ma, I ask to see the young lady of the compound.'

'My name is Miss Spencer... don't call me Ma.' The gateman looked at Miss Spencer. He looked at her voluptuous breasts and wondered why she was not married.

'Okay, Ma... *ehm*... Miss Spencer. I... please can you

allow me to see her?'

'Adeline? What do you want with her?'

Donaldo's eyes lit up. 'If that is her name, then yes. I have some… business to discuss with her.'

Miss Spencer coughed slightly. She could guess what 'business' this boy wanted to discuss with Adeline, who was never short of admirers. Still, he was brave to come so brazenly into the Chuba residence. Brave, or naïve, and naïvety could be a dangerous thing.

'Listen, I'd advise you to leave immediately,' she told him, 'here we follow rules, and the rules won't allow you to see her. Understood?' They were all quiet. The breeze swirled her skirt. It made a sizzling sound. The trees made a noise too. The weaverbirds were chirping and the rain had stopped. The compound was serene.

Then, just as Donaldo looked at Miss Spencer, then at the security man, and back at Miss Spencer, the door opened. As if the weaverbirds had called her out, as if they had asked her to come and behold the face she had been thinking about, Adeline stood tenderly by the doorway.

'Hi,' Donaldo said, his voice unsteady. He fidgeted. He felt like sprouting wings and flying away.

'Why don't you come in?' Adeline said, ignoring everyone. Miss Spencer looked at the security man and nodded for him to leave. As she stood watching the two, she allowed herself to think for a moment how beautiful they looked together.

Donaldo was still wet from the rain.

'No.' He looked down at his clothes; Adeline's eyes followed him. 'I am in no state to enter your home. I am happy just to know where you live. I am sorry for any trouble I have caused.' He looked from Adeline to Miss Spencer, whose expression did not change.

Adeline was surprised; she wanted him to stay. 'No. It's okay. I mean… we can get you towels. Please do come in.'

'Please, if you don't mind, I will leave now.' There was no way he could stay: he was shy and he was soaked through. He turned to walk back towards the gate.

'It is strange to come here and then refuse my invitation. I don't even know your name,' Adeline called behind him, 'you could at least return another day.'

He turned back to face her, the hint of a smile on his lips, and for a moment their eyes were locked together.

'My name is Donaldo, and with your permission, perhaps I can return tomorrow.' He glanced at Miss Spencer. 'If it is not any trouble.'

Adeline smiled. 'No trouble at all. I am Adeline. Until tomorrow then, Donaldo.'

He turned and walked away, never looking back.

That day, there were a lot of arguments in the Chuba residence.

They were gathered in the kitchen.

'I don't want that boy to come back, Adeline.'

'Why, Miss Spencer? Why?'

'Because it is not right. Your father… he made it clear

104

that no boy should—'

'I don't care about my father. I can't continue to be in this house every day, every year, without going out. I have no friends.'

'It is for your own good, Adeline.' Miss Spencer's heart thought otherwise. She was so confused.

The maids were in the kitchen too. Michelle said, 'Perhaps we shouldn't… I mean… you shouldn't deprive Adeline of the chance of making friends.'

Miss Spencer barked, 'Are you stupid, Michelle? Are you Adeline's father or mother? Now get out.'

Michelle hurried out of the room.

'All of you!' Miss Spencer screamed. The others followed Michelle, but they stood beside the dining room, eavesdropping.

Miss Spencer approached Adeline. 'Please, Adeline,' she said, her voice calm now, 'I don't want trouble.'

'Who will give you trouble? Donaldo?' Adeline said in a pleading voice. 'He looks gentle.'

'Ah. What will your father say when he finds out?'

'His father is Dad's friend.'

'All the more reason why you shouldn't see this boy. Your father won't like it.'

'I can't continue to please my parents all the time and displease myself.' Adeline sat down on a chair. 'Please, Miss Spencer. Please.'

Miss Spencer was silent.

'They don't need to know.'

TWELVE

The next day Adeline waited in anticipation, checking the window every now and then. Once, she had gone as far as the gate to look. Finally, when she had given up and gone back to her room, he came.

She was called down. She was surprised to see that they had brought him into the sitting room. She stood by the staircase staring at him.

'I am sorry to come late in the evening – if this is a bad time, I will leave.'

She came forward shyly. '*Mba...* sit down.' She wanted to say more, but it was as if her lips had been sealed with glue.

'You have a nice house.'

'Thanks,' she smiled at him, unsure of what to say next.

Donaldo sensed her uneasiness. 'Perhaps you would like to sit, too?'

'Yes, of course,' Adeline approached and sat down on the sofa beside him, turning her body slightly to face him. He wore a T-shirt and jeans. She couldn't stop admiring his long hair. They continued to sit silently. After a few moments a maid appeared.

'We have a visitor,' Adeline told her, grateful for the interruption. 'Get him some snacks, anything hot because it is cold.'

Donaldo smiled uncomfortably. She had not even asked him what he wanted, or if he wanted anything at all. He guessed that she wasn't accostumed to having visitors.

'So what do you do?' she asked.

'I am an artist.'

'A musician?'

'No. I paint. I draw and paint.'

Adeline was thrilled. 'That is so cool. I do some drawings. But I am only an amateur.'

'You will get better.' Donaldo's eyes fell on her neck and the creases around it. He swallowed. Adeline didn't notice.

'You studied that at college?'

'What?'

'You studied Fine Art?'

Donaldo hesitated, then said heavily, 'I did not go to college.'

He bent his head, and she was surprised to hear that.

'The harmattan has worsened,' Adeline commented awkwardly.

Donaldo nodded, grateful the conversation had steered away from his education, 'It must be the rain.

When it rains in January or February it makes the harmattan worse.'

'I wonder how it will be in the North.'

Donaldo didn't respond; he hadn't travelled out of the town since he was born.

Adeline switched on the television, hoping the distraction would calm her nerves. The maid returned with a tray carrying a drink, a meat pie and a bowl of groundnuts. She placed it on the table in front of them.

'Please, help yourself,' Adeline said.

'Thanks.' He pointed at the flickering set. 'You watch TV all the time?'

'Yeah. I enjoy watching TV,' she said. Another maid brought her a glass of juice.

They watched the television together in silence.

In the kitchen lounge, adjacent to the dining room, the maids and the nurse chatted with Miss Spencer while she cut up *ugu* for the stew they were preparing.

Miss Spencer said, 'I wonder if she is going mad. How could she bring him inside?'

'They look beautiful together,' Michelle said and giggled.

'If e go make small madam *happi* me I no see anything wrong for there,' Ngozi said. There was a water lily in bloom in a large vase on the table, and Miss Spencer stared at it as if it would reveal what they were discussing. Ngozi found a cloth and began to clean the flowers.

Miss Spencer said, 'What are you doing that for?'

'I think say you wan make I clean am. You just dey look am,' Ngozi responded.

'No, I was staring far beyond the flowers. Something tells me we are stepping into a big *booom*, *wahala*.' She made an awful sound as she said the word *booom*. They all laughed.

'Check the rice. She might want to eat with him. Adjust the cooker too,' Miss Spencer ordered and Ngozi went back to the kitchen.

'I love them… I really do. So much,' Michelle said.

'I wish na me be Adeline oh!' Ngozi's voice echoed from the kitchen.

'What is happening to all of you? Just the second time you are seeing that boy and all your mouths are wagging *kpam kpam kpam* like a typewriter.'

They sat at the long dining table. Miss Spencer, Donaldo and Adeline. The maids were desperate to know more about him, so they stood by the door leading to the kitchen and listened in. Donaldo felt exhilarated. Adeline felt full of gladness.

They ate in silence till Adeline asked, 'Do you like Miss Spencer's stew? She is the best cook in the whole world.'

'Yes. Yes.' Donaldo couldn't look at either of them. But the stew was good.

There was silence again.

By the time they had finished the meal, it was getting dark and they went back to the sitting room. Donaldo stared at the framed photos on the wall.

'You have a nice family.'

'Thanks.' Adeline picked up a novel on the coffee table, *Devil on the Cross* by Ngugi Wa Thiong'o, 'Have you read this?'.

'I don't read books. I find it difficult. I find it easier to draw and paint.'

'Hold on.' Adeline hurried upstairs. When she came back she was holding some sheets of paper. She smiled childishly and showed him her own drawings. 'They are just amateur sketches.'

She sat close beside him. He had never sat that near to a woman before other than Madam Vero. His heart began to run a marathon.

'What you draw. They... they look sad.'

Adeline looked at him. 'I feel sad, at times,' she admitted. 'I draw when I am bored. But I love to read. I have hundreds of novels.'

'Boredom brings out ingenuity and creativity.'

'*Hmmn*, you really have a love for art, then?'

'Yes. Every artist should.'

'Your father loves art too?'

'He was a footballer. Are footballers artists?'

'Well, I guess so.' She laughed.

'I inherited my love of art from my mother, Christiana.' He smiled sadly.

Adeline looked affectionately at him, she knew Chief Amechi's wife had died many years back, it was popular knowledge. 'Where was your mother from?'

'Palermo, in Sicily.'

'Oh. I couldn't have guessed that. Ever!' She giggled happily.

'Let me show you something,' He took one of the pieces of paper and on the other side sketched the tree by the window. In no time, he was done. She looked at it and marvelled.

'It's beautiful. Gosh, this is amazing,' she said, her eyes filled with admiration.

'I've been talking only about myself since I came here, Adeline. Unless you want to write a novel about me, I would love to know more about you.' Donaldo smiled at her and their eyes met briefly. His body trembled. He felt heat engulf him. He wished he could just sit there forever.

THIRTEEN

Simon Chuba was a civil engineer with the Ministry of Works in Awka in Anambra State. While in secondary school, he founded the Black Scorpions Fraternity and lured many students into it. The fraternity terrorized the other students, the school and all nearby schools. He beat up teachers and flouted school rules. And his brother, Evangelist Chris Chuba, bailed him out in times of trouble. Back then Chris Chuba was building his religious ministry and had just returned from the United States. So, whenever he wanted a rival pastor threatened, the young Simon did it for him.

Simon got whatever he wanted, even women, either by kind or by force. Only a few in the fraternity knew about his perversion for rape. Once, at the age of nineteen, he had raped a fourteen-year-old girl selling oranges. He called her into an empty building pretending he wanted to buy some fruit from her. He knocked her down and tore her clothes. The young girl's eyes were red and filled with tears and fear. And he liked the fear that had engulfed his prey. He entered her forcefully. The next morning, they found her dead body in the building. Years later, as he watched his niece Adeline grow into a woman, he knew he had to fight with himself not to commit a taboo.

It was a rule that two blood relations could not both be members of the Sacred Order of the Universal Forces. But, thanks to Evangelist Chuba's friendship with Chief Amechi, Simon was a hatchet man for the organization. He received contracts to assassinate those who threatened the existence of the organization in Nigeria, or any of its members.

The harmattan sun made the air hot. But inside the large library of Chris Chuba's home it was cool. Chief Donald Amechi and the Evangelist were seated on sofas. They had summoned Simon for an important and urgent assignment.

The Evangelist was the first to broach the issue.

'Simon, we need your help again. That is why we have invited you here.'

'If it's an assassination, count me out after the way I was treated the last time, with my name appearing in the papers.'

'Listen, Simon, it happened so quickly. Chief Donald and I were out of the country—'

'Do not tell me that, Chris! You have a lot of friends. Governors, presidential aides, ministers… Is the Chief of Police not under your control? Was he not aware that I was performing a duty for you?'

The Chief was silent. He knew that they had failed the young man in their last operation, so he wanted the Evangelist to appease his brother.

'It was a member of the Nigerian Intelligence Agency who had been following your activities – he was the one that caused the whole problem. That was why your name was among the suspects. But we took care of it. No one's mentioned the matter since. The case file was made to disappear. We are sorry,' Chris Chuba said.

Simon was silent.

'Look, Simon. That was in the past. We have reorganized now.'

Simon looked from his brother to the Chief. 'What is the job this time?'

The two men looked at each other. Chief Amechi spoke first. 'This could be dangerous if not well handled. We have a friend who we suspect could turn into a parrot.' Simon nodded. He watched the Chief – he had always admired his strength and influence. That day, the Chief wore a white gown made of *safari* and a red cap on his head, signifying his title.

'So who is it?'

'This man's name is Alhaji Umar Hassan.' Chief Amechi produced from beside him a thick brown envelope. 'All you need is in here. Your cheque, his photos, addresses in Abuja and in Sokoto, his vehicle number plate... all the information you need is here.'

Simon took the envelope and looked into it. He pulled out the cheque.

'Two million naira?' *This target must be a very important person*, he thought.

'Yes. You work alone on this. Alhaji Umar is the head of the Nigerian Port Authority. He has security and he is very intelligent. We had a meeting and he walked away from it, he understands the implications of that. You know what I mean?'

'Two million naira is not enough. For the head of the NPA.'

'Simon, *nawao*. We are in this together,' the Chief said.

'My target is an important man, Chief.'

'Do the job first, Simon,' his brother pleaded.

Chief Amechi stood, signaling that the meeting had come to an end.

That evening Simon drove back to his base at Awka.

Donaldo came out from the hut where he painted, his face radiant with joy. He clutched his board under his arm, and his leather bag hung on his shoulder. He passed the Island chapel, which was very close to his hut. It could hold about fifty people, and was built of unplastered mud blocks. The floor was made with hard clay, the traditional way. The roof was finished with thatch, and leaves from nearby gmelina trees covered the floor and the pews.

The altar was built in the form of a stage, raised off the floor, its walls extending to the roof. The long altar table was polished every Sunday. A tabernacle was fixed to the wall and enclosed with strong metal doors. To the side of the tabernacle was a lamp stand, and when there was a communion at the tabernacle, the lamp was lit. Donaldo would have made the sign of the cross as he passed if he had seen the lamp lit.

He had asked his father once why the chapel had never been replaced with a modern structure, and he had replied that he wanted to retain the archaic architecture the British missionaries had left behind. After the missionaries had gone the subsequent owners of the Island had always maintained the chapel as it was and just rebuilt the mud walls.

He walked to the priest's cottage and smelt the aroma of fish pepper soup. He knew Ite, the priest's servant, was preparing his master's favourite meal. He knocked at the oak door and pushed it open.

'Who is that?' a voice called.

Donaldo came in and put his art materials by the entrance. The cottage was rarely visited. The Islanders avoided it because they resented the old nagging priest.

The priest had been reading, *The Ritual Circumcision of Ezza People* by Rev. Fr. John Okwozey Odeh, and, on seeing Donaldo, he put the book aside.

'Welcome, Naldo. Your face glows. What makes you so happy?'

'Am I? I don't know. I am making a painting.'

'Of what?'

'It is called *Head on a Basket*.'

Ite entered the room carrying a bowl with bananas and groundnuts, which he set down on the table. Ite was a dapper young man in his early thirties, but still unmarried.

'Tell me about it, son.' The priest's voice was husky and it broke from time to time. He had lost a couple of his teeth, which also gave him a slight lisp when he spoke.

Father Simeon Iwunze had been a psychologist before he entered the priesthood and he claimed he had read about five hundred books on psychology alone. He was the special advisor to the Committee of Bishops in the country and was often consulted by powerful people in the state.

'*Head on a Basket*, you'd love it if you saw it. It's a huge painting, the size of your front door. I am painting on wood. It has a small basket and a large female head. There are shadows in the background and the image is well illuminated.' Donaldo picked up a banana from the bowl and began to eat it.

Father Simeon had baptized Donaldo. His godfather, Donaldo's uncle – his mother's elder brother from Palermo – had told him during his last visit some years back that his mother's wish had been that he be brought up not by his father, but by the old priest. Christiana Amechi had developed a deep love for Father Simeon, who was like a father to her; whenever she was beaten by her husband, she would run to the cottage for refuge. After Donaldo had to stop going to school when he was twelve, the priest became his teacher, though Donaldo rarely attended his lessons, discouraged by his father

117

who preferred him to focus on his art. As time went on he had avoided the priest. But since he had met Adeline, he felt the need to visit him again.

They talked about the painting, which Donaldo intended to donate to the Island to be put on display at his favourite restaurant. The priest said it was a good idea.

Ite brought the fish pepper soup and white *agidi* on a tray and went back to bring another glass of water. He also brought a bottle of whisky for the priest, which he would drink after his dinner.

'Come to the dining table, Naldo.'

The priest began to say grace, firstly to himself quietly, before continuing aloud, '… bless and sanctify this meal, which we, thy children, are about to take out of the abundance of thy grace, Lord.' He made a sign of the cross with his right hand, which was wrinkled and trembled slightly.

'This reminds me, Father. Why is it that whenever we want to eat, you say some prayers in silence, even in mass?' Donaldo served the food.

Father Simeon was quiet for a while. He drank some water and then said, 'Quite a number of prayers priests say, especially at mass, began as private prayers.' He took his plate of *agidi* and a fork and began to eat. Donaldo ate too.

When satisfied, the priest sipped his whisky and Donaldo watched as his Adam's apple jumped up and down. They said nothing to each other until the servant came and cleared the table.

The old priest began to talk about the origin of the prayers they said in mass. He wanted Donaldo's mind to always be occupied with the things of God. But the young man's mind wandered far away – it had always wandered. Before, he used to think deeply about his mother. He had not stopped missing her. But since he had met Adeline, he felt happier, he smiled to himself often, so as the priest talked about mass, Donaldo's mind was elsewhere. He imagined kissing the lips of the beautiful girl.

'Donaldo. Your mind is not here.'

'Oh, I am tired.'

'You work hard. All the time. You should go home now and sleep. Okay?'

Donaldo straightened his hair.

'I am fine.'

'And how is your father? Still determined to make you the greatest artist ever?'

Donaldo groaned. 'He is well, as always. Attending to some business.'

'Your father…' Father Simeon said in a whisper, his hand turning his glass of whisky around. 'Your father is a complex man.'

Donaldo looked at him.

'Donaldo, there is something that has been worrying me for some time now. Some rumours, not that I give much mind to such talk. But, they say your father is an occultist.' Donaldo's eyes widened in surprise. He stared at Father Simeon. For many years he had witnessed his father's odd behaviour, but he never thought other people had noticed.

'You scare me with statements like that, Father.'

'Do not be scared, son. God watches over you.'

'God is in heaven, Father.'

'Have faith, son. God is not just in heaven. He is here. Over you, beside you, behind you. He is in the space around us. Watching over us. The idea of heaven is to give you a sense that, up there where your eyes cannot reach and your hands cannot touch, there is where God is. But what is the definition of heaven? It is the vacuum. The void.'

'It is a shame God was not here when Christiana needed Him.'

The priest was taken aback by this statement. Donaldo looked down, sorry for his outburst.

Father Simeon opened his mouth to speak but he couldn't find the words.

'And what of Satan, Father?'

'Come to the sitting room. I need to relax my back.' The priest stood and stretched. 'My boy, the church teaches you that Satan is beneath the earth. As a kid they ask you to march on the earth hard so you can stamp on his head. But son, he is not there. He is on earth, beside you, behind you. He is everywhere around us. He is even human!'

FOURTEEN

The two brothers were inside the International Stadium in Lagos. They were sitting on the plastic seats surrounded by empty rows. They could see the two goalposts and the green field. A few people were jogging round the field.

Alhaji Umar Hassan turned to look at his younger brother, a man in his mid forties, who was holidng an envelope. Their eyes locked and Malik Hassan said, 'Is what they plan really jihad?'

The Alhaji shook his head. 'Jihad, Malik, means a lot of things. There are three categories of jihad in Islam: jihad of the soul, jihad against *Shaitan*, and jihad against the infidels.'

'So what they plan could be categorized as jihad against infidels.'

The older man shook his head. 'Malik, the world has changed. When jihad was fought during the time of the Prophet, peace be upon him, and after his death when caliphs took over the leadership of Islam, things were different. Islam was a new religion striving for prominence. Remember that back then a religious leader also served as the leader of the people. So the Prophet Muhammad, peace be upon him, was the religious leader as well as the people's leader... they needed to conquer new territories to expand their reach and win converts to the religion. Things are different now, Malik.'

'Do we as Muslims not need to strive to conquer more territories?' his brother replied. 'We need the Islamic caliphate back. Don't we? I believe that the Islamic world was better off when the caliphate was in existence. Alhaji, for thirteen centuries, the caliphate fused Muslims and Muslim lands as one, politically, economically and spiritually. Ever since the caliphate fell the Islamic world has not been united. But given what is happening around the world, in Africa, in the Middle East and Asia, we may succeed in getting back the caliphate. Who says it cannot be stationed in Nigeria? You never can tell, brother.'

Alhaji Umar Hassan shook his head – he had heard the same sentiment expressed by many young men recently. 'That was long ago, Malik. The world has outgrown that. There is the growth of technology, and the forces of economics have spread beyond individual states bound by the same religion or ideology. Besides, many people now do not even want to belong to any faith at all. Do you think it is the will of the Almighty Allah that people should be forced to follow our religion?'

The young man said nothing.

'One of the Hadiths explains that the Prophet, peace

be upon him, when he was returning after a war, had told his companion that they had left the lesser jihad and were returning to the greater jihad. His companion asked which jihad is greater than the war they had just fought and the Prophet, peace be upon him, replied that the jihad against oneself, jihad against *Shaitan* is the greater jihad.'

The young man had heard that Hadith before. He was silent. He was a brave man who liked war. He did not like the path his elder brother had chosen.

'What is happening across the world is not drawing people closer to Islam.' Alhaji Umar shook his head. 'It pushes them away. The religion of Islam is not under external attack, though some terrorist organizations will make you believe otherwise. The fact that some countries have attacked an Islamic country does not mean every Muslim should take up arms against Christians and non-Muslims. No. I tell you, the Western media totally misuse the word "jihad" to describe suicide bombers or any people striving against the interests of the West. In the past they caused a lot of disaffection among many Muslim countries, and now that some individuals in these countries have turned against the West, and are using violence, Western countries are claiming in their media that these people are fighting in the name of the Prophet Muhammad, peace be upon him.' He looked down and shook his head again, his eyes sad and his heart heavy.

'When I was at university in Zaria, I took part in and led uprisings against the Christians, as you know, brother. I thought I was doing the will of the Almighty,' Malik said.

'Yes, Malik. But remember, I warned you. Look, do you not have a brain? Do you never wonder what kind of God would command people to kill others? No. Allah is compassionate.'

Malik stared at his brother. And there was no doubt in his mind that there was fear in his elder brother's eyes. He wondered why he should be so afraid. He said, 'I would have been happy to hear of this plan, if it weren't for what you tell me now. '

The Alhaji smiled. 'Malik, do you now do God's work for Him? Who are you, a mere mortal to know the ways of the Almighty? Leave Him to judge everyone according to His choosing. There is no coercion in the worship of the true God, no coercion at all. The Qur'an says: "There is no compulsion in religion. Verily the right path has become distinct from the wrong path." '

'Whatever my brother says.' Malik looked away, and for a while there was silence as the two brothers watched some men who were exercising on the far side of the pitch.

Alhaji Umar broke the silence. 'I am going to be assassinated, Malik.'

Malik turned abruptly and looked at his brother, a sudden sick feeling in his stomach.

'I have no documents to prove all that I have told you, about the terrorism plans. But the men whose names I gave you – you must watch out for them.'

Malik looked at the envelope in his hand. Inside it were names, phone numbers and contact details, together with photos of Chief Donald Amechi and Sheikh Mohammed Seko. 'What are you going to do?'

'*Insha'Allah*, nothing will happen to me. But my heart is filled with fear, Malik. Yet I take solace in the teachings of the Holy Book. It says: "Do men think that they will be left alone on saying we believe and they will not be tested?" My hope is in the Lord.'

'Then may the will of the Almighty be done.'

Donaldo was in the sitting room that Tuesday afternoon when his father saw him from the porch and came in. He greatly resembled his handsome father, the only difference being his eye colour, the length of his hair and his accent.

'It's been a long time, son,' Chief Amechi greeted him.

'Good day, Chief.' Donaldo seldom called his father 'daddy' or 'papa' in his presence.

They shook hands and the Chief patted Donaldo's shoulder, saying, 'Sit down. Do you want a drink?'

Donaldo remained standing. 'No. I need sleep.' He hesitated before saying, 'This month is the anniversary of my mother's death.' He looked at his feet. If there was anything he feared in this world, it was the tall man in his presence.

Chief Amechi frowned. '*Ahh!* That's right. I don't need you reminding me. I miss her too, you know. Don't look at me like that. Life must go on.' His father sat on a large sofa. 'Yes, life must go on – in fact, you need to get your portfolio ready to show it to that company in Italy. I'm leaving tomorrow.' The bulky man lit a cigar. His expensive robe was radiant in the light spread by the coloured chandeliers.

As he sat drawing on the cigar and puffing out smoke, he wondered about his son. Many years back, he had discovered that his son had an extraordinary artistic talent, so he encouraged that passion and turned him against everything else. He made sure his son visited no one, had no girlfriends, and attended no parties. He was happy Donaldo did not love women, for he believed that women had destroyed so many great men.

He knew Donaldo would be a great man and exposing him to the world might destroy that potential. He watched the smoke as it played with the breeze in the room; he watched it as it curled around the only picture of Christiana, which stood on top of the television. Oh how he hated that woman.

FIFTEEN

A Toyota Hilux drove into the Centre for Islamic Knowledge. Some men, dressed in *gallabiya* and carrying Kalashnikovs, were posted around various parts of the massive compound and they watched the vehicle as a young man with a well combed afro got out. They watched him closely as he scanned the compound, then brought out four large bags from the back of the truck. No one approached him. And the man did not notice the men carrying guns. A visitor would assume that this place was a school, but what kind of school had such massive buildings?

Then Sheikh Mohammed Seko emerged from his quarters and strode towards the man. Abouzeid tucked his pistol into his trousers and marched after the Sheikh.

'*Hahaha*, Shedrack! Shedrack!' the Sheikh called.

The visitor spotted the Sheikh and rushed up to hug him. People watching wondered if he was the man they had been waiting for before the attacks could begin.

'*As-salamu 'alaykum*, Shedrack Obong!'

'My Sheikh. Look at you. You look so good.'

'Oh, praise be to the Almighty Allah, Shedrack.' He turned and faced Abouzeid. 'He is the one I have talked about all this time, Abouzeid.'

Sheikh Seko's deputy stretched out his hand and Shedrack took it. He motioned to some of the gun-toting men to carry the visitor's bags. They led him to a very modest room with just a mattress on the floor, a transistor radio, a rail for his clothes, and walls painted with Islamic calligraphy.

The Sheikh, Abouzeid and Shedrack all sat on the mattress. The Sheikh said a quick prayer of thanksgiving.

'How was your trip?'

'It was fine.'

'How is America?'

'Fine. Fine.'

'Abouzeid, go and get him some food.'

Abouzeid hurried away, his heart filled with anger as he wondered why Sheikh Seko trusted a man whose name was Shedrack.

Shedrack said, 'This place is huge. I'm impressed.'

'Yes. *Allahu akbar!* We have a lot of soldiers ready to target our strategic locations. We have been waiting for you.'

'How many do you have?'

'Close to three thousand, but as soon as we start our attacks more young people will join. There are incentives too.'

'I will build some explosives for the attacks. But

then we need to test the soldiers. We need to organize an attack – say, an army base or a police station or a school.'

'Very good. I will start the preparations immediately.'

Donaldo busied himself trying to finish the drawings that his father would take to Italy. The sculptures were all ready; some of them were gigantic works so would have to be transported in crates.

It was late afternoon when he gave up and called Adeline's mobile. They had talked on the phone several times since they met.

'Hi.'

'Hello, Donaldo, how are you?' Adeline answered happily. She was grinning from ear to ear.

'I am very well.'

'Good. Your call woke me. I was sleeping.'

Donaldo imagined how she would look lying down, her eyes closed in sleep. 'Hope your enjoyed your siesta. I wanted to say hello.'

'Donaldo, why don't you come and see me?'

'What about your parents?'

'They are not around, just Miss Spencer, but I'll take care of her.' She hung up before he had the chance to object.

Donaldo changed into jeans and a T-shirt. Then he went down to the garage and drove off.

As Donaldo drove to the centre of the town, he thought

back to when he was in primary school. How he used to be alone, especially after the death of his mother. He remembered how one day his teacher called him *ogbanje*, one who is reincarnated, possessed by spirits and waiting to die and be reincarnated again. Whenever the car dropped him at school, he would watch the car recede then he would walk away, into the thick Mile 4 forest. One time he missed school for a whole week. He did not tell his father about it, nor did he tell Madam Vero. Then his teacher came to the mansion and complained to his father, saying, 'He hasn't been to school for a week, Chief. Even when he is in school, he keeps to himself... like... Some say... Sir, some say he is *ogbanje*. He talks to nobody...'

Donaldo remembered standing at the staircase, eavesdropping. He was ten. His father did not ask him questions; he beat him with his belt mercilessly.

Alhaji Umar Hassan was driven to Kafurzan by his driver at 4pm. Outside the gate of the Centre for Islamic Knowledge, they were stopped and had to wait for fifteen minutes, enough time for Sheikh Mohammed Seko to ring Sheikh Kabiru Ibrahim and inform him of the development.

They had to park the jeep outside the gate and then an armed man escorted the Alhaji and his driver into the compound. They were taken to the side of one of the blocks and frisked. Then the Alhaji was taken to where the Sheikh sat at the back of the mosque. The Sheikh stood up as soon as he saw the Alhaji.

'Alhaji, *As-salamu 'alaykum!*'

'*Alaykum as-salam*, Sheikh. You have a big place here.'

'*Alhamdulillah!* Please sit down.'

Alhaji Umar Hassan sat on the mat, facing the Sheikh. He was scared but he willed his heart to be strong. His driver was sitting on a wooden bench in front of the mosque and a guard stood a few metres away from him.

'We have some *fura da nunu*—'

'No. Never mind. I am fine.'

'Are you sure? We have *kunu*. We can get you some. Fresh *kunu* made some minutes back.'

'You are so kind, Sheikh Seko. But I am okay.'

'How is your family, Alhaji?'

'*Lafia*. They are fine.'

Mohammed Seko stared at the Alhaji's clothes, a long garment sewn from expensive brocade material. A black cap was on his head. Sheikh Seko said, 'I hope you come in peace, Alhaji?'

'Sheikh Seko, you are my brother. Of course I come in peace.'

'Then may Allah guide your path.'

'Sheikh, we belong to the same faith. I have come to you as your brother. I acknowledge that I was part of the plan but I now realize the ramifications of what we planned and the motives of our friends in the South. I want to plead to your conscience to abandon this war.'

Sheikh Mohammed Seko had a smile on his face as

the Alhaji was talking.

'Sheikh Mohammed, we have had a little argument before about jihad. You are convinced that what you are doing is jihad for Islam, so permit me to bring to your notice the conditions in which jihad is prohibited. And, Sheikh, I believe that you will agree with me that what we have planned falls within these conditions.'

'Go on, Alhaji.'

'Jihad is prohibited if it will cause destruction to the Islamic world and if it doesn't fulfil the prerequisite that Islam must be under attack before one embarks on jihad to protect it against attack and aggression. We are not under attack, at least not in Nigeria. Some Nigerian states even have Sharia law in place. Sheikh, if you go ahead with the plan the Government will order war against the North and bomb Muslims. Our nation's soldiers don't respect human rights, so you will endanger our brothers and sisters. Jihad is prohibited if it fails to lead people in the good path.' Alhaji Umar Hassan was counting off his points with his fingers. ' "Invite to the way of your Lord with wisdom and fair preaching, and argue with them in a way that is polite." This is the way we are taught, Sheikh.'

The noise of children playing football in the compound distracted the Sheikh.

'Are you following?'

'Yes, Alhaji.' The Sheikh was still smiling.

'This jihad will cause destruction to our people. We are bringing war to our own land. If you bomb schools and hospitals and libraries and police stations in the North, are you not destroying the infrastructures? Our own infrastructures?'

'Yes. We destroy the infrastructures, but Alhaji, infrastructure is nothing compared to what we will gain – an Islamic region. Perhaps, *insha'Allah*, we might succeed one day in making Nigeria an Islamic nation.'

'How do you ever think that will be possible? A country of over one hundred and fifty million people with diverse ethnic groups and faiths?'

'Nothing is impossible with God. When the Messenger of Allah, peace be upon him, began in Mecca, and later migrated to Medina, did anyone ever believe that he would later on conquer Mecca? When he left Mecca, he'd wanted to go to the hill town of Taif, but the people mocked and snubbed him saying, "If you were sent by Allah as you claim, then your state is too lofty for me to address you, and if you are taking Allah's name in vain, it is not fit that I should speak to you." Yet, these people later accepted Islam.'

'Sheikh Seko, you are not the Messenger of Allah, peace be upon him, and we will never control this country with violence. Our young men will fight and die while the children of our friends in the South are living safely abroad, studying to become leaders of this country.'

'Alhaji, we will win in the end, fame and fortune will be ours. You are shying away from your responsibility.'

Alhaji Umar gave a knowing smile – he had always

known that the Sheikh was not fighting for faith. He was a greedy man, drunk in his quest for fame and fortune. He scoffed to himself. Sheikh Seko noticed his change in demeanour, and stared at him deeply in the eyes, as if challenging the sanity of the Alhaji.

'Alhaji, until we restore full Islamic law we have not done the will of the Almighty.'

'And the will of the Almighty is done by the sword?'

'It has always been by that way. Human beings respond easily to instructions at the sight of the sword.'

Alhaji Umar Hassan shook his head and the two men looked at each other in silence. They understood that each had chosen their own separate path and no rhetoric or preaching would change their hearts. Alhaji Umar got to his feet.

'When the Government forces come, they will burn down buildings, shoot men and women and children. They will shoot children running away from attacks. They will shoot them in the back. They will rape our young girls. And some wealthy men like Dr Bode Clark and Chief Donald Amechi will make millions of dollars from security contracts. When that time comes, I want you to remember my words today.'

The road was very quiet, except for a few old men and women on bicycles, riding home, holding torch lights. It was evening now, and Donaldo had taken Adeline out in his car to get away from the ever watchful eyes of the staff, particularly Miss Spencer.

Adeline was jubilant, talking excitedly about various things.

'Who taught you how to drive?'

'My uncle. My mother's brother. He visited two years back. He lives in Palermo. Do you want to learn?'

'Yes! When do we start?'

'*Haha!* So keen? Okay, we'll have our first lesson soon.'

'Of course, soon.' She rolled her eyes dramatically. 'So where do we go now?'

'To my hut.'

'Your hut?'

'Just wait and see.'

Donaldo accelerated and she squealed. She felt like a bird – free. She looked out to the heavens through the window. What could be sweeter than freedom?

They drove to the Island and parked near Donaldo's hut. Adeline was happy and her face shone with joy. They got out of the car and, using a torch, followed the concrete path lined by flowers that gave out an overpowering fragrance. She noticed gmelina and many fruit trees.

'Wow! I love this place. Where is your house?'

'It is not far from the chapel. Welcome to Williams Island.' He hesitantly placed his hand round her waist, afraid of what she might say, but after initial resistance she leaned close to him. He turned to face her and she looked into his eyes, and behind all his bravado, she still saw naïvety. She saw sweetness and fear that was rather provocative.

'What?'

'What?' he repeated, mimicking her voice, then laughed, took her hand and led her to his hut.

'Look over there, where you see flickers of light. There is the chaplain's cottage. He is an old man, and my friend. You will meet him one day.'

'Oh, I'd love to.'

They were very near to the hut when she saw a sign on a board hoisted to a pole: 'Out Of Bounds. Not Safe.' She stopped.

'What's wrong?' Donaldo asked.

'The sign.'

'Don't be afraid. It's just to ward off intruders. It's my sanctuary. Now, even if you walk through the valley of the shadow of death, you should fear no evil, for I am with you. Isn't that what it says in the Bible?'

She laughed.

Donaldo showed her the barbed wire that surrounded the perimeter. He unlocked the small gate and with the torch she saw the trees and the swings. She saw the tables and the wood he was carving. He switched on the lights outside the hut.

Adeline saw that the little hut was just made of mud. The roof was thatch and, when they went inside, she noticed that the floor was mud too.

She was surprised. 'Is this your studio?'

'Yeah.' There were a lot of paintings, sketches and sculptures scattered around.

'Oh wow. My heart is racing. These are fine. So professional. You are so talented, Donaldo.'

He smiled shyly. 'Chief is taking a lot of my work to Italy. He wants to contract me to a well known firm.'

'Oh?' She dropped the sketches she was looking at and stared at him.

'Yes. If the contract goes through, I'll travel to Italy and work for the firm as an artist for a few years.'

'Donaldo! You're leaving me?'

He didn't know what to say. 'Well… for all I know the firm won't agree to the terms my father is insisting on. So I may not be going.'

Even Donaldo could hear the lack of conviction in his voice. He was intelligent enough to recognize his own remarkable talent. Adeline had realized it too. Her eyes glistened. He wanted to hold her, but his heart warned him against it. He looked away.

'With paintings like these, they are bound to sign you, Donaldo,' Adeline said. He looked at her and saw a tear fall slowly down her face. It was his cue. He approached her and hesitantly put his arms around her.

'Listen, Adeline. I assure you, even if they accept me, I will decline.' He gave her a reassuring smile.

She sat down on a bench.

'Can you draw me, Donaldo?' She took his right arm. 'Please, I will hang it in my room.'

Happiness mixed with nervousness filled his heart. After over a minute of silence, their hearts beating against their chests, Donaldo said, 'Lie down on that swinging bamboo bed.'

SIXTEEN

Tuesday, 23rd February 2010

That night Donaldo painted Adeline. He thought she was the most sublime creature he had ever seen. Adeline's eyes gleamed at him. Her black hair was held with a golden fillet and thrown down her back. Her elbow was on the bamboo bed and her other arm was on her lap and her slender legs were crossed as if intertwined with the night. Her black smooth skin made Donaldo swallow with desire.

Her face was turned to him. Her thin dress deliciously outlined the contours of her body. A torrent of passion rushed through him and his long fingers held the gold-coated pencil loosely. He began to sketch her, paying attention to the way her breasts swelled beneath the fabric, how her chest rose with every breath, the way the material clung to her hips.

After some time he sensed she was starting to stiffen and he suggested that she get up and relax her muscles. From the sketches, he finished up the work while she stretched the full length of her body and began to approach him. Heat rose in him and he asked her to sit again.

He smiled, looking at her and then at the picture.

'Are you through?' she asked.

He nodded, stood and shook the tension out of his hands. His face was sweating and he removed his shirt to cool down. Adeline approached and looked at the drawing, astonished. It looked more real than her. The work made her remember the first picture of the Blessed Virgin Mary her mother gave her as a gift – she had adored that image but the one she was holding now had a more powerful, secular energy and felt more real than that of the Blessed Mary.

'Donaldo!' She could not say more. He could see she was shy and feared she sensed in his strokes the sexual tension that he fought as he created the piece.

'I am sorry.'

'No, Donaldo, it's sweet,' she said and her eyes drifted from the image to his eyes. Donaldo had intimidating eyes. Grey, and sensual. Whenever he looked at anyone, that person would bend their head or look away. Madam Vero always found it difficult when he stared at her. He instilled a kind of fear in people. When he was a kid, his eyes had helped to fuel his teachers' suspicion that he must be *ogbanje*.

'You like it?'

'No, I love it!' She smiled, overwhelmed. 'It's perfect, Donaldo, thank you! I love you,' she said before she could stop herself.

It took him by surprise. His father had strict rules about women, and he suddenly realized how serious this had become. 'We must leave now. It is late and your people will be worried.' He hurriedly packed his work away into the large locker and locked it. He folded the newly made image of Adeline and carefully placed it in a drawer.

'What about the painting?' she asked, hurt and ashamed.

'I will add some detail to it tomorrow. Then frame it and bring it to you.'

'All right.' She was annoyed with herself for her outburst. She was worried by his sudden change of attitude and felt she might lose him. He switched off the lights and turned on the torch and led her back to the car.

Madam Vero served her master a cup of Nescafé. He wore black jeans and a white long-sleeved shirt, which made him look even taller, and his newly shaved chin made him seem younger.

Chief Amechi sat on the sofa facing the television while Madam Vero hung around waiting for orders. He looked at her finally and beckoned her to come nearer.

'Who is the girl my son is carrying around in his car, Veronica?'

Madam Vero was shocked. She looked at him and then at the huge guard seated by the door.

'I don't understand, Chief?' Her hands were behind her back and she was uneasy. She had lived with him for a long time and was like a wife to him, so she understood his temperament.

'I just saw my son driving with a girl in the front seat.'

His stare was enough to tell her that he was serious. He was demanding answers.

'*I met a girl today…*' Madam Vero recalled.

She finally said, 'Chief, she could have been any girl from the village, probably needing a ride home, they are so careless these days.'

'I want to know who he has been visiting.'

'Chief, we both know your son very well, he doesn't visit anyone but that priest. And you are embarrassing me. Do you think I would allow any girl into this house, flouting your orders?'

Madam Vero turned to walk away and the Chief looked remorseful. He loved her in his own way, for caring for him, his son and his household.

'Wait, I am sorry. But you know how much I value his future. His talent. Women will destroy him like they did to other great artists before him.'

Madam Vero turned back towards him, 'But you will end up destroying your son yourself, *agwagom gi*, I have told you.' They stared at each other and she walked out of the room toward the kitchen. She was one of the few people in the world with the power to walk away from the Chief and live to tell the tale.

Once in the kitchen, she noticed she was breathing very hard. She drank some water. Fear gripped her. She knew better than anyone the consequences if Chief Amechi discovered his son had a woman in his life.

Chief Amechi was still on the sofa waiting for his son to

return home that night. He had changed into pyjamas and stretched out his legs on top of the glass coffee table. All his years as a footballer had kept him in good shape. The door clicked open, and Donaldo walked in.

'Where have you been, son?'

'To the café,' responded Donaldo and he headed for the stairs. His father called him back.

'When did you start visiting the cafeteria?'

'I was bored.'

'Have you finished the drawings?'

'No… I will do that tonight.'

At that instant, his father sprang to his feet, 'You are a fool, Donaldo. You are toying with your future and talent! I saw you tonight, with a woman in your car. Perhaps you were taking her to the café, or somewhere else. Have you started messing about? And you forgot to complete the work. I am supposed to take it with me tomorrow.' He was facing Donaldo. Madam Vero was now standing by the door to the sitting room, ready to run in and intervene.

'There was no girl in my car!'

'Don't you dare raise your voice at me, you fool! You are just like your mother. Liars! You will end up throwing all your efforts to the mud. You are a fool, Donaldo!'

Donaldo said nothing and just stared at his father. The mere mention of his mother made him weak. It made him hate his father even more.

He summoned courage and said, 'How dare you insult my mother—' At that, his father swooped on him like a kite about to carry off a chick. He punched his son on the nose. Donaldo fell down. He was about to hit him again when Madam Vero ran in.

'You will kill this boy, Chief!'

'Stay out of this, woman!'

Madam Vero held his hands, forcing him away from Donaldo. Donaldo just stared. His nose bled. He wiped it with the back of his hand.

'I hate what you are doing to him, to this house!' Madam Vero was shouting.

'Listen, boy. Women have led to the death of so many great men. Name them. You know the list. Be careful. Otherwise, you will join the list.'

He turned and stormed out of the room. Madam Vero rushed to Donaldo and tried to help him but he pushed her away.

'I hate him! I hate you! I hate everyone.' He walked out of the room. It was a lie and Madam Vero knew it.

He did not answer his phone that night when Adeline rang. The next day, he did not answer because he was afraid she might ask him to come over. He did not want her to see him like this – swollen face and bloody nose.

Whoever joins himself to another in a good cause
shall have a share of it,
and whoever joins himself to another in an
evil cause
shall have the responsibility of it, and Allah controls
all things.

Surah 4:85
The Holy Qur'an

SEVENTEEN

Alhaji Umar Hassan woke up in the morning feeling happy. While his heart was not completely at ease, he knew that at the age of sixty-eight he had lived a long life, and a good one for the most part. He had enjoyed life. On the matter of the jihad, he trusted his younger brother to take action if he died. He regretted that he had no taped conversation or a single document to prove what he knew. But Malik had the names of all the members of the Sacred Order who were a threat to his life.

That morning, as he got up, his happiness enhanced by the fat young woman who shared his bed, he went into the bathroom, turned on the shower and stood under the warm, cleansing stream of water, letting it fall all over his head and body.

The knock on the door had come several times before the woman lazily raised herself from the bed and, using the duvet to cover her nakedness, walked to the door. Without making enquiries she threw the door open.

She opened her mouth to ask the hotel attendant what

she could do for him when the young man pushed her into the room. She hit the ground so hard that cries of pain escaped her mouth. Her hand dropped the duvet, revealing her voluptuous breasts at which a gun was now pointing.

'Shhhhhh!' The intruder placed the forefinger of the hand he ate with on his lips. Alhaji Umar Hassan heard the woman's scream and rushed out of the bathroom, a towel wrapped around his waist and water dripping from his body. He saw the man who was in the room.

'Simon!'

'Alhaji!'

Fear like he never knew gripped him. 'Spare my life. I plead with you, Simon. Oh Allah! Have mercy on me, Simon.' The Alhaji was facing him. The naked woman was crying and crawling backwards in fright, till she was in front of the Alhaji.

'How much did they give you? I will double it. I will triple it—'

The intruder cocked the Bersa Thunder 380 semi-automatic pistol in his left hand. The Alhaji began to say the *Shahadah* rapidly: '*Ash-hadu an laa ilaaha illallah Wa ash-hadu anna Muhammadan rasulullah.* I bear witness that there is no God but God and that Muhammad is His messenger...' And the bullets came. They travelled in a split second. His forehead opened and the bullets entered. His brain splattered on the woman, on the bed, on the table, the chair and on the wall.

The gun had a silencer, but the woman's wails pierced

the intruder's ears. He shot her once in the chest, between her breasts. And her head rested on the spread out legs of her lover.

Chief Donald Amechi's convoy drove up to Akanu Ibiam International Airport in Enugu, and as he boarded the flight to Lagos en route to Italy, his phone rang.

A familiar voice spoke, 'It is done, Sir.'

Chief Donald Amechi smiled sinisterly.

'May the Almighty God bless all your endeavours, Simon.'

And then he rang off.

EIGHTEEN

Friday, 26th February 2010

It had never been hot in Katsina like it was that afternoon. Five Toytoa Hilux trucks sped recklessly into the fenced compound of the Centre for Islamic Knowledge and parked at the back of the quarters. Over fifteen young men, dressed in army camouflage and carrying guns, stepped out and walked up to their leader who was standing in front of the mosque.

There was no wind. Everyone was sweating as the radiance of the sun burned down on the brown sand.

'*Izzay el-sehha?*' Sheikh Mohammed Seko asked.

'I am fine, brother. *Khalas*, it is done,' Abouzeid responded. He approached the Sheikh and they shook hands. The other men stood watching, their heavy AK-47 rifles hanging on their shoulders and in their hands.

The Sheikh approached the men and shook their hands one after the other.

'*Alhamdulillah!* Today we have opened a new history in Nigeria. Today our actions have made the souls of our ancestors, our fathers, rest in peace with Allah.

The infidels who are a threat to the religion of Allah bleed. What a great honour you do to the world with your actions! Do not ever think that the actions you take today will go unrewarded. *Chchchchh!*' He made a sound with his tongue in between his teeth. 'No. Allah sees all things. He rewards us according to our deeds. And what greater reward is there than that due to a mortal who paves the way for the religion of the true God? None. It is a delight that we have lost no man. It is a sign that the Almighty is our guide. Abouzeid, please bring me my Holy Qur'an.'

Abouzeid hurried away. He returned shortly with the Holy Book and handed it to his boss. By then over forty other young men, smiling and talking happily, had joined the group. The Sheikh opened the Qur'an and began to read out loudly: ' "Surely those who guard against evil are in a secure place." You, standing here today, are the ones the Holy Qur'an talks about. It reads: "In gardens and springs, they shall wear fine and thick silk, sitting face to face; thus shall it be and we will wed them with Houris pure, beautiful ones".'

The joy of the men resounded through the whole compound, disturbing the children in the classrooms.

Then the children's voices rose in crescendo up to the heavens as they recited *anasheed* in their classroom, unaware of what was happening in front of the mosque.

'I cannot thank you all enough. What do I have to give? Nothing. But your rewards are in heaven. My duty is to make the earth as comfortable as possible for you

149

while you await a greater comfort in heaven. Comfort that no man could ever fathom or explain. Abouzeid will give each of you a parcel. You are dismissed. Go in peace and with the blessings of the Almighty!'

The men filed away. They were going to return their weapons.

'Brother, I owe you my life—'

'Do not say that, Sheikh,' Abouzeid replied. 'Who am I without you? You brought me out as an *Almajiri*. And gave me education and a better life.'

'May Allah guide your path. Give each man twenty thousand naira. I must go back to my studies now. In the evening, I will make the announcement. Jama'atul al-Mujahideen Jihad must take responsibility. Do we fear for a cause we have chosen?'

'No.'

Sheikh Mohammed Seko's *masbaha* with its ninety-nine beads of coloured amber rattled as he crossed his hands behind his back. He began to walk back to his quarters, Abouzeid following behind him.

Oh, how I draw nearer to my destination. Fools. Fools. They believe whatever they are told, he thought and smiled to himself.

'You are happy, my brother,' Abouzeid said.

He turned and faced Abouzeid and took his hands. 'Thank you. Thank you.

NINETEEN

Adeline sat on the sofa reading Ayi Kwei Armah's *The Beautyful Ones Are Not Yet Born*. Her parents had returned. Her mother was in the kitchen making supper.

Her father watched a recording of one of his evangelical missions in Ghana. As he watched, he envisioned himself changing the world, turning it into the kind of world he wanted – a world where he would be equal to the Pope or even greater. He wanted to be worshipped and adored. He was already accomplishing his dreams. He preached about a world where men and women adored Christianity and honoured Evangelist Chris Chuba as a representative of Christ on earth.

He had always preached that he was a messiah sent to heal people of all illnesses and diseases. He pressed his message hard on all the ears that listened to his sermons every day that to see God, you must obey Evangelist Chuba. You must listen to his words, his sermons. You must follow his church, The New Christ Mission International. You must abandon your own denominations and religion.

He felt he was destined to do what he was doing, because he now controlled people – people from every corner of the earth.

If he called for donations, they rolled in from different

places. He had foundations and old people's homes. He had clinics and hospitals and orphanages in almost every country. In Africa, he cared for homeless people. In Europe, he cared for drug addicts and those living with HIV and AIDS.

He preached against violence and adored discipline. He condemned gay marriage and fought against it with his great influence. He advised world leaders and men of God. Old, poor women across the world would call his hotline and donate their last penny to his church after his sermons. His schools scattered all over the globe were free of charge. He was generous, or so people thought, but they paid a great deal from their voluntary donations. And as he watched the video, he was happy with himself. At least he had succeeded where others had failed.

He had a lovely home, a lovely wife who would cry if he asked her to. She would jump if he wanted. A daughter who was the epitome of the life he wanted people to lead – one of chastity, discipline and an unwavering love for Evangelist Chris Chuba. Those were his words. Sprawled on the cushions, he smiled to himself.

His wife walked in and announced, 'The food is ready, darling.' Whenever the Chubas were in residence, the maids worked harder to please them. Everyone in the house prayed more. And every morning, by 5.30am, they would gather in the sitting room to pray until they had pulled down heaven or the angels in heaven covered their ears.

Adeline joined her parents and Miss Spencer at the dining table. She greeted them before they dished up the *esusa* soup and pounded yam. It was a rule that she greeted her parents before and after eating. The Evangelist said grace for almost four minutes before they began to eat.

During supper the Evangelist studied Adeline. 'I have noticed your temperament has changed. Why are you so happy?' he asked her.

'And she looks more beautiful,' her mother added.

Miss Spencer looked at Adeline. She winked.

'So how do you like the presents?' her mother asked. She was an attractive, statuesque woman and her gown was made of *Ankara*.

'The presents are fine. Thank you!'

After the meal, Mrs Chuba prayed for a minute. Miss Spencer served red wine.

'So when do I start college, Dad?'

'Soon—'

'When is soon? I have stayed at home for a very long time. I need a change of environment.'

'A change of environment? Very well, next year, you will complete the JAMB form and sit an entrance exam for Madonna University.'

'Dad! That place? It's like a convent. No one can visit you, or if they do they only give your visitor a few minutes with you. The students are like inmates in a prison yard. You can't even use certain mobile phones.'

'And what is the problem with that? Are you expecting

visitors?' He looked inquisitively at his daughter. 'It is a highly disciplined instutition, that is true, and that is what I want… discipline, discipline, oh Jesus, discipline! That is what I preach. And that Catholic mission college will guarantee it.'

Fear gripped Adeline – she had hoped to join a local college, she could not go away, not now she had found Donaldo. 'But Dad, I thought you hated Catholics.'

'I appreciate anyone who will groom my daughter to the standard I want.' He coughed. Miss Spencer quickly poured water for him. Their eyes met. She looked away.

'But Dad!'

'Adeline!' It was her mother who spoke now. 'Listen to your father. He will never lead you astray. He won't advise you wrongly. He is a special advisor to many world leaders. Do you know that your father gives advice to the President of the United States of America? Please, my daughter.' She reached for Adeline's hand, but she removed it, distraught.

Miss Spencer felt sorry for the girl, and spoke up. 'I think Adeline has a point. All through her life, she has lived a secluded life. She has never experienced freedom. She has always been either at boarding school or at home. Going nowhere—'

'Carol Spencer!' Chuba shouted. 'Mrs Chuba and I will be the ones to decide what is best for our daughter. Be quiet, you idiot!' He regretted the words he had used immediately. *How could I have allowed Satan to push me into calling her an idiot?* he thought. 'Leave! Leave before I… I commit another sin!'

Miss Spencer got up and left.

Turning to Adeline, he said, 'I will speak with the priest who runs the institution, and you will be admitted.' Turning to the maid Ngozi who was clearing the table, he said, 'Now, get my Bible.'

Determined not to cry in front of her parents, Adeline excused herself, went to her room and locked the door. She was glad that her parents were leaving again in two days.

Mrs Chuba stared after her daughter long after Adeline had left the dining room. She regretted scolding her child, but wished Adeline could understand what a great life her father could offer her. She turned back to look at her husband, his face contorted in concentration as he read from his Bible, and she sighed.

The story of Chris Chuba and his wife, Franca, was a long and complicated one. When he joined the Sacred Order, his church was gaining worldwide popularity and he had just bought many hectares of land at Abakaliki and built the Sanctuary – a complex containing a big church, a mansion with rooms for all his pastors, a pastoral school, an orphanage, a boarding school and a day school. The Sanctuary had a double fence and every sports court you could think of. People came there for pilgrimage. It had cheap but well equipped lodgings. Chuba would carry out power packed crusades, ministering to people and healing the sick, claiming that he had powers to heal people suffering from HIV and AIDS.

It was at the time when the Sanctuary was newly built that he met Franca, who was twenty. She was a Catholic but she often came to his church to give talks. He met her on one of these occasions and admired her. She was beautiful, fair and tall. She was an angel and he called her that.

He found that she possessed all the qualities he desired in a woman. Full breasts and pointed nipples, a flat stomach and rounded buttocks. He was delighted with her. She was the woman the angel of God had ministered to him that he would meet.

After they talked, he visited her at the quarry where her mother worked. Franca was from Ezza, one of the clans in Abakaliki known for being industrious. The family were devout Catholics, and as a result were determined that their daughter would not marry the wealthy Evangelist. Franca herself would not even dream of it.

'You are as beautiful as a butterfly. But you are poor and unkempt. By the time I take you to America and you have been looked after by beauticians, you will look like the Queen of Sheba,' he had told her. Franca had refused. He tried for two months. Three months... Still, she declined his offer.

It was then that Chief Donald Amechi bought the quarry. Chuba told him about Franca. He came up with a plan. The Chief ordered one of his men to hide some money inside her mother's head pan – the pan she used to carry quarried stones to a large heap from where they would be sold.

Franca's mother was accused of stealing the director's money, and was about to be burnt alive by a mob as was common; when a thief was caught, he or she would be burnt alive with used tyres before the police arrived, so as to clamp down on robbery and to prevent thieves bribing their way out of police custody. Chuba, who had been watching from the manager's office, came out and stopped the beating. He reimbursed the money and took the woman away.

'You should thank your God I came to buy gravel,' he said to her.

'*Idike*, thanks!' she cried. She was very grateful to Chuba, who took the shaken woman to his house. She had never entered such a luxurious home before. She took a hot bath and was served white rice, chicken and sauce, given new clothes, wrappers and a huge sum of money. She felt like dying.

His plan only partially worked – Franca's mother pleaded with her daughter to marry the Evangelist, but Franca still refused.

Chuba kept trying and Franca kept turning him down. Months later, his desperation reaching new levels, on Chief Amechi's advice Franca was kidnapped by masked men and dumped in an abandoned building before the same men alerted the police and ran away. The police came and found a corpse beside her. She was charged with murder and detained.

Chuba allowed her to stay in detention for two weeks while instructing the police to feed her. Then one day, he came to see her.

'I always come to bail detainees who have no one to care for them. What in God's name are you doing here, my angel?' he said. Franca was so relieved and, sobbing, narrated her ordeal to him. If only Chuba could save her?

'I will help you. But first, you must help me,' he told her.

'I will do anything, Sir.'

'I heard that you have been charged with murder. You could be hanged.'

'Please help… help me,' she begged.

'Marry me. You see, I told you that God has destined us to be together. I was in time to save your mother and in time to save you,' Chuba said. She was quiet, resigned to what she knew she had to do.

She was released and given the same treatment as her mother back at his house. He then sent her overseas for beauty treatments and training in the art of preaching and lectures on counselling. Soon after, Franca became Evangelist Chris Chuba's wife, and in time a great evangelist in her own right. They developed the church together.

Since then, she did whatever he said. He would threaten to reopen the murder case if she disobeyed him. Chuba made sure his wife had no money of her own.

Three years after Franca gave birth to Adeline, she was diagnosed with fibroids and had to have a hysterectomy. 'Pregnancy and breastfeeding will make you lose your angelic shape,' he told her as she recuperated. 'It's God's will. Perhaps He doesn't want you to lose your beauty for the love He has for me.'

Franca knew her husband was evil but she could not leave him. So she grew to love her husband and his work, just like he said she would – his company, his wealth, his status and the international travel. She was adored by other great women of the world, advised wives of world leaders and attended global women conferences.

She loved her daughter and wanted to make her happy but there wasn't any time for that. Although she loved her husband, there were three things she could not excuse: his treatment of Adeline, their only child; the beatings she received from her husband; and his aggressive style of lovemaking.

TWENTY

Chief Donald Amechi and Evangelist Chris Chuba sat in the gazebo. The Chief had just returned from Italy and was in good spirits. They sipped from glasses of Rémy Martin. Oranges were in blossom and their fragrance filled the air. Soon, another man joined them, Chief Amechi's manager. He was short, with a stomach as large as a water tank. He was holding a copy of the *Sun* and there were copies of the bestselling daily on the table in front of the two men.

'Oh, you have copies of today's paper? It is terrible. The attacks in the North. This new organization Jama'atul al-Mujahideen Jihad. What people!'

'*Hmmn*,' the Chief responded. Chuba remained silent.

'How can this be happening now in Nigeria? The election is almost around the corner. What will happen with all these bombings and shootings and burning of churches?'

'God is faithful. His hands grip us tightly. He will never fail us,' Chuba replied.

When the manager had left, the Chief turned to Chuba, 'It is working.'

'Yes, there is no way another Northerner will rule this country for years to come. See, they are burning churches, schools and police stations. The Sheikh and his men have achieved more than we had anticipated. And the fools do not even realize that the terror they commit is only in their own backyard, that it benefits us, not them. Everything they destroy is in their land. People will hate the North and Islam even more.' Chuba laughed loudly and raised his glass to his friend.

Chief Amechi said, 'I have been in Italy and the news of the terrorist attacks in Nigeria was everywhere. We are giving Al-Qaeda a run for their money.' The two men laughed sardonically.

'Soon, the Government will get angry. Out of frustration, they will damn Transparency International, the United Nations, Human Rights Watch, and retaliate with military force. They will kill Muslims, and then every Northerner, Muslim and Christian alike, will hate JMJ. And a Southerner will win the next election. Even the Northerners will vote for us.'

'Very true, my friend. May God guide you with wisdom.'

'Sheikh Ibrahim is a good man. He is effective with the general administration of our affairs in the North. I will make a recommendation to the Universal Temple for his promotion.'

Chuba responded, 'Oh, what a good heart you have, my lord.'

Donaldo was at the priest's cottage. He was feeling extremely unwell with severe stomach pain. Father Simeon had given him some medicine and advised he rest at the cottage. Since his father's return from Italy all he had heard was how well the negotiations had gone. Even without a final answer from the firm, the Chief was planning for Donaldo to travel to Italy, and the young man was feeling anxious and frustrated.

He sat in the sitting room from where he could look at the priest's portrait he had made. Father Simeon was extremely proud of it and had invited many powerful friends and members of the church to admire the work. News had quickly spread about it.

'The Bishop will commission you soon to make paintings for the Pastoral Centre in Abakaliki.'

'That would be nice. I will charge him less, for he is a holy man.'

The priest was aware that whenever Donaldo was angry, just the mention of art was enough to light up his face. Another thing made him happy: the teachings of the church.

The priest had always hoped Donaldo would enter the priesthood. His mother had been a very devout woman, but he feared for Donaldo under the influence of his father. They spoke about the priesthood, communion and the importance of faith, until the priest grew tired and sensed Donaldo's concentration also faltering.

'Get me cold water, Ite, please,' he instructed and the servant left. When the servant came back, Donaldo asked, 'What is the purpose of putting fragments of the Sacrament into the chalice during mass?'

'What I say as I perform that act will answer your question. *Haec commixtio, et consecratio corporis et sanguinis Domini nostri Jesu Christi fiat accipientibus nobis in vitam aeternam. Amen.* May the mingling and hallowing of the body and blood of our Lord Jesus Christ be for us who receive it a source of eternal life. Amen.'

As the priest was saying Amen, a young, uneducated man in Sokoto drove an explosives laden car into the state police headquarters. Deep in his heart he was saying some prayers.

...may the mingling of my blood with theirs cleanse the land of the infidels. May the religion of God be established on earth...

And the car hit the front door of the gigantic building. His flesh was engulfed in flames, burning with the bodies of over fifty policemen and cell inmates. Some of the victims were devout Muslims. Later that evening, Sheikh Mohammed Seko drank some *kunu* with Shedrack Obong and blessed him for his benevolent heart.

TWENTY-ONE

Simon Chuba was in his elder brother's house in Ishieke. He was dressed in black trousers, a red top and trainers. A long chain with a pendant of 2Pac's head was hanging round his neck.

The air-conditioner was on, and its cooling breeze made him want to grab Adeline. But since his arrival, she had been noticeably avoiding him. They met briefly when her father called her to come and say hello to her uncle, but then she had quickly disappeared.

The two men were not talking to each other. The Evangelist was reading his King James Bible, while his brother stared at the religious and history books stacked on the shelves that lined the walls. Whenever they were together, they did not talk much, discussing only the business that brought them together before going their separate ways.

A large black rat stood nibbling at the corner of a cardboard box. It paid no attention to the men in the room. If they watched, it was none of its business. Soon they would leave it alone to enjoy the palace. And as it shifted to the other side of the carton, the knife came, so swiftly and silently that it pinned the rat to the box even before it could move. It gave a slight squeal and died.

Chris Chuba raised his head, just in time to see the rat Simon's jack-knife had pinned to the box. He looked at his brother. Before he could speak, a third man entered.

They stood up and shook his hand. Chief Amechi wore a three-piece Bob & Bros suit. His full hair was well combed.

'Sit down, Chief. We have been waiting for a long time.'

'I had to take care of some business. Simon, good to see you.'

Simon replied without any emotion, 'Thanks. I leave for Awka, today. So let's talk, Sir.'

'Chief Amechi, Simon has been of great help to our success over the years, so I trust he will not disappoint this time.'

'Of course, I know. Simon,' the Chief said as he looked at the younger man, 'this might be the toughest assignment since you became our partner. I will get straight to the point.'

The maids had been advised not to bother about drinks. The room was soundproofed. They discussed how the Minister of Justice would be assassinated.

They had anticipated that Simon would be shocked at the mention of the name, but his face registered no expression, no surprise. The Minister was another stumbling block that must be removed. He was a bone in the throat of some highly placed senior brothers.

'... I want a clean job. There should be no traces. No mistakes. No mentioning of the job to anyone. You are to carry out the assignment alone. I don't care how you intend to do it, but that will minimize risks—'

'I know my job very well. I do not need anyone to tell me about it. Your own job, Sir, is to give me the file and my cheque and I am out of here.'

Chuba smiled; few people spoke to Chief Amechi in that manner, he loved his brother's nerve.

'This is the document. All you need is here. If you have questions, call my special line. The Evangelist is not to be disturbed on this particular assignment. Understand?' The Chief handed an envelope to Simon and looked at the Evangelist, who smiled and nodded his agreement. 'You report only to me.'

Chief Donald Amechi stood. 'I will leave now. We will create diversions as soon as this job is done. All arrangements for that are being made.'

'Thanks, Chief. Simon will do a great job. I should hear about his death on the news within the next two weeks. May God bless you and bless this assignment,' Evangelist Chuba said, raising his right hand to give blessings like a priest.

The men shook hands. The meeting was over.

When the Chief left, Chris Chuba turned to his brother and said, 'Simon? *Ka o di*, God speed.'

Adeline kissed Donaldo. It was tender and her lips were full, soft and satisfying. She had only seen him a few times when work with the church was keeping her parents busy, but their relationship was already blossoming, and they talked often. The phone was her one luxury her father scarcely monitored.

'Donaldo! Look at the chapel. It is poor, yet it radiates a kind of holiness and sanctity.'

'*Hmmn*,' he replied, lost in thought on the rock on which they were sitting. Donaldo saw Adeline as a gift from his mother. He recalled years back when his mother's voice last spoke to him.

'What is wrong, Donaldo? You look distracted.'

'It's Christiana, my mother. You made me remember her.'

'Tell me about her.' She caressed his neck.

'She was lovely… fair and pretty. I remember she was very pretty. I still see her in my dreams. My father…' He stopped and looked away, as if looking into her eyes would prevent the words from coming out.

'My father used to beat her till she became too frail to fight him. I watched all the time…' He stood and moved away from the rock. The memories were too hard. They tortured him. 'She was always out of the house at the clinic. After every fight she would say to me, "I'm going to Enugu, I will buy you something on my way back." They'd help her climb into a car. Sometimes, I'd watch from the window. Then, one day, I saw him push her down the stairs. She was pregnant. She rang me the next day and said she was in Enugu, for business. She wanted me not to be afraid. It was the day she promised me a teddy—'

Adeline put her arms around him. She noticed the hint of tears glistening in his eyes.

'The next day, she died. It was only a matter of time before he killed her... I was so young, only six years old, I felt so helpless watching her fall, Adeline.'

'How did you know she was pregnant? You were young then.'

'I was looking through some of their things once searching for my mother's belongings. There was the doctor's report on the cause of death. It said she was three months' pregnant. He killed her, he killed them both. I saw my mother bleeding. I saw the guard rescue her... and then she said to me that she was leaving for Enugu.'

Adeline kissed him to stop him from talking; she could see the pain in his face as he remembered his mother's death. It was the first time he'd discussed the incident. They went towards the riverbank and lay down in the grass, Donaldo holding Adeline in his arms, caressing and kissing her gently. He looked at her, knowing he had never before experienced the emotions he was feeling at her side. They lay there for what seemed like ages – touching, kissing, exploring, their shared inexperience only adding to the joys of discovery – until the sun began to cast its shadows on the horizon, and the birds watched him enter her.

That evening, when Donaldo returned from dropping off Adeline, his father announced during dinner that Donaldo had been hired by the Italian firm. Donaldo frowned momentarily, but his father noticed. Chief Amechi was mad. He demanded that Donaldo prepare for his journey to Italy, but Donaldo knew that the dream of going to Italy to start a career as a renowned artist was never going to be fulfilled. He had found happiness and joy here, more than he ever knew. Just when he was beginning to see light shine in his life, his ever controlling father had dealt him this deadly blow. He knew he would not agree to leave the thing that mattered most in his life. He didn't care if the dreams of his father for him to become an artist in the league of Picasso or da Vinci worked out or not.

The argument that night was fierce. Madam Vero sat quietly and said nothing.

'I never said I am not going,' Donaldo said and drank some water from a tall glass tumbler.

'You are indirectly saying you are not. Listen, son, you are all that I have. You are not going to inherit my wealth as a failure. I was never a failure. I have always succeeded where others failed... Over my dead body will you mess up my name!' He pushed past his son, knocking off Donaldo's plate of food and glass as he left the room.

The next day, Chief Amechi took Donaldo to Abakaliki town, to his big rice mill. One car was in front while two others followed as backup. Donaldo sat in the back of a Toyota jeep with his father in silence. When they passed girls, Donaldo would stare. The Chief noticed, but said nothing.

Chief Donald Amechi was not into women. His power and status in the Sacred Order had been his only passion and there were rules he must keep.

At the rice mill, the noise of the milling machines was deafening. Peasant women carried rice husks in big sacks on their heads to the disposal site, far from the mill. Donaldo watched with keen interest, wondering why his father had suddenly brought him here.

Donaldo watched as his father supervised the work. He stared at milled rice of many varieties heaped on large mats. The rice mill was the biggest in the country and his father had once told him that people from Togo, Ghana and Cameroon came to the mill. He shipped the rice to Europe where it was further treated and repackaged and exported all over the world, including back to Nigeria where it had originated.

At his office at the top of a three-storey building, Chief Amechi sat in a swivel armchair. For hours, he checked files, read financial reports and asked questions of various managers who came in and out. Then men who had violated rules of different kinds were brought to him. He heard their cases from the appropriate managers and fired them. Donaldo was baffled when Ogiji's father came in to be dismissed from work. He was among the last three waiting to be sacked.

'You are a co-ordinator?' the Chief asked.

'Yes, Chief. At the Distribution Department, Sir.'

'And you are also in charge of sending rice husks to the ceiling sheets factory?'

'Yes, Chief.' His tone was subdued and he looked bedraggled.

'The report here says you refused the orders of the general manager to send trailer loads of husks to the ceiling sheets factory on the 20th of October last year—'

'No, Chief.'

'Will you shut up! Who are you to talk while I do? Your action cost us money.'

'Chief… Sir, two trucks were at the mechanics. The trailer wasn't working. It's not working now still. So I conveyed the husks with only one truck… Sir, I couldn't finish the work that day with only one truck.'

'When he was asked to send the husks, he delayed till later in the day, Sir,' Mr Ogiji's boss said.

'Sir, I had to wait for the truck to return—'

'Be quiet! I think if you knew what you were doing, you would have ensured that there was always an available truck. When you give an excuse, I lose time and money. So assuming we do not have a truck can't you make arrangements to hire one?'

'I am sorry, Sir.' The defeated man cast a look at his son's friend, and Donaldo felt helpless.

'There is no repentance in hellfire, you know. Is that not what your Bible says? Mr Man, we cannot continue to work with you. There are so many people that need this job and can do it better. You are fired!'

'Sir?'

'Get out!'

Mr Ogiji's mouth opened and closed in frustration, then he hurried away.

'Chief,' Donaldo whispered. His father bent over to hear him.

'He is Ogiji's father.'

'Ogiji?'

'My friend. The one who comes to the house sometimes. That is his father.'

Chief Amechi sighed. 'Son, this is business... we will talk about it at home.'

All the sacked staff were asked to vacate the factory residence within two weeks. Donaldo grieved for his friend's father, while his hatred for his own father grew in leaps and bounds.

TWENTY-TWO

It was two weeks after the death of Alhaji Umar Hassan. Malik Hassan stood in front of his brother's grave and recited *Surah Yasin*. He wore a sparkling white *quftan* and a red cap.

He closed the book in his hand and prayed. '*Inna lillahi wa inna ilaihi raji'u*. We come from Allah and to Him we shall return. May Allah grant you paradise, elder brother.'

When he was done, he walked to where his red Toyota 4Runner was parked and drove off. He was sure that his contact in Chad was finalizing arrangements for the arrival of his own *mujahideen*. As he drove out of the cemetery, he thought, *they will pay one after another, just like my brother, with their blood.*

The next day, Sheikh Mohammed Seko was visiting his father's home. He was eating dinner when a red jeep drove into the compound and stopped. Three of his father's wives came out of the zinc-roofed bungalow to watch the car that had just arrived. Their heads were covered with black *nicob* and there were some girls wearing *hijab*. Small children played in the dust, singing and clapping.

Before Malik could alight from the jeep, several young men surrounded him carrying AK-47s.

'*As-salamu 'alaykum!*' he greeted, trying to hide his fear. 'I am Malik Hassan, the brother of Alhaji Umar Hassan. I have come in peace.'

Sheikh Seko was listening through the open window. *Why has Alhaji Hassan's brother come here? Why did he not visit the Centre if he's come for business?* he wondered. He collected his pistol and tucked it into his trousers under his white long-sleeved *gallabiya*.

'What do you want?' one of the young men asked.

'I've come to see the Sheikh. He was a friend of my brother.'

The Sheikh came out and beckoned to the guards to bring the stranger, who wore a *quftan*. His head was not covered and he was well shaven.

'*As-salamu 'alaykum*, Sheikh Mohammed.'

'Brother of my friend. *Masha'Allah!* To what do I owe this visit?'

Neither man offered the other his hand. They stood inches apart.

'I need to speak with you alone, Sheikh.'

'Come.'

Malik Hassan followed him to the back of the house, where they sat down on a mat. The two men were silent for a moment. Malik could see the men hovering about in the compound.

'Sheikh, my brother was murdered!' he burst out.

'I know. It was in the news. Accept my condolences. Allah gave him to us. He took His servant.'

'Sheikh, my brother was killed by the infidels.' Malik Hassan watched the Sheikh's reactions closely.

Sheikh Seko fought to keep his demeanour calm while his thoughts were roving. *What is he saying? Is he trying to weigh my reactions?* 'The infidels kill everyone now. All the assassinations and robberies in this country are the handiwork of the Igbos, and the thieves in the South-South part of our country. The Yorubas are ethnic bigots and criminals who steal with the pen more than with swords and rifles.'

Malik Hassan lowered his voice. 'Sheikh, I have come to tell you that I know what is going on.' He deliberately paused before continuing, hoping to unnerve the Sheikh. 'I know the good job you are doing for our faith. The infidels who killed my brother are suffering for it. I am glad that you are paying them back this way.'

Sheikh Mohammed Seko had doubts that the man had merely come to congratulate him on his jihad.

'What can we do for you?' he responded.

'I felt that I must come to see you. My brother talked of you. He held you in high regard.'

The Sheikh rose and this time they shook hands.

'May Allah guide your path!'

As Hassan drove off, the stars followed him. And

darkness came. That night, Sheikh Mohammed Seko was perturbed, for he had heard of the escapades of Malik Hassan when he had entered the University of Zaria. Malik Hassan had graduated four years before him, but his reputation was still strong during Mohammed Seko's time there.

All Donaldo's efforts to persuade his father to reinstate Mr Ogiji were in vain, until his father gave him a condition – if he signed the contract with the art firm, he would reinstate the man and promote him to manager. Donaldo refused. He gave his friend's father some money, with which he rented a new apartment for his family and began a rice retail business.

On the day Malik Hassan paid a visit to Mohammed Seko, Donaldo sat on the edge of his bed. Madam Vero sat beside him, chatting with him, while rubbing a towel soaked in hot water on his chin. His father entered.

Chief Donald Amechi looked around the room admiring the many paintings. He lowered his eyes at Madam Vero, who placed the towel back in the bowl and carried it out. At the door, she turned back and glanced at Donaldo. He smiled at her.

'How are you?' Chief Amechi asked. Donaldo said nothing, but watched his father. It was there, that day, and at that very instant, that Donaldo began to nurture a sinister thought inside himself.

'Well, I have arranged for the contract to be extended. I called Italy last night and told them you have a problem and that you cannot sign the contract right now. They consented.'

'I sense there is more.'

'You still have to travel to Italy. I don't know what has entered your head, son.' The Chief paused. 'Let me tell you a story.' He came and sat on a chair by the bed. 'There was once a man who was a political genius. He was wicked at heart. The worst was that he was a soldier. He led a country, a great nation, and maimed his countrymen. He killed his friends and dined with his foes. He hated intellectuals and sent many of them into exile…' He looked at his son to check he was listening. 'He had great powers, but he wanted to rule forever. He wanted to graduate from a military leader to a civilian president. And rule till his death. He was revered by many leaders, and abhorred by many too. Others envied him.

'He achieved all his desires. Then he said to himself one night, "I have achieved all I ever wanted in my life, and now to become the civilian president of this great nation will give me much honour." That night, he died. He died in the hands of a whore. An ordinary whore. A woman killed the man that not even world leaders could reach. You have heard of this General. This story of his death in the hands of a prostitute may be true or not, but it explains what women can do to a great man. You must be careful, Donaldo. So many have ended at the hands of women. So many.'

Donaldo was silent. He feared the look in his father's

eyes. He looked away and said, his voice quivering, 'I have no woman.'

'*Aagh!* You think I do not know, come on. Spare me. Have you forgotten who I am? If I can fool Americans and Europeans with all their intelligence, if I can have a say in who becomes the President of this country, why do you think I do not know the affairs of my own son? You must be damned to think so!' He laughed fiendishly. Donaldo stared, but the worst was yet to come.

'I know who she is. You have made the wrong choice, my son.' The words came as a surprise.

'You know?'

'Of course! *Hahaha!*' Donaldo had never seen him laugh. Once when Donaldo laughed at a joke Madam Vero had made, his father had shut him up and said, 'A man only laughs on two occasions, on his birthday and when his wife is delivered of a baby.'

His father continued, 'Do you think there is anything in this world that I cannot find out if I wanted to?' The atmosphere in the room became even more tense, and Donaldo suddenly felt suffocatingly hot. 'Even things in the spiritual realm, my son. There is so much you cannot understand, unless of course you are told. You have made the wrong choice. Do not allow yourself to be the one that will lead to her fall.'

Malik Hassan's men arrived from Chad three days after he visited the Sheikh. They camped in the house of his late brother's friend in Maiduguri. The host, a Nigerian

Senator, was providing the resources that would be used to avenge his political godfather.

Abouzeid received highly classified information from Chad the same day the men arrived in Nigeria. He hurried to Katsina from Kano where he had gone to visit Sheikh Kabiru Ibrahim.

TWENTY-THREE

Wednesday, 17th March 2010

Abouzeid sat with Sheikh Mohammed Seko in his room; he had just finished briefing him about the men who had arrived in Nigeria on the orders of Malik Hassan. He then said, with hatred in his heart, 'I do not trust the other fellow with us... Shedrack. I do not trust him.'

'Why not, brother?' the Sheikh asked.

'I still wonder why a Muslim bears this Christian name.'

The Sheikh smiled. 'Brother, there is a lot you do not know.'

'My Sheikh, the job we do is a very difficult one. If I am not trusted enough to know all the details of this job, then I might not discharge my duties well.'

'You are trusted, Abouzeid.'

'I lead the soldiers to war. I strategize and fight in battles. I need to know the plans. I need to be able to protect my Sheikh.'

'You know the plans, but Abouzeid, sometimes all we need is to follow orders. I follow orders too, and mostly

I do not ask questions.'

Abouzeid was silent. Sheikh Seko didn't want him to start having doubts, so he said, 'What is the meaning of Islam?'

'Submission.'

'Good. Not just submission, Abouzeid. It is total submission.'

Abouzeid did not respond. Who was he to question his Sheikh's wisdom? He stood and said, 'I am sorry, Sheikh Mohammed. I trust in you.'

When Abouzeid turned to step out into the blazing afternoon sun, Sheikh Seko said, 'Shedrack is a Christian turned Muslim. His Islamic name is Adam.'

'Why doesn't he use it?'

'We need to keep him from the ever suspicious eyes of the Americans.'

'Why?'

The Sheikh smiled. 'Remember the phrase *Al-harb khida'a*?'

'War is deception.'

'Precisely.'

Two days later, Sheikh Seko and Shedrack walked down the empty street leading from the village market to the Centre, talking in hushed tones.

'The things you asked for from Sheikh Kabiru Ibrahim arrived today in a truck. The brothers in the South made arrangements for plenty,' the Sheikh told Shedrack.

'*Alhamdulillah!* And you are sure they have everything? The ammonium nitrate fertilizer, the black powder, the sodium chlorate… everything I need to make a C-4 bomb.'

'The delivery is there, they said they have it all.'

'Then, with your permission, I would like to go immediately to look at the supplies.'

When they reached the Centre, they hurried to the back of the building where the truck was parked. Shedrack hauled the crates down with the help of two other men, while Sheikh Seko watched. He took an inventory.

'Right, we need to move all these to the lab, and I will need the assistance of a few skilled men. We are going to make various explosives, so I need to trust the good sense of the men I work with, and I will need a place where we can also test what I make.'

'There is a place in the forest, not far from here. It is an unfinished building, abandoned years ago.'

'Great. I need to prepare. But let me sort out these things first.'

TWENTY-FOUR

Tuesday, 23rd March 2010

Sheikh Seko, Abouzeid and Shedrack, with four other trusted men, gathered in the makeshift lab that had been set up in the abandoned building. Inside they had installed five long tables where most of the IED components were stacked. There were crates on the floor. Shedrack's upper body was bare. A nervous sweat appeared on his brow and his back glistened.

Sheikh Seko was curious. He had asked Abouzeid to be present so that he could learn what the physicist was doing.

'This seems easy.'

'Yes, IEDs are easy to make, once you know how,' Shedrack said, 'and the most important thing about this is that the materials for making them can be found everywhere. They can be purchased without raising any suspicion.'

Sheikh Seko smiled, his prayer beads dangling from his hand. 'Good!' He patted Shedrack on the back. 'Well done, brother. You make me so proud.'

The men watched Shedrack as he explained how the explosives worked. 'They have provided car batteries. We will use these to produce the ones we will plant and activate with a remote but for the ones we will plant in vehicles the vehicle batteries will supply power. Power is vital to get an IED working. The power supply will provide electricity to the trigger switch. This.' He pressed the switch. 'So the *mujahideen* will press the switch down like this.' He demonstrated. 'Then the electrical detonator will explode to set off the main charge… its work is mainly to provide enough energy to the main charge. When this happens our main charge will explode with a blast powerful enough to kill anyone within the immediate vicinity, and the shrapnel will add to the number of casualties through injury. It will send a very loud and very clear message, I guarantee.'

The men clapped their hands and slapped each other's backs.

'So what are we using to transport them and to avoid detection?' the Sheikh asked.

'Several options, Sheikh. We will use vehicle borne IEDs, we will pack IEDs in plastic containers and drop them in target areas and our *mujahideen* will set them off. If we want, our *mujahideen* can use these detonators anywhere within a one and a half kilometre radius of the target.'

They stared at him in admiration.

But then Abouzeid frowned and said, 'Sheikh, since we have the option of dropping the bombs in target locations and activating remotely, do we need soldiers to strap these to their bodies?'

Before the Sheikh could reply, one of the four soldiers present said, '*Kai!* No. I am going to be one of the first volunteers.' He looked the Sheikh in the eye. 'I will be the first person to await the others in paradise.'

The Sheikh turned to the young man who spoke. 'Musa?'

The young man looked imploringly at Sheikh Seko. 'Please, Sir. What I have seen here today makes my heart bold and ready for the fight to liberate our people.'

'Musa, this is not a decision one must take in haste. You have to sleep on it—'

'Sheikh, I am ready to do this.'

Sheikh Seko was satisfied that his grooming was proving successful. 'Listen, Musa, go home and sleep on this. Remember you must not say anything about this to anyone. This goes for all of us. No one should mention this to anyone. Not even the location of this place.'

The following night, Simon Chuba made his way to the back fence of the Minister of Justice's apartment. The fence had a live wire running along the top. But he was prepared for that – the documents had outlined every security feature in detail.

The Minister was a grey haired man in his late seventies. He had served as Minister during President Obasanjo's administration. The Minister was known by everyone as a no nonsense man and had been retained by the current President. He was a man of integrity, so the men of the Sacred Order of the Universal Forces knew that to succeed in their plans they would have to eliminate him. Besides, he had begun to institute investigations through the Department of State Security into the activities of Chief Donald Amechi, especially the recent alleged illegal importation of arms into the country.

Simon Chuba checked his watch and waited. They had earlier contacted the power company and he knew that there would soon be a temporary power outage that would allow him to bore a hole in the fence before the emergency generator could kick in. When the lights went out, he worked quickly, until the hole was large enough to admit him, then he entered with his head and shoulders till his hands found the ground and he slipped in. Then he retrieved his backpack and hurried to the back entrance of the building. He found the kitchen window. He slid it open with the aid of his knife. He was faced with a security grille but he was prepared. Simon took out a handsaw from his backpack and began to saw through the metal grille till it gave way. He lifted his slim body and his head entered first. His hands found the kitchen sink and the rest of his body followed.

He pulled out his torch and lit up the kitchen. He listened. Everywhere was quiet; he opened the door and found himself in a spacious lounge. He could see the stairs before him, and moved up them slowly. As he reached the top he came to a door, just as the plans had shown; he pushed and it opened. He entered a lobby; he walked down to the room at the end. He waited and listened. Nothing but the faint snore of an old man. He tried to open the door but it was locked. If it was locked with a key, he could pick it, but if it was bolted he would have to burst it open. He prayed for luck as he picked the lock. When it opened, he smiled, and drew out his Bersa Thunder 380 with a silencer already in place. The room was so large that the bed in the centre looked small. The assassin could see two figures in the bed. He approached the bed where the Minister lay with his elderly wife.

He collected a spare pillow, placed it gently above the man's head, not allowing it to touch the Minister. He pressed the nozzle of the silencer to the pillow. He pulled the trigger once. The old man's head blasted as his legs kicked up and he lay quiet. The small pop the blast generated and the kick did not wake the sleeping woman. Rather, she turned lazily towards her now dead husband and began to snore. He smiled, realizing it was her snores he had heard.

Simon Chuba didn't shoot the woman. He turned and hurried out of the room, closing the door. Then he headed down to the kitchen and opened the door. He saw flashlights from the security quarters and heard footsteps approaching the backyard, probably for a regular security check because of the power shortage. It wouldn't be long before they noticed the hole in the fence. He hurried to the fence and crawled out.

TWENTY-FIVE

Friday, 26th March 2010

Easter was approaching with great speed. Lots of preparations were being made on the Island. Chief Amechi was inspecting his businesses. He also wanted to attend the burial of the Minister of Justice, two days after Easter.

Donaldo and his father went to shop at a supermarket in Abakaliki. The Chief had been insisting that his son accompany him on his various errands under the guise of spending quality time together before his trip to Italy, but they both knew it was a lie. While there, they met the Chubas.

Evangelist Chuba was dressed in a shirt tucked into well-starched plain trousers. He walked side by side with his wife, Miss Spencer and Adeline.

Donaldo watched the men exchange hugs. His father then hugged Adeline and her mother. Adeline felt like killing him for what he had done to Donaldo and to Donaldo's mother. Now she knew everything.

'You are grown up now, Adeline,' Chief Amechi said.

'Thanks.' She and Donaldo avoided each other's eyes. He leaned on a rack of goods and watched other shoppers go past. He could see the Chubas' guards scattered all over the mall.

'Your daughter is now a grown woman... I guess it's time I came to see if she would agree to marry me,' Chief Amechi joked. When Adeline was much younger, she used to call Chief Donald Amechi her husband and everyone would laugh. This was because he had bought her a gift on her seventh birthday and called her his wife.

'No... no! You are an old man. Besides, you are an Islander. My daughter won't marry anyone who lives there!' Mrs Chuba said. She laughed with her husband and Miss Spencer. Donaldo would have smiled too, if he hadn't known that his father was aware of his relationship with Adeline. He wondered if he should tell her.

'Why wouldn't she marry someone who lives on the Island? It's a nice place,' the Chief said.

'Because it is surrounded by water. One of these days, with climate change, floods will swallow all of you,' Mrs Chuba joked.

'No. Our God is not that of the white men. Things like that don't happen in Africa,' said Chief Amechi.

'God is God,' Chuba retorted. They laughed.

'Donaldo, how are you?' Mrs Chuba asked.

Donaldo came forward.

'I am fine.'

'Donaldo has grown up too,' Evangelist Chuba said.

Chief Amechi was proud. 'Oh yes. His art is now world class. He is a genius in that field. Nothing and no one will prevent his success, he is meant for greatness.' Chief Amechi looked briefly in Adeline's direction. She noticed it, but thought her mind was playing tricks on her. Donaldo stepped back and Miss Spencer joined Adeline.

Evangelist Chuba excused himself and the Chief, telling the others they had much to catch up with, the boring business of old men, and that the others should continue shopping.

Donaldo quickly hurried away. Adeline's eyes searched for him as she walked down the supermarket aisles.

'It was a fine job, that of the Minister,' Evangelist Chuba said, in a lowered voice.

'I trust your brother. The police and the Security Service will investigate the case forever.'

'Any information about the terrorists?' Chuba asked.

'So far, everything is going smoothly. The young men have grown in number. The pay is good. They have a new sport and believe that they do the will of the Almighty, so recruitment is not a problem. Our friends in the North have silenced all their enemies. We will win almost all the seats in the Senate and in the Lower House, the governorship positions, everything. Sheikh Kabiru Ibrahim has told me that the local government election in Sokoto in the next two months will be used to reward those men who have been sympathetic to our cause.'

Chuba was quiet, listening. He leaned closer and whispered, 'They are doing great in Katsina. But what about other nearby states?'

'Did you not hear of the Kano bombing? Sheikh Kabiru arranged it and Shedrack built and transported the bomb there. Their base in Kano is bigger than that in Katsina but we have chosen to make the operation clandestine for now… that is even better. The Government has concentrated their efforts in Katsina, but they do not know that we have a bigger establishment in Kano. We are working in Sokoto and Zamfara. Maiduguri is too hot. But we will get there.'

'Why is Maiduguri so hot?'

'There are a lot of other smaller groups operating there already.'

'With different motives?'

'Yes, different motives and fighting for different causes. But we will bring them into our fold as soon as the backing comes from Afghanistan—'

'Oh! The training?'

'Yes.'

'And the funds?'

'Turkey, Yemen, Syria, UAE and the US.'

'Great.'

'Yes. Alhaja Amina Zungeru and Professor Yerima Musa are working on it. Amina has been of great assistance from her base in London. Women are extremely valuable. They can achieve what men would never even dream of.'

'I didn't know she was in this.'

'There is much you do not know, brother.'

'The more I know, the more headaches I have. It is better for me.'

'On Good Friday, the Government will pay JMJ a lot of money in an attempt to stop the attacks. We hear there is a lot of international pressure on them. They are looking into negotiations.'

The two men paused for some shoppers to pass. They walked to a more secluded part of the shop.

'What is the option?' the Evangelist asked.

'Are we not the Government?'

'So do we negotiate?'

'Do you negotiate with death? We receive the money and order the Sheikh to hibernate the boys for a month or two or even three. Then they will announce a provocation and start all over again. Look, brother, the way I see it, things won't calm down till after the elections. When we are sure of where we stand.'

Evangelist Chris Chuba took a deep breath. 'May God be with us,' he said.

'He is with us, brother.'

Chuba noticed his wife standing at the other end of the aisle waiting for him. The Chief said, 'There is a problem.'

'What?'

'Alhaji Umar Hassan's brother has received help from Chad.'

Chuba was silent. As his wife approached them, Chief

Amechi took his friend's hand in a handshake and in a louder voice said, 'Join us for lunch on Easter Sunday.'

'That will be our pleasure,' the Evangelist responded.

The next Monday, Donaldo was at the chapel for the Easter confession with his father. The crowd was bigger than usual. He sat in the back pew. Rain clouds roamed the sky, and thunder roared like a group of hungry lions. The breeze made the gmelina trees outside the chapel swirl about and birds flew across the chapel as if to join in the confession.

He watched his father kneel to pray before confession and he watched as the priest entered the confessionary. His father was the first to go to the priest and kneel down. Donaldo checked his watch. His father spent about seven minutes there, and he wondered what sins he was confessing. His heart asked him to stop. He was committing a sin by even thinking like that.

Donaldo's heart was beating faster than usual: how could he confess fornication? He was afraid the priest might tell his father. His uncle from Palermo had taught him to trust no one, not even priests. *They could whisper*, he thought.

'Next!' He heard the priest shout after banging on his seat and saw no one coming. Donaldo was startled and hurried up. Some girls in the congregation admired him as he trudged to the confessionary.

'Forgive me, oh Father, for I have sinned through my own thoughts, my characters and words,' he said. His voice was sober. 'Father, I lied so many times—'

'Please, my son… when was your last confession?'

'A couple of months back, Father…' He had forgotten the actual date '… I called the name of my God in vain… I missed mass.'

'Son, can you tell me how many times you committed each of those sins?'

Donaldo was uncomfortable. One thing bugged him and he wondered whether to confess it.

'I missed mass about ten times, Father. I called my God's name in vain so many times. Father, I, I stole money from my father twice… I gave it to someone who needed it.'

The old priest's voice came abruptly, 'It's a sin to steal. No matter the cause. What is the fifth commandment?'

'Thou shalt not steal, Father.'

'You see. You must report yourself to your father and ask for forgiveness. Understand?'

'Yes, Father, I understand…' After a pause, he said, 'All these sins and others I don't remember, I plead for forgiveness from the Lord.'

'Say five decades of the rosary for three days. Don't miss mass again, son.'

'Yes, Father.'

'The act of contrition,' the priest reminded him. He said the act of contrition. The priest blessed him and knocked at his seat. Another person was already coming as the priest lifted his arm to bless Donaldo.

That night Donaldo was troubled, as he did not know how to tell his father that he had stolen from him and his heart pricked him for failing to confess his whole sins before the priest. For the first time in many years, he watched television with his father. He pleaded with him to include Ogiji's name on the list of people to be sent for training on modern rice milling. Chief Amechi agreed, to his son's utmost surprise.

'I will agree because you have agreed to travel to Italy,' his father said. Donaldo stopped smiling.

TWENTY-SIX

Easter Sunday, 4th April 2010

The Chubas sat with the Amechis at the long dining table. The food was served by Madam Vero, whose own family had come for Easter, but they were eating in the kitchen; only her daughter helped her serve the food. Donaldo watched Adeline. He wanted to grab her and kiss her and caress her. He played with his food, even though he was hungry.

After dessert, they all moved to the sitting room.

'So, my dear, what do you do now? I believe you have graduated from university, right?' Mrs Chuba asked Donaldo. Adeline felt like closing her mother's mouth. Miss Spencer gave Donaldo a knowing look. He kept quiet.

Chief Amechi cut in, 'Donaldo does not waste his talent at college. When he finished primary school, we noticed he had an extraordinary gift for art. An expert saw Donaldo's great potential and advised that I shouldn't send him to school any more. He said Donaldo would do better if he could focus on art and be trained by special teachers from all over the world. So Donaldo studies art, away from distractions that would dilute his natural talent. He has been taught by international professionals and they all said he knew even more than they did.'

'That's wonderful,' Mrs Chuba said, 'but won't that make him less social—'

'*Hey* no! Does a man need to be social? What a man needs is money and fame and power. And he is on the verge of achieving that.' The Chief smiled at his son. Donaldo said nothing. Mrs Chuba knew that her husband and his friend cared only for wealth and power.

'The Lord is good. *"And I will lift thee from Egypt and put thee in the land full of honey and milk"*,' the Evangelist chanted.

'Donaldo is so good that if he were to paint your daughter, you would mistake her for one of the angels of God,' Chief Amechi boasted. His words made the Evangelist uncomfortable.

After the meal, Donaldo asked permission to show Adeline around the Island. Chief Amechi, fully aware of his son's true intentions, tried to object, as did the Evangelist, trusting no one with his daughter, but Madam Vero and Mrs Chuba insisted they let the young people be. Chief Amechi conceded, but knew then that something had to be done if he was to protect his son's future.

Alone near the river, Donaldo and Adeline held hands. He wanted to put his arm round her waist, but thought better of it, in case his father should send someone or the Chubas came for their daughter. Fear still gripped him over his father's words, but he tried to put it out of his head, focusing on Adeline, who looked so lovely.

To hell with my father, he thought and turned Adeline to face him. Then, looking round one more time to check that they were alone, he took out a small box from his pocket that he had been carrying around for some time.

'Adeline,' he said, 'I am a mad man now… I am madly in love. I do not sleep at night. I can't do anything without thinking of you. My heart pounds at the very thought of you. Sometimes I wonder if my heart will fail me.' He went down on one knee.

'Donaldo! What are you doing? Someone might see us…' Her voice trembled.

'I believe that this madness is a good one. I am in love. I am in love with the most beautiful girl in the world. And if that is madness then I want to be mad for the rest of my life.' He took out a ring from the box. Adeline's hands went to her mouth. 'Please marry me, Adeline. Please.'

Adeline was so overwhelmed that she was left speechless. He placed his mother's ring on her finger. She kissed it before kissing him.

When they finally released each other, their eyes scanned the whole area for anyone watching them. There was no one around. They stood there for a while, hand in hand, until Adeline regained her composure, and said, 'Let us hurry back. I don't want our fathers to get suspicious.'

As they walked they talked, and as they approached the house Adeline removed the ring, placing it safely in a handkerchief in her purse.

'So, how many kids do you want?' she asked him.

Donaldo laughed joyfully and, with a final stolen kiss, they walked back into the house to join their families.

The following night, as Chris Chuba was changing into his pyjamas, the phone rang on his private line and he picked it up, glad his wife was with Adeline. He locked the door.

'Hello!'

'The Brotherhood greets!'

'May His reign be forever,' the Evangelist responded.

The voice at the other end of the line was silent for a few moments, then said, 'You are aware, Evangelist, that every seven years you are required by the Brotherhood to make a special and solemn offering as proof of your loyalty.'

'Is my loyalty to the Brotherhood in question?' Chris Chuba was taken aback. He had never been prompted about his offerings before, and he certainly needed no reminder of his duties.

'Should it be?'

'No.' Chuba began to worry. 'Forgive me. Seven years have passed so quickly. I will arrange a contribution—'

'That won't be necessary. The Tais has already decided upon a suitable offering, something that will guarantee the Brotherhood's satisfaction with your loyalty.'

'I see.' Chuba's palms began to sweat. It was rare for a specific offering to be ordered, and it was never good.

'Have you not been blessed beyond the imagination of the angels in heaven?'

'Of course I have been blessed. I cannot ask for more—'

'Good. As you know, family life can be such a distraction for a man as great as yourself. The love of family can make it difficult for a man to act in the way he was created to, with logic and reason. There can be no greater show of strength than to learn to sacrifice even one's own family for the greater cause. And no greater honour for those we love than to play such a vital role in the success of our Brotherhood.'

Chuba could not speak, his mouth was dry and his hands shook. He thought of his wife and slumped onto the bed. He knew her increased fame and success as Evangelist Franca Chuba had raised eyebrows among his peers, and everyone knew how he obsessed over her. He waited for the inevitable.

'Your daughter will do the Brotherhood the honour. I hope you understand?' the voice asked heavily and the line was silent. The voice was never questioned nor argued with when it made such demands.

Chuba felt his chest tighten. He looked up and almost let out a cry – he did not recognize the terrified man who looked back at him from the mirror opposite the bed. It soon became blurred just as he noticed the stinging in his eyes. *Adeline? But why?* He had never even considered it might be her, he did not understand.

'Peace... and love!' the voice concluded. 'May angels guide you. And may evil not swallow you.' And with that, the line went dead.

TWENTY-SEVEN

Saturday, April 17th 2010

Alhaji Abu Rabiu Mukhtar's convoy travelled from Abuja to Jigawa. As they approached Dutse, they were flagged down by mobile police officers who had laid a blockade on the road. The Alhaji wondered if the policemen were blind not to notice his convoy. He was a very wealthy man and his compound in Dutse was three times larger than a football pitch. It sheltered hundreds of *Almajiri* and was where almost the whole community came for their lunch every day. With the lift of a finger, thousands of people were ready to kill in his name.

It was a four-vehicle convoy. He was in a Rolls-Royce. The first vehicle was a Toyota Hilux, filled with armed policemen. The second was a Prado jeep carrying two of his friends and some of his aides. The vehicle behind the Rolls-Royce was a BMW, occupied by two aides and two armed policemen. The police officers who had blocked the road spoke to the man driving the Hilux and removed the blockade. It passed and gained speed, followed by the jeep, and then the blockade was closed again. The

Rolls-Royce hit the blockade as the policemen opened fire on it and on the BMW, which collided with the back of the Alhaji's car. More men appeared from the nearby bush and began to fire at the Hilux and the jeep.

Through the window they shot the driver of the Rolls-Royce. They shot the two policemen in the BMW and dragged out the men in the back of the Rolls-Royce. They were bleeding.

'Alhaji Mukhtar!' one of them called. The Alhaji was wounded in the shoulder. He was numb. Other approaching vehicles were turning back swiftly and colliding with each other. Some of the assassins were still engaged in a shootout with the policemen in the Hilux.

'Alhaji Mukhtar! This is for Umar Hassan!' the assassin shouted, and fired four times into the man's head. Alhaji Mukhtar's skull shattered and his brain mixed with flesh and blood and splattered all over the highly polished Rolls-Royce. The assassins ran into the bush and disappeared. In all, three men survived, including the aide, who had heard the assassin's words.

Professor Saturday Effiong was reclining on a cane-chair in the evening, the day after the death of Alhaji Mukhtar. He had just returned from work at the University of Calabar Teaching Hospital, and was sipping a glass of orange juice, reading the papers, when he saw two men stroll down the alley and approach the front of his massive duplex.

His chained dog noticed the men and began to bark roughly. He dropped the newspaper on a chair and sat up.

'Good evening, Sir.'

'Good evening, gentlemen,' he responded. 'How may I help you?'

One of the men noticed his pockmarked face; it matched their target. The taller one said, 'We are friends of Alhaji Umar Hassan.' Professor Effiong made to stand and when the man drew out his silenced pistol the Professor's eyes widened.

'Alhaji Umar sends his best regards.' And the bullet hit the Professor's forehead once. It opened like a door, admitting the bullet. He fell backwards and his legs were thrown up and landed with a thud. A yelp of agony escaped his mouth before he died.

The Professor's security guard, who doubled as the gateman and who had admitted the men, convinced that they were doctors, saw what happened. He drew out his gun but one of the men was already running towards him, so he shot at the assailant twice but missed. The assailant dodged beside a hedge and they began to exchange fire. Another bodyguard ran out from the quarters, carrying an AK-47, but the tall assailant – Malik Hassan – was already close by, and before the bodyguard could fire a shot, he was gunned down. The gateman withdrew behind the building close to the gate. The two assailants ran towards the gate, expecting him to shoot but he didn't, so they opened it and were free.

Adeline's hand trembled as she dialled Donaldo's number. As the line was ringing she wondered what she was going to say – the news she had to deliver was very important.

'Hi, Donaldo. Can I see you straight away?'

'Are you okay?'

'There is big trouble, Donaldo… can I see you now?'

Donaldo's heart fell inside his stomach; he had never heard her sound so worried. 'How will you get out? Aren't your parents around?'

'No. Please!'

'All right,' he agreed.

Donaldo picked her up from her gate and drove her to his hut on the Island. It was still sunny that evening and there was no breeze. The grasses refused to swirl in different directions. The dried leaves on the ground did not drift into the air. It was as if the *asha* birds in the treetops caused everything to stay calm. Even the tiny insects were quiet.

Donaldo made her sit down on one of the stones outside the hut. She was nervous. He was worried, as he had not been able to see her since his proposal and feared what his father might have done – there had been a big fight that night after the Chubas had left. His father knew something had happened, and had only promised to 'take care of it'.

'Donaldo, I am finished.'

'Adeline, you are killing me with suspense. Tell me. What's wrong?'

'Donaldo…' She stood up, but her legs buckled. He

caught her before she fell and she sat down again. He was holding her tightly.

'Adeline!'

'I… I… I have not had my period,' she told him.

She wept. He was confused.

'Okay, but what do you mean?'

She stared at his face, at the silence in his eyes.

'I am pregnant, Donaldo.'

'Jesus!' he exclaimed. He moved away from her and sat on a stool. His mind began to revolve around his life. Donaldo remembered the death of his mother, her unborn child. He remembered his father's brutality. He remembered Madam Vero, her soft and calm words. His brain stopped working. He was in another realm.

'Donaldo!' He startled. 'I am sorry.' She was crying. 'What are we going to do?'

'I don't know, please… I am confused,' he finally said. Tears were in his eyes. Beads of sweat dropped from his jaw to his chest. She stood and came to him.

'Do you love me, Donaldo?'

'You know the answer.'

'Then marry me, Donaldo, marry me now.'

'How?'

'We are already engaged, we can just marry sooner.'

'It's impossible for now, you know that.'

'Why?'

'My father.'

'I will call my father… no… no, I will call my mum and tell her. They will talk to him.'

'No!' They were quiet again. 'Wait, please, tell no one. Just wait for a while.'

'My dad will kill me.'

'Don't worry. He will not.' He hugged her tenderly and their lips met. And he began to kiss her, gently first, then more urgently. Perhaps, if they stayed like this, just kissing, the pregnancy would disappear, the nightmare might just vanish.

Adeline did not want to tell anybody, not even Miss Spencer. She withdrew from everyone. She did not talk with Miss Spencer or with the maids, she went to bed earlier than usual, and she cried quietly and secretly. She called Donaldo and he said he was still thinking – he sounded harassed and the fear that had begun to ravage her increased. She knew she had to do something, and Miss Spencer was the only person she could trust.

TWENTY-EIGHT

Saturday, 24th April 2010

In a large sitting room in a mansion in the centre of the ancient city of Kano, six men were sitting on very soft leather cushions. Outside, people were going about their business. At the gate, a man was working in a small kiosk, where he traded in snacks, cooking spices and stationery. Inside the house, the men were silent, each pondering the latest development.

Abouzeid broke the silence. 'That operation was carried out by professionals. That is all I can tell you. Based on the description I know the man who led it. I trained him in Chad, and I have received confirmation that he is in Nigeria.'

'How good is he, Abouzeid?' Sheikh Kabiru Ibrahim asked.

'If I trained him, it means he is good. In fact, he was one of the best people I ever trained. Mia is a very ruthless boy. Very ruthless. That is bad. Very bad. May Allah guide everyone!' Abouzeid shook his head several times.

'Two people now. Alhaji Mukhtar and Professor Saturday Effiong. What is their plan? To wipe us out?'

'My contact said that Malik Hassan's plan is to punish us in revenge for his brother, then start up another group. He is recruiting.' Abouzeid lowered his voice. 'He has mentioned Sheikh Mohammed Seko to the Department of State Security. How he did it I do not know.'

'I know. I know. The day State Security got the information, we were informed. We have men there. That is not a problem—'

'There is a bigger problem, though,' Abouzeid cut in, 'they want to assassinate the Sheikh.'

'Are you sure of this? *Kajiko*, did you hear me?' Sheikh Kabiru Ibrahim was noticeably disturbed.

'*Ustaz*, would I lie to you?'

'Do we have a solution?' another man spoke up. He had been quiet until now. It was Dr Bode Clark.

'By Allah's help, we do,' Abouzeid said.

'And what is it?' the Sheikh asked.

'Tell the Government to block the Nigeria–Chad border. But not before I have travelled to Chad. We will hold Mia and his men in Nigeria. Invade their camp and bomb it. Then they will scatter and in that confusion, I will contact him from Chad.' The men in the room stared at the young man.

'Why contact him from Chad?' Dr Clark asked, cleaning his glasses with his sleeve.

'Because I will be holding his family hostage. He has a young wife waiting for him at home.'

209

Donaldo was at the dining table. Since the day Adeline had told him her news, the only time Madam Vero saw him was when he came down to eat. He'd stopped going to his hut or even sitting in the living room.

'Ma? If I do anything stupid... what do you think Chief would do?'

Madam Vero was surprised. 'Disown you, maybe, I don't know; your father is mean. But it all depends on the degree of stupidity. If it is bad enough, your father is capable of anything.' She looked at him and noticed the seriousness in his face. He played with the pounded yam and avoided her eyes. 'Why do you ask, Donaldo?' she added quickly.

'Nothing.'

'He loves you, Donaldo, *inugo*? You hear?' She wore an *Ankara* blouse and her hair was plaited and tied with a rubber band, but some tufts of grey hair still sprouted out.

He washed his hands and headed for his room, closed the door behind him and stripped. He walked to the bathroom and filled the tub. When it was full he submerged himself in the water. Madam Vero had never lied to him before, and she was right. His father *was* capable of anything. He would kill him. If he destroyed the Amechi name, he was in deep trouble. He willed his brain to think faster.

At the Chubas' house, alone in Miss Spencer's room, Adeline made Miss Spencer swear never to tell anyone about her love affair with Donaldo.

'Do you love me?' Adeline asked.

'Of course,' Miss Spencer answered, surprised.

'And my happiness is your utmost concern?'

'Yes, my dear.'

'Then swear in the name of the Blessed Virgin Mary that you'll never tell anyone, and that you'll ensure that the staff will not tell anyone, no matter what. Unless I ask you to do otherwise.'

'I don't know why you are saying all this. Come here. Sit down.'

'No. Do you swear?'

Miss Spencer was worried. 'Okay... I swear.'

'Even if I die?'

Miss Spencer was shocked by the statement. She knew Adeline very well, so something must be wrong.

'Yes, of course,' she laughed nervously, locking and unlocking her hands in her agitation, 'but you are not going to die, petite Adeline. What is wrong with you, why all this? Are you sick, my dear?'

'No... but if you want my happiness, you must tell no one.'

Miss Spencer was uncomfortable. *What could be the problem?* Adeline had been acting strange and she was losing weight. If taking the oath would make her happy, Miss Spencer was ready to do it. She had always prayed in her room every night for God to grant Adeline peace of mind.

'Oh! So, you are afraid one of us would reveal your

little secret to your parents. No, Adeline! How could we?' Adeline just stared at her. 'But will you cheer up and be happy if I do as you request?'

'Yes... please.' Adeline's eyes were blinking.

'I swear... if that will make my angel happy.' She touched the holy statue to seal the oath. She saw new light appear in Adeline's eyes and hugged her.

When Donaldo told Adeline what he was thinking, she cried. God had not answered the prayers she had made every night and all the rosaries she had offered to the Blessed Virgin.

'Donaldo, please.' But he said nothing. He was afraid of what he had suggested – abortion was a grave act – but he was more afraid of his father. Even if his father did not kill him, he would lose everything, including his home on the Island. He would also lose his chance to become a renowned painter. He was afraid of Evangelist Chuba too. He hated himself for his cowardice.

'This baby,' she touched her stomach, 'is the result of the unquenchable love I have for you, Donaldo.'

'But it must not get in the way of our future, Adeline.'

'What future, Donaldo? What future is brighter than our own child? She will be beautiful—'

'She?'

'Yes. I saw her in my dreams. I call her Menora. You gave her the name in my dream. She was in the hut with us. You held her—'

'Stop it, Adeline! You are driving me mad.'

She began to cry again and he went to her and held her, stroking her back.

'I am sorry. You are right, how could I have suggested such a thing?'

She looked up, hopeful. 'I will not abort my baby, Donaldo. I am ready to face anything. Besides, abortion is evil, a crime, it is murder. I can't do that, please. I will go to hell.'

'Hush, don't worry. We'll work something out.' Donaldo held her and soothed her, but he knew deep in his heart that the baby could not be born while Chief Donald Amechi lived.

And if an evil whisper comes to you from *Shaitan*,
then seek refuge with Allah.
Verily, He is All-Hearer, All-Knower.

Surah 7:200
The Holy Qur'an

TWENTY-NINE

Thursday, 29th April 2010

Mia Ngarta needed to undertake the strenuous journey back to Chad. His family lived in a squalid hut at Tibesti, close to the Aozou Strip. When he got the information that they had been kidnapped by a terrorist group, that they had his beautiful young wife, he took five of his men and hurriedly left Katsina. At the border, the Joint Security Tax Force, made up of soldiers, the Nigerian Immigration Service and mobile police officers, arrested all of them. Abouzeid had supplied his name and details to Dr Bode Clark who in turn sent it to his men at the Department of State Security.

That afternoon, news spread across Nigeria that six terrorists were apprehended as they tried to escape to Chad. When they were paraded their faces were covered with hoods. But instead of six men, only five were paraded. The report said that one of them, their leader, had tried to escape and had been shot. He was Mia Ngarta. But he did not attempt to escape. He never even imagined that he was going to be arrested, nor did he know that his friend, Abouzeid, had been in Nigeria for some time.

That evening, as people were glued to their television screens, praising God that some of the terrorists had been captured, Donaldo sat thinking about his predicament. He loved Adeline, there was no doubt in his mind about that, but he was in danger – his life was in danger. He knew the only outcome was death if his father found out about Adeline's pregnancy, for him, for his baby – or perhaps there was another option. He recalled that the Hausa people were known for their skill with poisons and charms. Donaldo rushed to find his car keys.

He parked on the kerb, got out and leaned against his car. A Hausa man with tribal marks on his face that stretched to his jaw was roasting *suya* by the roadside. Donaldo bought some *suya* from him. He noticed that there was no one else around. He sat on a dirty bench and began to eat the meat.

'Aren't you afraid working here, at this lonely road junction all alone?' he asked the *suya* seller.

'I never be dey alone. Na now people dem dey comot. I no dey fear any person,' the Hausa man responded. The smoke from the charcoal stung Donaldo's eyes, but he was careful not to rub them because of the juices of the peppery beef on his fingers.

'So what if thieves come... beat you, take your meat and money?'

'Dey no go go free. I get machete, dagger and… *haba*, I go kill them.'

Donaldo looked up at the dagger. 'It's not sharp. How can your dagger fight men who might come with guns? Be careful, brother. Make sure you go home early.' He took another bite of the meat and, looking around again, he continued, 'or do you have poison on the dagger that could be more lethal than a gun?'

'*Oga*. Me I get charm, wey be say if I rub am for my dagger, *kai* for three minutes, anybody wey e cut e don die be that. No gun pass that one na.' He shook his head and made a disapproving sound with his clenched teeth.

'What?' Donaldo's eyes widened. How could God be so kind and merciful?

'Oh… *walahi*, I swear, I know wetin I talk. E beta pass gun self. *Kajiko!*'

Donaldo's whole body tensed and his breathing quickened. The weight of what he was proposing began to dawn on him. 'You are sure that it kills in three minutes?'

'*Haba!* You e doubt me? If I e enter your body. If say na small small, e go still kill the persin.'

Donaldo thought about it, then said, 'You get am? The poison, you get am here?'

'*Haba oga*, wetin you go carry am do if I sell am give you?'

'Do you have it? You get am?'

'Yes. I get am here.'

'Let me see it.'

The Hausa man eyed the young man. Then his eyes wandered to the Volkswagen Bug. He turned and rummaged in his leather bag and brought out a tiny container. He handed it to Donaldo who stared at the contents, his heart beating like a drum.

'How much?'

The next day, Donaldo met with Adeline and they discussed the pregnancy again. He told her that he had changed his mind and he would find a professional to arrange everything. 'It will take just a short time,' he told her. I have made enquiries.' But it was a lie. He knew nothing about abortion. All he knew was that if she agreed, he would travel to town and then make enquiries. He wanted her to just give her consent, to save them both from a far more dangerous fate. 'Please, Adeline, consider our future. We are still too young.'

Adeline sobbed, desperately hurt by his change of heart. 'I cannot kill the baby. You are mad, Donaldo! You said you loved me! Remember that? How can you ask me to do this?'

He tried to touch her but she turned and ran.

'Adeline! Adeline!'

She ran without looking back.

'Please come back!'

He feared that he might not see her again. He knew then that there was only one solution.

THIRTY

It was around 8pm.

Adeline and Donaldo walked down the rugged path leading to the hut. The leaves that fell from the *dogoyaro* trees were damp and the soil was wet from the drizzle that had stopped only minutes earlier. The breeze could set a man's heart on fire and it caused her milk-coloured dress to cling to her slim, dark body.

As she walked, the fillet holding back her hair glittered in the moonlight and her ponytail swayed from side to side as they walked down the path she had become so used to.

They said nothing to each other as they walked. Thoughts hung in their hearts. She had refused to respond to his calls after their last meeting, until at last she had agreed to meet him. But it was not the same. It was as if the sound of the bush pigeons prevented them from talking as they used to, as if it prevented them from holding hands like they used to. And if it were not for the beautiful songs of a nightingale, it would have seemed as if they walked through the valley of death.

Donaldo stared at her. She was quivering because of the cold and he was tempted to offer his jacket. *But, no, not tonight*, he thought.

'Have you made up your mind, my sweet?' he asked. She turned to him ready to reply but a frog in the nearby pond croaked and she said nothing. The crickets chirruped continuously, filling the air as if beckoning on the night.

'Do not look at me as if you have never seen me before.'

'I'm not.' She looked away.

'Now, you tell me... what's your final decision?' he asked. He stopped abruptly and thrust his hands in his pockets.

Adeline spoke up. 'I never believed in love, but you taught me to. I never knew what it was, but you coached me. You gave me what my parents couldn't. But I can't do what you ask of me. It's absurd to think of it.'

'Please, darling. Think of my future, *our* future. I'm going to be a world famous artist, and the next heir to this wonderful island. Then we can have as many children as we wish, we can be free. But your decision now is risking all that. You know how much I long for this future of ours to come true. I have dreamt about this future with you ever since we met. I never told you, but my father knows about us. I am afraid of him. I can't allow him to know about this baby, he will try to hurt us. With your decision, you force me down a path I don't want to take.'

His voice shocked her; it was different, ominous. She was scared by what she could see in his eyes, which used to be so lovely.

She shook her head. 'I am sorry, but you're being selfish. Why don't we talk about our future together? Why do you want me to suffer now because... because—'

'Adeline, it is not what you think. My father is evil. He will kill me. He will kill us!' He came closer, but she stepped back.

'I can't do it. It is better for my baby to die in his hands. No! I cannot. I know I'm young. Inexperienced. I know the problems we are going to face. But please, let's face them together like one strong body. Like you always promised me.' She began to cry. It was for their future, he had said. But she knew it was because of his ambitions as an artist. Because of his father.

He approached her again and this time she came forward until they stood an inch apart. His hands were still in his pockets.

'Donaldo.'

Just as the vibrations of the crickets increased, she fell on his lean body and buried her head in his broad shoulders, her hands flung around his neck. Insects provided love rhythms with their noise. Even the leaves gave out a sweet muffling sound. The moonlight glimmered more brightly, so bright that she could easily see the drawings he had left outside on the table.

It was then that he drew her face to his and kissed her softly. And as she opened up her lips to savour the kisses, to return the sweet kisses she could not resist – she felt it. It was only a sting, but it had gone deep.

'What was that?'

She pulled away from his embrace. The pencil with the needle attached was in his hand – it had pierced her neck.

'What was that? What did you do to me?' Then the poison hit her. Her hands clutched his jacket as she started to fall like a piece of cloth thrown from a tall building.

She struggled to keep hold of him. 'Why? Why are you doing this?' She stared at him, shock and confusion in her eyes. He just stared back in fear.

'But… but I love you. I always told you I… I did,' she said, feeling herself weaken as the poison took effect. She slumped to the ground but still clung on to Donaldo's ankle.

Then silence came. The leaves became calm. The bullfrogs went to sleep. Darkness enveloped the world as the moon retired slowly.

'I love you, Donaldo,' she whispered, until finally her grip loosened completely and she stopped breathing, her eyes staring vacantly.

He felt goose bumps all over his flesh.

'I love you too. Adeline, I love you so much. But you are stubborn… you won't understand. I do not want to ruin my future. I am afraid of my father, Adeline,' he cried, *if only she knew why she must die.* He fell on his knees beside her long black legs.

The leaves howled in disbelief. The clutch pencil was still in his hand and he gripped it tightly. A bird gave out a loud startling screech; the heavens growled and commanded the clouds to produce a sudden lightning bolt which was followed by a clap of thunder that silenced the insects. It was as if rains were waiting to start, but nothing happened. Everywhere became very quiet again. The world fell silent like a graveyard at midnight.

With a trembling hand, Donaldo closed Adeline's eyelids. Then he thought about his next problem, the disposal of her body. Which would be the greatest crime of all.

SECTION III

FRUIT OF EVIL

… no murderer ever left the scene of a crime without leaving some physical evidence of his crime behind him.

A Taste of Death
P. D. James

THIRTY-ONE

Friday, 7th May 2010

Donaldo was roused from his thoughts by a knock on the door. He had been remembering how he had met and fallen in love with Adeline and how she had died. His face was covered in tears and he hurriedly wiped them away with his bed sheet.

Madam Vero opened the door. She knew he had been crying.

'What is it, my son? What is it?'

She came to him and touched his forehead with the back of her hand. She touched his cheek and his neck. 'Are you all right? What is bothering you, Donaldo? Please tell me.'

He managed to smile. 'I am fine,' he said.

Madam Vero wasn't convinced, but she shrugged and said, 'Your father wants to see you downstairs.'

Chief Donald Amechi's library was large, full of hundreds of books, mostly old books on medicine and psychology, science, the humanities and art. The walls

were covered with framed photographs and memora-
bilia from the Chief's sporting years in England, Italy
and Spain all those years ago. A cabinet contained all
the medals he had won and three silver trophies. They
looked resplendent; it was these trophies that Donaldo
would always come to look at. He admired his father's
success despite his wicked heart.

Donaldo tapped on the door quietly and entered.

'Good evening, Sir?'

'I heard you've not been all right.'

'I am fine, Sir.' He sat down and stared at the medals.

'Your forehead has lines. You are ageing, son. What's
bothering you? Is it about going to Italy?'

'No, Chief. I am fine. I am looking forward to it.'

Chief Donald Amechi was surprised at his son's
change of heart. He smiled warmly; everything was
falling into place.

'You will leave soon then. In the meantime I have arranged for you to work in Port Harcourt. It is a short resi-
dency before you leave, to make the change easier on you.'

This announcement took Donaldo by surprise. He
had been keen to leave ever since the news broke out
about Adeline going missing. 'I didn't know there was
going to be a change of plan.'

'It's fine. Listen, you are going to be making big money.
Plus royalties from any of your works sold. Everything
is here.' He touched a big brown envelope on his desk.
'Our family lawyer will be here tomorrow to give you all
the details.'

'All right.' Donaldo did not sound very happy.

'Donaldo? Your work is the best on the international market right now. The whole world is watching you. You have an agency to represent you now. They are waiting to see you... in fact, as I speak, they are asking: "Who is Donaldo?" It's time to release you to the world. I have kept them waiting for so long... so long, son... you will enjoy this.' Chief Amechi's eyes glowed. 'You will be like Rembrandt, Michelangelo. Can't you see?'

'I want to be me. I don't want to be like anyone else.'

His father just smiled.

That evening, just before darkness began to cast its shadow, a car drove into the Chubas' compound. Before the man seated in the back got out, the Evangelist was already downstairs, ready to welcome him. The two men hurried to embrace each other and walked over to the gazebo. Chris Chuba was still wearing the outfit he had worn to visit Chief Amechi earlier in the day. Professor Yerima Musa was dressed in an Armani suit, black shoes and wearing spectacles. They sat down.

'I am delighted that you have come, brother. You cannot imagine how hard these past days have been for me.'

'Oh, I understand, I understand. It is a terrible shame... what has happened is so dreadful.'

'Thank you for your concern. How was your trip?'

'It was fine.'

'And London?'

'Fine. London is fine.'

The Evangelist looked around before leaning closer to the Professor. 'My brother, I am confused. Who would dare to act against any one of us? And to take my daughter after she has been requested. There is something worrisome here.'

'I hear that the patience of the Brotherhood is running out. I hope we find Adeline before then.'

The Evangelist flinched at the mention of his daughter's name. Fear and guilt engulfed him. 'Professor Musa, sincerely speaking, I do not know what to do. I swear I know nothing about this.'

'*Uhmn.*' The Professor nodded.

'The day we got the news about her disappearance, you know, we thought our contact had kidnapped her like we ordered. I had travelled to Canada as instructed to give them the chance to snatch her. Then when I came back I found out that there had been a car accident. The men died. The hand of fate is working against me. Now, she is missing. And my fear is that the Brotherhood will think I know where my daughter is. The Universal Temple will think I have hidden my daughter.'

The Professor waited a while, then responded in a gruff voice, 'The Tais knows more than you do. They are aware that you would never go against the Brotherhood in anyway. The Universal Temple is aware of your unflinching loyalty. Do not worry, Evangelist. But you have to hurry.'

'Thank you so much, brother. Thank you,' the

Evangelist said, relieved.

'That is why I have come. If there is anything I can do to assist, please tell me.'

'Professor, Chief Donald Amechi suggested we hire a private detective. He has made the contact.'

'The disappearance of your daughter is a setback that occurred at the worst possible time. The sacrifice must not delay for long. So the Chief's suggestion is a good one. We must hurry, Evangelist.'

'The Nigerian Police Force are the worst investigators in the world.'

Professor Musa laughed a little. He moved nearer to the Evangelist and whispered, 'Our enemies have her. Perhaps the late Alhaji's friends planned this. She will come back to you, which is why I agree with Chief Donald that we need a foreign detective.'

The Evangelist frowned. He saw his life dangling from a thread. He could see the hand of the clock of his life ticking away.

Donaldo Amechi was rummaging through his belongings searching for his gold-coated clutch pencil. He couldn't recall what he had done with it after he had killed Adeline. He sat on the bed and cast his mind back to the moment. He could see Adeline's body crumple to the ground still holding on to his jacket. He remembered that at that time he still had the pencil in his hand – but where was it? Then he hurried back to the hut to search for it.

THIRTY-TWO

Saturday, 8th May 2010

Around 4pm, a tall, dark, good looking man, dressed in a very expensive blue suit, walked into the Shoprite mall in Abuja. He wore a silver watch and black shoes that had been well shined, glistening in the mall's artificial light. There were a few young men dressed in private security uniforms whose duty it was to look for shoplifters and one or two armed police at the car park gate. There were no bomb detectors at the gate or at the entrance to the mall. A few minutes after he entered the busy shopping centre, he made his way with difficulty through the crowds and stood in the middle of the mall, surrounded by shoppers – mostly women, children and young people. He began to recite to himself, his mouth moving slowly. Then his hand slipped into his suit jacket and he screamed from the top of his voice, '*Allahu akbar!*' The explosion occurred.

The martyr was blown high up to the ceiling of the mall and shredded into pieces. The explosion shook the foundations of the building and people were thrown with great force against walls, windows, columns and their fellow human beings. Shops were engulfed in flames. Then for some seconds the whole place was calm, until a huge pillar cracked and gave way, and the beams, the ceiling and the roof came crashing down. Over a hundred people were lying on the floor, unconscious in pools of blood. More than a thousand others began to wail in panic, knocking each other down as they made their way out of the blazing shops and the tumbling building, screaming the name of God in various languages.

Just as the news went viral all over the world that the massive shopping mall in the capital of Nigeria had been attacked, Evangelist Chris Chuba, unaware, paced in his garden, his hands behind his back, his head bowed in worry. That morning, he had had a meeting with the Commissioner of Police and discovered that the police hadn't made any headway. A young officer had suggested that he employ diabolic means.

The Evangelist recalled what the officer had said. 'Sir, we have tried all means and we do not have any idea about the whereabouts of your daughter... we do not know what happened to her, whether she is dead or alive. So, I suggest that we go see Baba.'

'Who is Baba?' the Police Commissioner had asked.

'He is a powerful diviner in Ijebu Ode—'

'Officer Ajeore, stop! Chris Chuba is a man of God!' the Commissioner interrupted.

'But Commissioner, Sir. I am not saying he should

go… I can travel to Ijebu Ode for him. I will do the consultations for him. If she is still alive, we will know. If she is dead, Sir, we will know…' Everyone was silent. The Evangelist was thinking about it, but he was worried they would doubt his faith if he consented. He had often heard of Ijebu Ode and the might of the powers of the diviners there.

'If she is alive, Baba will tell us where she is. And how to find her.'

'Thanks, officer. But I think God will take charge,' Evangelist Chuba said.

'As you wish, Sir.'

The officers saluted and left.

Turning to face the Commissioner the Evangelist said, 'I am thinking of employing a private detective.'

'That isn't a bad idea, Sir. But I think my men have covered everything.'

'I am aware. But I am still not satisfied, I must do more.'

'Very well. You can always direct the detective to come to us for information. We will always be ready to assist. There is a good private investigating firm in Lagos. I can give you the details.'

'No, there is no need for that. I am sending for someone from Ghana.'

'Ghana?' The Commissioner laughed. 'Are they better than us? What do Ghanaians know? I thought you were going to say somewhere like the United States.'

'I have a good source. This man in Ghana is recommended.' The Evangelist rose. 'Good day, Mr Commissioner. And may God continue to bless you.'

So as the Evangelist paced, he worried about the officer's words. *Should I ask him to go to Ijebu Ode?* He dialled the number for Chief Amechi.

'Peace and love, brother!'

'Peace and love, my lord! My heart is troubled.'

'Your heart is in turmoil. Indeed it should be.'

'How much time do I have?'

There was silence for some time, then Chief Amechi said, 'Between seven to fourteen days. They can come for you any time before the fourteenth day.'

Evangelist Chuba shivered.

'Someone suggested that I consult some diviners at Ijebu Ode—'

Chief Amechi was shocked. He must stop him from doing that. 'Why? No. The mantra forbids that... Listen, I have contacted the detective I told you about.'

The Evangelist sensed unease in his voice. 'But my lord, what about the Sacred Order? Can they help me locate her? The Temple has the divine powers.'

'The burden is not that of the Sacred Order. Everyone has his task. This is your cross. Do you disturb the Tais with your worries? Has the Order not treated you well all these years? I hope you do not intend to travel to the Temple. Remember you will receive no audience. Their anger is running high. The clock is ticking away.'

'Thank you for your counsel, my lord.'

'Peace and love, my brother!'

THIRTY-THREE

Evangelist Chuba sat under a canopy tree, drinking juice and eating Cabin biscuits. A newspaper and his Bible were by his side and his eyes occasionally drifted to the gate.

Just as Mrs Chuba came out and sat beside her husband, the gateman rushed to the gate and opened it. A Mercedes E-Class pulled into the compound, and a sturdy man of average height stepped out of the car. He looked around to appraise the luxurious compound. The visitor wore woollen trousers, a white striped shirt and black shoes. He had on a pair of sunglasses, a fez and a gold watch. One of the guards took his luggage inside. The Evangelist walked over to welcome him, shook his hand and led him over to the garden seats.

'So, you are Detective Kwame?'

'Yes, Sir. I am sorry about your daughter.'

'Please, do sit down, Mr Kwame. This is my wife... Evangelist Franca Chuba.'

'My pleasure meeting you, ma'am.'

Mrs Chuba nodded briefly and asked, 'What may we get for you, detective?'

'A cup of coffee will do. I guess you people have coffee in this part of the world?' he asked with a smile. He touched his moustache while surveying his hosts. Mrs Chuba instructed one of the maids to bring a cup of coffee.

'Nigeria is a nice country.'

'Is this your first visit?' the Evangelist asked.

'Yes, I had a wonderful journey. Lagos is a beautiful place. I took a taxi around town for a couple of hours while waiting for my flight to Enugu. I loved all the jostling. It reminded me of New York.'

'Oh! Nigeria has been experiencing steady but continuous growth. Soon, we shall get there,' the Evangelist said proudly.

Kwame's eyes were caught by the newspaper; he picked it up and looked at the headlines. 'Terrorism is tarnishing the image of the giant of Africa,' he said.

'What can we do? The world is full of evil.'

'Ghana is a nice place too,' Mrs Chuba said.

'Yes. But of course, we cannot compare with you. You are years ahead of us—'

'That is right. But if Nigeria is succeeding and Ghana is failing, or any other African country is failing, it means Nigeria is failing too. Don't you think so?' the Evangelist asked.

Detective Kwame considered these words, his head tilted to one side while he stared at the Evangelist. 'I think… you are correct. But tell me, how has the family been coping?'

'Brother Kwame, we have been in despair. We fear our daughter may be dead,' the Evangelist said, his eyes blinking rapidly.

The detective sat back in his chair, resting his hands on the arms, and said, 'Give me a brief rundown of events so far. How you heard the news, the efforts of the police. Her friends. Her close relations… Who and where she visits. Any discoveries so far… no matter how minute you might think them to be.' He turned to see the maid approach with a tray of biscuits and his coffee.

They were silent as the maid placed the tray on the stool beside the Evangelist.

'Thank you. How is lunch coming on?' Mrs Chuba asked.

'Almost set, Ma. In fifteen minutes, Ma.'

'Have you tasted Nigerian *banga* soup?' Mrs Chuba asked Kwame.

'No, ma'am. I can't wait.'

Kwame got to work that very day. His method of questioning was detailed and to the point. Each person was interviewed separately and thoroughly. Kwame compared his notes with those he had been given by Officer Leonard who had been introduced to him soon after his arrival.

He found out that none of the staff knew when Adeline left the house. He also tried to establish her mood before the disappearance. Some said she was not in the best of moods. Others said she was okay. Miss Spencer said she was fine. Demola revealed something that she did not tell the police.

'Sir, one day, some days before small madam got missing, she was vomiting—'

'How many days before her disappearance?'

'Like four days, Sir.'

'I didn't see it in your statement to the police, beautiful girl?' He looked her in the eyes.

Demola grinned.

'They didn't ask me about her mood, Sir. Is it not good to answer only what you are asked?' She was admiring the detective.

'How did you know?'

'I am her nurse, Sir. We are to answer only what we are asked.' She grinned at the detective again and Kwame grinned back.

'So the vomiting, my dear? What do you think about it?'

'There are many reasons why one would vomit. I don't know why she vomited.'

'You are a nurse. So don't you think if she was sick, she would have told you? Maybe she was hiding something from you… like pregnancy?'

'No, Sir, Adeline can't be pregnant. She has no boyfriend.' Demola became uneasy. 'May I leave now?' she added quickly.

Kwame was startled at her sudden change of mood.

'You can go, my dear.' She stood to go. At the door, he called her back. 'It's been a few days now, Demola. Maybe if you sit down and think, you might come up with some other things about Adeline.'

She said nothing.

'You loved Adeline?'

'I still love her, Sir. Adeline is a nice person.'

'Then you should help me find her for you. She may be in danger wherever she is, Demola.'

'If I remember anything I will let you know.' She hurried away.

Miss Spencer and the girls gathered in the kitchen; she was trying to find out what they had said to the detective. Demola didn't tell her that she'd told him that she'd seen Adeline vomiting. Miss Spencer's phone rang.

'Excuse me,' she said and hurried to her room. She locked the door and went into the bathroom.

'Hello, Donaldo.'

'How are you, Miss Spencer?'

'I am fine, but you don't sound good. Are you okay?'

'I am worried. Very worried about Adeline.'

'Me too. I don't know what happened, Donaldo. She didn't come to see you that evening? She told me you were waiting for her outside.'

'No. No. I wasn't waiting for her. I can't lie to you.' But he did exactly that. It hurt him to lie, but Miss Spencer was the only connection he had left to Adeline, the only source of redemption. Maybe through her love and forgiveness the nightmares would cease.

Miss Spencer took a deep breath. She had been willing her mind not to think that Donaldo might know Adeline's whereabouts.

'Donaldo, things might work out fine now. There is a new investigator. His name is Kwame... he is from Ghana.'

'Oh.' He paused for a few seconds. 'When did he arrive?'

'This afternoon. He is trying to find Adeline. He has a great reputation, I am sure he will solve this in no time.'

'Please keep my identity a secret. You know that if her father discovers that she was seeing me, he will feel betrayed. Things will turn out worse.'

'I know. I know. My God. I am so afraid, Donaldo.'

'Adeline would want us to be strong. She wouldn't want her parents to know about me no matter what.'

'Yes, of course.'

Detective Kwame was a soft-spoken, gentle man. He walked gracefully, never appearing to be in a hurry. He often stroked his moustache and carried a comb in his pocket which he would run through his hair. The maids were all in love with him and gossiped about him.

That night, Officer Leonard Omelu came to see him again when he left work. The two men met in the Chubas' sitting room.

'I am passionate about this case,' Leonard told Kwame. 'It's puzzling. A girl disappears without a trace and everyone claims she has no friends and she wasn't seen leaving the house.'

'We can't talk here. Come to my room.'

In the guest room Kwame brought out the copies of the police statements that Leonard had given him earlier and his own notepad.

'I don't want to talk in the sitting room because I don't trust anyone.'

'Good. Do you get the feeling that there is a kind of conspiracy going on here?' Leonard wanted the detective to speak his mind. 'Kwame, the day this girl was reported missing, we came here to talk to the staff, but each of them answered our questions as if they had been prepped before we came on what to say and what to leave out. If we pushed too hard, the Cameroon woman, *ehm*, Miss Spencer, would say that we were embarrassing or intimidating her staff.'

'I see.'

'Then when we took the security guards to interrogate them, nothing new came up. I think something fishy is going on here.'

'I believe, Leonard, that they are scared of something more than interrogation. Something I cannot pinpoint. I think something is going on in this house that they are frightened to say in case they are punished.'

'Exactly.' Leonard was impressed with the detective. He liked working with intelligent people.

'I've got some new information anyway,' Kwame announced. 'The nurse, Demola, said that a few days before the girl disappeared she saw her vomiting.'

'What else did she say?'

'Nothing more. I wonder if the girl was pregnant and has eloped with her lover.'

'Well, we found a letter in her room. A love letter, but when we showed it to the Evangelist he tore it up—'

'What?'

'Yes. He claims the girl had no friends, and certainly no boyfriend—'

'So the letter was going to contradict his claims?'

'Yes.'

'How stupid – does he want us to find her or not?'

The two men looked through the statements spread in front of them.

'This girl,' Kwame tapped Adeline's photograph, 'this girl is so beautiful. There's no way people in town won't know her. I think we can get more information from people outside this compound than we have from the staff here.'

'So what are you thinking, Kwame?'

'We need to come up with a publicity strategy.'

'But her photograph has been in national dailies and on television every day.'

'Not that kind of publicity. How many people in this town have access to the dailies or the national TV or cable network channels? We need to come up with something simple. Tomorrow we will scan this photo and print lots of copies and pay some boys to paste them on the walls of public places with a notice.'

Officer Leonard smiled. He was beginning to like Kwame even more.

'Leonard, someone in this town must have seen that girl around. She is eighteen. At that age, girls are adventurous, with boys and so on. Especially if they are being controlled by their parents. We need to find someone who thinks they have seen this girl before, either alone or with someone. That would be of great help.'

THIRTY-FOUR

Monday, 10th May 2010

Officer Leonard Omelu drove Kwame around town after they had printed Adeline's photo in a printing shop because the District Police Office had no scanners or printers. The notice had Adeline's colour photo with a message:

> If you know anything about Adeline Chuba
> Come forward. Reward: N100, 000

He added his mobile number at the bottom. Some young boys were paid to paste the posters around Ishieke and to drop them in hotels and restaurants. The next day they were to do the same in the nearest town, Abakaliki.

Late in the afternoon, Leonard and Kwame sat on Leonard's bonnet talking in front of the Chuba residence, when Leonard's phone rang.

'Hello? Yes, I can hear you. Yes, I am in charge of the case. Good. You saw my name and phone number on the poster.' Leonard looked at Kwame. 'Yes, yes. You saw her once. With a boy? Okay. How can I meet you? Please, no, don't worry, I won't arrest you. I am not a police officer. I am a private investigator hired by her family…' He knew that if he told the truth it would put the caller off. 'Please, this girl might be in danger…' Leonard began to get into his car. Kwame hurried to the passenger's side. 'I am on my way. Please hold on. I will be with you in… five minutes.'

Leonard drove like someone on the run from hired assassins. They parked outside a small café and hurried inside. Kwame dialled the number and saw someone behind the counter answer their phone, then he rang off and walked up to her. Leonard followed. She was a middle-aged woman. She was dark, dressed in a blouse and skirt but wearing a cooking apron over the top. Her hair was covered with a scarf.

'Sir, good afternoon. Please come.' She indicated a door behind her and led them to the kitchen.

Leonard spoke first. 'My name is Leonard. This is Kwame. We are not policemen. He is a Ghanaian. I am a Nigerian. We were hired by the family to search for the missing girl.'

'Sir, I am scared because if you give information to the police they will arrest me as a suspect.'

'We know that, but we assure you that we won't do that… you see, this girl has been missing for several days now and no one seems to know what has happened to her. Her family claims she doesn't leave the house.'

The woman was surprised.

'What?' Kwame said. He had been studying the woman for signs that she was lying.

'They say she doesn't leave the house? I don't think that's true, Sir. You see, that girl is very beautiful. That is the problem with beautiful people. Everywhere they go they are easily noticed.'

'I agree.'

'She came here once with an elderly woman.'

'Can you describe the woman for us?'

'She was plump and busty with chocolate coloured skin.'

The two detectives knew who she was talking about.

'What did they do?'

'It seemed they just came to hang out. The girl was behaving strange. She was staring at people as if she had never seen humans before. I noticed this because she was so lovely and you know... we women, we notice when we see a gorgeous woman.'

'That's very interesting.'

'There is something else.'

'What? Please tell us.'

'I saw her again... here... twice.'

Leonard and Kwame took a deep breath. God was on their side.

'She came with a boy... a very handsome boy. In fact the boy was even more beautiful than the girl. I noticed them because this is a small place and we don't get that many customers. And I liked the girl because of her looks and lovely figure. And the boy too.'

'Was it the first time this boy came here?' Kwame asked.

'Yes. Well, I don't know if he had been here another day…' The woman paused. 'I think he came here another time before the day he came with the girl. But I am not sure. Please… I can't say what I don't know.'

'This boy came with her twice, you say? Around what time did they come?'

'It was always in the evening, seven or eight o'clock.'

The two men glanced at one another.

'Describe the boy, please… just like you described the woman.'

'That's easy because he didn't look like one of us—'

'What do you mean by that?' Leonard asked.

'He looked mixed-race. Long hair, chocolate skin and a straight nose. He looked like a foreigner. I have never seen someone like that before… I remember thinking how perfect they were. Both of them.'

Leonard smiled, and Kwame said, 'Thank you so much, Ma.'

The woman grinned. 'So?'

'Oh, the reward? I assure you, if what you have told us turns out to be useful information, which I believe it is, you will receive due reward, even more than the money promised.'

'When?'

'I will call you.'

'Please don't cheat me, Sir.'

Kwame placed his hand on the woman's shoulder. 'In Ghana we are sincere. Trust me.'

When they got back in the car, and Leonard sped off, he said, 'Kwame, you are brilliant.'

'Do you know the boy?'

'Yes.' He laughed so loudly that Kwame thought he was going mad.

'Oh… this is just beginning to get interesting.'

'We need to get back to the Chubas' house. We need to interview that cunning woman… that Miss Spencer or whatever they call her.'

'What is it, Leonard? Who is the boy?'

'The first day we investigated, a mixed-race young man came to the house, said he was supporting the family. He was very nervous. I think that is the boy this woman just described.'

'So, let us go and question him!'

'Wait, Kwame, relax. It is not so simple. The boy, it will not be easy to talk to him. His father is a very powerful man. He is the son of the Chief of the Island. We must be very careful with these people.'

'Chief of the island?'

'Yes. Williams Island we drove past this morning. He is one of the most powerful men in this country. As powerful as the President. We need to get to the residence and talk to Miss Spencer again, now that we have further information… now that we know that she is hiding something from us.'

'I sensed the maids were hiding something too,' Kwame added.

'I agree.'

'Then I will find out. From now on, everyone in that house is a suspect. Including Evangelist Chuba and his wife,' Kwame said.

Leonard laughed. 'That day, when I asked the boy a question, Miss Spencer answered for him. I thought nothing of it then. But now… oh my God.'

Evangelist Chuba came back from visiting one of his churches. It was late, but he was feeling wide awake and energized. He removed his jacket and walked to the bedroom. Franca was already in bed, wearing a thin nightdress, the covers thrown off her. He looked at her for a while, allowing her beauty to take effect. Her rosary was beside the pillow. He knew she'd forgotten to hide it. He grabbed it and ripped it apart. The beads bounced and rolled across the room. The rattling sound woke Franca.

'*Hey!* What's that?' she asked sleepily. 'Oh, welcome home.'

She raised her head and saw the scattered beads of the rosary. She said nothing. Her husband was removing his clothes.

'Get undressed,' he said and unbuckled his belt.

She was not surprised. It was an act she had got used to. 'I am not in the mood.' She rubbed her palms over her eyes.

'But I am in the mood.' His trousers were already down. He pulled down his underwear revealing the clear sign of his desire. As he leaned over the bed to remove her nightdress, she said nothing.

His hands travelled up her smooth legs. His breathing became slightly more urgent. She flinched.

'I am your husband. Both of us know what the Holy Book says on this. So just do as I say!' He pulled her white lace pants past her hips, and then down the length of her legs. Climbing on top of his wife, he slid into her as she let out a sharp cry.

That same night, two men arrived in Ishieke. They had driven all the way from Kano. One of them was Malik Hassan. They drove a big black jeep with a federal government number plate. The seats had been slit open with a knife, and guns and bullets concealed inside and then the leather had been sewn back up. They pulled into a small hotel and checked in.

THIRTY-FIVE

Tuesday, 11th May 2010

Chief Donald Amechi's private phone rang and he hurried to his library and locked the door.

'Good morning, Chief.'

'Good morning.'

'We are aware of what has happened to the Evangelist's daughter.'

'Yes. But God is in charge.'

'If we can be of assistance, do not hesitate.'

'Thanks. Your concern gladdens my heart.'

'The enemy of my friend is my enemy.'

'Thanks.'

'Do we make a move with a martyr?'

'Yes. In the upper and hallow chamber we have begun our own move.'

'Then ours will facilitate yours.'

'Exactly.'

'Pay attention to the news. We want to send you a congratulatory message.'

Chief Donald Amechi understood what that meant.

The caller rang off.

As Sheikh Mohammed Seko hung up, he pondered what may have happened to the Evangelist's daughter. Could it be that their enemies had made a move against them?

Shedrack Obong approached him.

'The attack will be carried out tomorrow,' the Sheikh told him.

Shedrack was surprised. He removed his marijuana joint from his mouth, and a curl of smoke came out with it. 'It is just a few days after the other attack.'

'Yes. Our friends have begun to plant the seed to impeach the President in the Senate and the House of Representatives.'

'Oh, I see. Then it is imperative that we make a move because with the attacks coming every few days, the President's impeachment plot will have a jolly quick ride.'

'Exactly, so prepare the explosives.'

'Where do we attack?'

'Lagos. The Government think that the South is safe. Let us take them by surprise.'

Donaldo was in the chapel on the Island. The birds chirped as they sat in the branches protecting themselves against the hot afternoon sun. The memories flooded back; how it all happened played in his mind like a movie.

That night, after she died, he was so weary from the thoughts that crowded in on him that he had no strength to stand up. He sat there, staring at her with tears streaming down his face for what felt like a lifetime. He could barely breathe for the guilt and anguish were strangling him. Then he remembered what she had told him once: *Donaldo, I would love us to get married in that chapel...*

He gathered the last strength in him and carried her lifeless body. She was so heavy. He wondered that someone so light when alive could be so heavy in death. Her skin was already beginning to feel cooler than the Island beach. He laid her at the altar. Tears were in his rheum-filled eyes. Mucus ran down his nostrils, saliva filled his mouth and his lips trembled.

He ran back to the hut, collected a shovel, and quietly dug a shallow grave by the altar of the chapel, just in front of the tabernacle housing the sacred body of the Lord.

His whole body shivered. The hand that held the shovel felt limp. Regret and fear convulsed him. He looked at her beautiful corpse, paler than usual, yet pretty even in death.

'Darling, I am so sorry for what I did. If only God in heaven could give me a second chance, if only He could give you life just for a minute for me to tell you how sorry I am. Since you died at my own hands, the same hands that I used to caress you, I pledge to respect your spirit all the days that I remain on earth. I will always pray before you. And will always kneel at this altar.' He knelt down, exhausted, sobbing.

'I have no other way of saying sorry but to bury you here, where you'd wanted to marry me.' He bent over her and wept. When he was done, he gently placed her in the grave. He collected the golden fillet that held her hair. It smelled of her skin. He sniffed it and tossed it into his pocket. 'Rest in peace, my darling.'

And there Adeline lay, buried close by the tabernacle, at the holy altar of the chapel of the Roman Catholic church. He covered the grave with soil and collected some dried leaves and scattered them over it. It takes evil to commit another evil and another evil to commit a sacrilege.

Donaldo hurried to the hut. The silhouette of the strange figure that lurked behind walked away too, wearily, turning just once, to stare and then continue.

Donaldo was sobbing. He knew that Adeline was cold beneath the earth at the altar. He made the sign of the cross, and stood. Just then, he heard his name.

'Donaldo!'

He froze.

He turned slowly.

'It's been a long time, my boy. Who were you talking to?'

He took a while to reply. 'The Virgin Mary... telling her about my trip to Italy.'

'Italy?'

'Yes.' He wiped his eyes with his sleeve.

'That is good. Telling her before you tell me.'

'I was coming to see you, Father.'

'Come, let's walk down together.' The old priest walked slowly down the path, his back bent as if he had a hump.

'Father, remember that work *Man on Glass* I painted few months back? It has been sold for a million dollars.'

The priest turned and stared at him.

'God is great! Christiana must be happy in heaven. You know, Naldo, I knew you would be great. The day they brought you here for baptism, your father and mother, you were special.'

They walked on quietly for a while.

'So you have changed your mind about going to Italy?'

'Yes. I think it is the best thing for me.'

'*Hmmn.*' The priest looked suddenly concerned. 'I will always pray for you, my son.'

As Donaldo and Father Simeon talked in the cottage, Chief Donald Amechi and his bodyguard were being driven in a Toyota Sequoia jeep to Abakaliki to visit the State Governor. A backup Honda Pilot was a few metres behind the Toyota. When they reached Mile 50, close to the Bishop's Court, a Volkswagen Golf parked at the roadside suddenly moved and blocked the jeep. The driver slammed on the brake frantically and swerved, then the right side of the jeep hit the Golf and the two cars skidded a few metres to a halt as a large man, dressed in jeans and a polo shirt, his face covered with a white mask, leapt out of the Golf carrying a

9mm semi-automatic handgun. He fired three shots at the windscreen of the jeep, but the bulletproof glass didn't shatter. The bodyguard jumped out and used the door as a shield. The assailant shot the guard in his right shoulder, rushed towards the jeep and shot him twice more at close range. The driver of the jeep ran across to the other side of the road firing at the assailant to draw his fire away from the Chief.

Chief Donald Amechi got out from the other side, pulling a shiny silver 1911 Colt .45 ACP from beneath the seat. He squatted beside the rear of the car, waiting. Just as the assailant turned to shoot at the driver, two men, carrying semi-automatics, were rushing towards the scene from the Honda. One saw his boss and ran to him, while the other covered him. The assailant shot at the driver but missed, hitting a fence post and shattering the wood.

The assailant took cover behind the jeep's bulletproof door and shot at the guard nearest to him and missed, while the other guard ran with the Chief to their car. The remaining guard saw the Chief's driver trying to escape when the assailant's driver emerged from the Golf and shot him in the back, then shouted at the assailant to pull back.

The assailant ran to the Golf, while the driver shot twice at the guards to cover him.

'Let's go!' he screamed.

The driver got in and sped off.

Franca Chuba wore a singlet and long skirt. Her hair was bound in a hairnet. She, Miss Spencer and her husband were having lunch that afternoon with Kwame. When the plates had been cleared away by the maids, Kwame's words hit all of them like a terrorist's bomb. Chris Chuba's eyes sparkled with rage; he could not look his wife in the face.

'Did you know that Adeline had a boyfriend?' Kwame asked. They were dumbfounded. Fear gripped Miss Spencer. Since the day Kwame arrived, the staff had been having secret meetings and monitored the man's moves. Miss Spencer had taken all the drawings and paintings that Donaldo had made for Adeline to a friend in Abakaliki for safe keeping.

'*Isi gini?* What did you say?' Mrs Chuba asked. She removed the toothpick in her mouth.

He turned to Miss Spencer. 'Have you ever had a male visitor, maybe in his early twenties, a tall, handsome guy?'

Kwame also had a toothpick, and he played with it while looking challengingly into Miss Spencer's eyes. The two maids present only stared at each other. Michelle wanted to excuse herself and return to the kitchen, but the detective ordered her to stay put. Franca looked at Miss Spencer in shock, the woman in whom she had special trust. If Miss Spencer had told her that Adeline had no male friends, it meant she had no male friends.

Kwame turned to Chris Chuba. 'Sir, we believe that Miss Spencer here once took Adeline to the Citi-chef café in town. We also believe that a young man took Adeline to the same place twice afterwards.'

'Spencer!' the Evangelist said sharply.

'Is that true?' Mrs Chuba asked.

'I took Adeline out to Citi-chef once. But that was that.'

'Spencer, did you arrange a boy for my daughter?'

'*Haa!* How could you say that, Sir?' Miss Spencer cried.

Kwame and Leonard had questioned Miss Spencer the day before when they got back from the café. She had admitted to going with Adeline to the café once for some meat pie, but said that she wasn't aware that Adeline had ever met with a young man.

'Now, tell me, all of you maids, just how often did Miss Adeline leave my house?'

'No one visited her and she didn't go out unless I went with her,' Miss Spencer answered, flashing an almost imperceptible look at the two maids. She looked at Franca Chuba directly in the eyes, hoping she sounded convincing.

'Was my daughter ever visited by a boy before?' Evangelist Chuba asked Michelle, noticing that she was looking nervous.

'I… I don't think so—'

'No, Sir,' Miss Spencer interrupted. But in her heart, it was as if a pestle was pounding some melon in a mortar and she wondered how long she would be able to keep lying.

'For Christ's sake! What are you women hiding from me?' the Evangelist shouted, rising to his feet in fury. Then his phone rang.

'Hello!' he barked.

After some seconds he shouted, 'What? Okay. Thanks for the information.' Everyone was silent. Kwame stared at him. Evangelist Chuba quickly dialled Chief Amechi's number. Looking at the others in the room he explained, 'I just got a call to say that Chief Donald has been attacked. His driver and guard are dead!'

Mrs Chuba let out a startled cry. The maids hurried out of the room with Miss Spencer.

'What about the Chief?' Mrs Chuba asked.

'It seems he wasn't in the vehicle. His line is ringing.' Chris Chuba was sweating. His hands were shaking. *What on earth is happening to us?*

'Hello, Evangelist!'

'Are you all right? Where are you? Were you in that vehicle? Did you—'

'My friend. Do you doubt the Brotherhood for my safety? I was in the vehicle. But the assailant didn't get me.'

THIRTY-SIX

Around 5pm, a man drove a white Hilux truck with the number plate of the Nigerian military into the car park of Games, a massive shopping complex in Lagos. The man, dressed in an expensive suit, walked into the mall. It was crowded. He headed into one of the large stores, picked up a plastic shopping basket and put some items off the shelves into it, then made his way to the checkout.

He queued up with other customers, and began to mumble to himself, quietly at first until his voice began to pick up volume.

An elderly woman behind him asked, 'What are you saying, young man?'

As the man turned to face her, the last thing she heard was 'Amen'.

The suicide bomber pulled at the wire protruding from the sleeve of his jacket and his chest erupted into a ball of fire. The blast killed seventy-six people, and the body parts of the elderly woman mingled with those of the bomber.

Donaldo began to feel a biting pain in his chest shortly

before he travelled to Italy. It felt as if pepper had been rubbed all over it. Once, he vomited blood in his hut and felt as if his tongue was being pulled out of his mouth.

He wondered what was wrong with him. He hid his condition from everyone. He did not want to tell his father because he would take him to hospital and he hated hospitals because his mother had died in one. He hated injections too. But the pain worsened by the day. He was worried. Perhaps it was a punishment from the girl he loved, the girl he'd murdered. He knew he had to find a way to earn her forgiveness, to let her soul rest in peace.

It was early in the evening, the sun was setting, but people could still drive without headlamps. He was driving back from Mr Ogiji's house, who he'd been to see in the afternoon after leaving the priest's cottage. He hadn't yet heard about the attack on his father because he had left his phone at home. Then the chest pains came on and he drove faster. His eyes were closing, and he just wanted to get home and relax, but he was afraid he might faint and crash the car.

He pulled over by the side of a long, quiet road. He felt the taste of blood in his mouth. He rushed out of the car and vomited.

He didn't notice as a car stopped and parked behind his Volkswagen. 'Hey! You okay? Just calm down. You'll be fine,' a voice said. And a hand rested on his shoulders. 'What's wrong? Have you got food poisoning?'

'No, I am fine. I am fine.' Donaldo stood and faced a tall broad shouldered man.

'I was driving to the Island when I saw you.' The man offered him a handkerchief.

'Thank you. I am headed there too. I am grateful you stopped.'

'Why are you vomiting blood? You need help. What is your name? Maybe I can take you the rest of the way.'

'I am… Donaldo Amechi.'

The man's heart skipped. 'My God, you are the Chief's son? Come with me in my car… I will send someone for yours later.' He held Donaldo's shoulders. 'Come with me.'

'Who are you?'

'I am Simon. I am Evangelist Chris Chuba's brother.'

Donaldo's heart skipped too. He was facing the man who once tried to abuse Adeline. He remembered how she had sobbed when she had told him about it on the phone and how he had wished he could've been there to hold her. He was sure that Adeline had given him this opportunity to appease her by killing the man who'd tormented her for so long. Donaldo felt that Adeline had suffered not just from the hands of her parents but also from the trauma of the attack by her uncle.

'*Uhmn*, I think I can drive—' he said, before groaning in pain for the benefit of Simon.

'No. I insist. I was going to see your father. You must be in shock from his attack this afternoon. What are you doing off the Island? Today is not a safe day for you to be out here alone.'

Donaldo registered what the man had said. 'Attacked?

Is he hurt?'

'No. He escaped. Haven't you heard? My God, come. Come. Let us go.'

Donaldo would have been happy to hear that his father was dead. But a more pressing opportunity was at hand and he had to act fast.

'Okay, a minute, please.' He hobbled to his Volkswagen and opened the glove compartment, groaning again, louder this time. Simon Chuba came behind him to offer help.

'Lock your car. Let us go.'

Donaldo turned and drove the knife into Simon's stomach. Before Simon's brain could take in what had happened, the knife was out and thrust in again with greater force. Adrenaline kicking in, he knocked Donaldo down with a blow and staggered, then fell. Donaldo sprang up as Simon was pulling back, losing blood, clutching at his stomach.

'What... did I do... to you?'

Donaldo kicked his stomach and he screamed in agony.

'Help! Help!' He coughed up blood and tried to crawl away from his attacker. Donaldo felt suddenly overwhelmed. Hate. No, more than hate, power. He bent down and stabbed Simon in the neck to curb his screams.

'This is for trying to rape Adeline,' Donaldo growled, spittle flying out of his mouth in his rage. He stabbed the dying man once more, in the groin. Simon Chuba's eyes bulged, he tried to scream but there was nothing but a gurgle as he choked and drowned in his own blood. Donaldo walked back to his car, breathing hard. The pain in his chest was a little sharper but he ignored it, adrenaline still coursing through his veins. He got behind the wheel and sped off.

THIRTY-SEVEN

The news of Simon Chuba's death spread like wildfire through Ishieke town. His body was found sprawled on the ground by a young couple who parked behind the abandoned car to grab a quick kiss.

They drove fast to the expressway and alerted some passers-by, who called the police. Officer Leonard Omelu rushed to the scene with three of his men. Kwame had asked him to inform him if there were any reports of crimes, as one could relate to another, so Leonard called Kwame and he joined them just before the ambulance from Abakaliki arrived.

'He is Evangelist Chuba's younger brother. I was with him just a couple of hours ago,' Kwame told Leonard. Then they heard the siren of the ambulance.

'Any idea where he said he was going to before he left the house?' Officer Leonard asked.

'I didn't even know he had left the house.'

The paramedics covered the body with a cloth and took it away on a stretcher.

When Kwame came back to the house, the maids were still awake because their master had not gone to bed.

Evangelist Chuba was sitting on one of the double sofas, his legs crossed, watching the news, waiting to talk to Kwame. He had just been speaking on the phone to Chief Amechi about the bomb attack in Lagos and had told him that Simon was on his way to the Island to discuss how to tackle Malik Hassan.

Demola opened the front door for Kwame and was surprised that he was with Officer Leonard, who was dressed in police uniform.

Kwame and Leonard found the Evangelist watching the television.

'What is it?' he said, thinking that they had news about Adeline.

Kwame asked, 'Where did Simon say he was going to when he left your house?'

'He was going to the Island to see Chief Amechi who was attacked today. I couldn't go since I am not feeling well, so I asked him to go and check on the Chief and find out if he is all right.' The Evangelist sat back on the sofa. 'Why do you ask? Is everything okay?'

'Sir... there is no easy way to say this... I am afraid Simon is dead. He has been murdered.' The words came out of Leonard's mouth more easily than he had thought when he had been wondering how to break the news. 'I am sorry for your loss, Sir. Rest assured we will do everything to find the killer.' About a minute elapsed. No one said anything.

Demola had been eavesdropping, something she did all

the time. She ran to Miss Spencer's room and informed her, but she was surprised when Miss Spencer did not show any concern.

'How did you hear?'

'Officer Leonard came here with Kwame. I heard everything.'

'Thank you for letting me know. Now, I want to sleep.' She turned to face the wall, and smiled. Though Adeline had never said anything, Miss Spencer knew how afraid she was of her uncle, and Simon had a reputation for liking his women young. Many times she had tried to broach the subject with Adeline, who refused to talk about it. She had once seen Simon standing very close to his niece – he had jumped when he saw her, only to relax on realizing it was only his niece's maid. She had hated him since that moment.

That night, Sheikh Kabiru Ibrahim sat with Sheikh Mohammed Seko in his father's sitting room. The older Sheikh had come to congratulate the men on the success of the two bombings. He had brought many gifts for the commanders of the operation.

'How many soldiers do we have, Seko?'

'In the Centre we have less than a hundred. But around Kafurzan and in other neighbouring towns we have close to ten thousand.'

'Great. Great.'

'The incentive is good. Beside there is no greater incentive than knowing that you do God's work.'

'Well said, Sheikh, well said. In Kano alone we have three thousand. In other states in the North we have a total of about four thousand.'

'We have been sending our soldiers to the South for over a year now. There are over ten thousand men scattered across all the states in Southern Nigeria,' Sheikh Seko said.

'*Alhamdulillah!*'

'Who made an attempt on one of the *Ustaz* in the South?' Sheikh Seko asked. He was drinking *kunu* from a small calabash plate.

'May Allah be praised that the Chief survived the attack. *Alhamdulillah!* He is a nice man. Sympathetic to our cause. He should have been born a Northerner. A Muslim.'

An elderly woman brought in the food. It was *jollof* rice with fried meat.

'We know who did it. Malik Hassan!'

Sheikh Seko's *kunu* spilled from his mouth.

'*Haa!* Pardon my manners, *Ustaz*.'

He cleaned his *quftan* with his handkerchief. The sound of children outside drifted in through the window. They were dancing around in circles and singing:

Young boy young girls listen to your father
Young boy young girls listen to your mother
You must obey what Allah says
You must obey what the parent says
Always ask them first what you want to do

For Allah will love you and they will love you too

Young boy young girls listen to your father

Young boy young girls listen to your mother…

'He has stepped on the tail of a lion.'

'He will be taken care of. A bounty has been placed on his head.'

Kwame was in his bathtub, which was filled to its brim with foamy water. He was lying still, just thinking about everything that had happened.

Perhaps Adeline is dead. Or being held by someone more dangerous than we think, the person who killed Simon. And are these crimes related to the Evangelist? The thoughts whirred around his mind as he tried to put them in order.

His mind drifted to Evangelist Chuba and his reaction when the news about his brother was broken to him.

Evangelist Chuba was in his study, speaking with Chief Donald Amechi.

'If Simon was killed by one of our enemies, it means we are not far from the target,' he told the Chief.

'Could it be Malik?'

'My guess is as good as yours.' The Evangelist rubbed his temples.

'We need more security. First Adeline, then the attempt on me, now Simon. I will talk to the Tais, we must get more intelligence on this. In the meantime, tell your men to beef up your security.'

Chuba nodded. 'The police said they are waiting for the results of the autopsy to determine the blade used – it might help with the investigation. The Commissioner called me a couple of minutes back.' The Evangelist's voice was hoarse and he trembled slightly.

'You see, Chris, I don't think we need to involve the police in this matter. The investigation might lead to where we don't want it to.'

Chuba considered for a moment. 'What do I do, then?'

'Call the Commissioner tomorrow after the autopsy; the information it provides may be useful to us. Then, tell him to forget the investigation. In fact, call him tonight and tell him not to involve the press.'

'Will he agree?'

'He has no option. Who made him Commissioner?'

THIRTY-EIGHT

Thursday, 13th May 2010

Officer Leonard and Detective Kwame drove to the Island to interview Donaldo Amechi.

'I got a call from the Commissioner this morning,' Leonard said. 'He said that we should concentrate our energy on looking for the Evangelist's daughter, that we should forget about Simon Chuba.'

'Why?'

'He said that he thinks it's a distraction. That if we could find the person holding Adeline then we may discover who killed Simon.'

'That's bullshit. It could be the other way round, Leonard.'

'Yes, I told him so. But he wouldn't listen. Kwame, you don't understand this country.'

'It is corruption. A lot of things are amiss here.'

'Yes. But for me that corridor is still open. Simon Chuba was brutally murdered. We owe him a duty to find his killer.'

'Did your men take fingerprints and collect evidence

at the scene? I would like to see the lab results.'

Leonard replied carefully, 'Kwame, this is not the US or the UK. Things are done differently here. Here we do not rely on science so much as intuition. They may have some evidence but, please, don't go demanding big scientific investigations, you understand?'

Kwame thought about that as they got to the Island gate.

There were trees scattered within Chief Amechi's compound and a deep forest started at the back of the white mansion. There was no gate, but the detectives could see at least five Alsatians chained near the house. The dogs began to bark fiercely at the unfamiliar car.

The two men parked and hurried to the front door and pressed the bell. After a minute a woman in her fifties answered.

'How may I help you?'

'Good day, Ma. My name is Leonard. I am the DPO in charge of the Ishieke Police Division. This is Kwame, my partner.'

'Ha. *Oga*, welcome, Sir.'

'Thank you. We are looking for your son, Donaldo.'

'My son? Donaldo's mother died years ago. In any case, he is not here, he travelled yesterday.'

'What?'

'Yes. What is wrong? Is everything all right?'

The two men stared at each other.

'Yes, Ma. Everything is fine,' Leonard replied. They

wondered why the woman didn't ask them in. Her bulky frame blocked the entrance, indicating that she preferred that they remain outside.

'Why do you want to see him?'

'We need to talk with him about the missing Chuba girl. We understand that she had visited here with her family before.'

'Oh yes. At Easter. We all ate together. What is so special about that?'

'Ma, they are young people, and young people talk to each other. We just wondered if she may have told him anything that might help us find her.'

The woman said nothing. She studied the two men.

'Where has he gone?' Leonard asked.

'He travelled to Port Harcourt. His father was attacked two days ago—'

'We heard. It is a pity.'

'You must excuse me now, I have something on the fire.'

She tried to close the massive door but Kwame's hand went to it. 'Hold on, Ma'am, when is he likely to return?'

'I don't know. Speak with his father when he returns. Both of them travelled together. But I think Donaldo is starting a new job there. His father might be back tomorrow. Excuse me.'

The thick door closed with a thud.

The two detectives stood for some seconds, silent, disappointed. Then they got back in the car and, as Leonard drove out, he suggested they drive around the Island to explore before leaving.

As they drove around, they couldn't help admiring the beauty of the Island – the jacaranda and gmelina trees, the tall neem trees, the brightly coloured flowers of the Pride of Barbados. They passed a small golf course, then a rice field, which Kwame had never seen before. Finally they saw a signpost leading to the chapel, so they parked and followed the path.

As they walked they discussed the announcement they had heard on the car radio – impeachment motions had been moved in both Houses of the National Assembly against the President for his failure to contain the spate of terrorist attacks in the country. Kwame laughed when he saw the small chapel. He could not understand why the Island with all its wealth would still be using a hut as a chapel that housed the Blessed Sacrament. Kwame noticed that the lamp by the tabernacle was lit so he picked up a Bible from one of the dusty pews and walked to the sanctuary and knelt down. He opened the Bible to the book of Psalms and read. Then he walked to one of the pews close to the altar, and sat down, forgetting that it was covered in dust. Outside, Leonard was throwing stones at some birds in a moringa plant.

Kwame loved the chapel. He was a Catholic and took great solace in his faith. He took a deep breath and was about to stand when he noticed something glittering by the pew in front of him, partly covered by leaves. A breeze from the open door had revealed it and it sparkled in the sunrays shining through one of the windows. Kwame reached out for it. His heart beat faster.

He hurried outside and cleaned it with his handkerchief to reveal a surface like a kaleidoscope.

'Leonard, look!'

The officer turned and came to him at the entrance to the chapel.

'What is this?'

'I found it there. Inside the chapel.'

'A golden pen?'

Kwame said, 'No. It's a golden clutch pencil. One of those refillable types architects use to draw building plans.' The sun caught it again and it radiated like a rainbow. 'Who would be using a golden clutch pencil round here?'

Leonard shrugged. Kwame twisted the pencil to see if any lead was left inside, but instead of lead a long needle came out.

'Jesus!'

'What is it?'

'Someone has replaced the lead with a needle.'

Leonard took the pencil and admired it. 'Who would put a needle inside this beautiful thing?'

'Whoever the owner is, he must be wealthy. This is pure gold.'

As they left the Island, Kwame still studying the pencil, he remembered one of the Psalms he had read while he knelt by the sanctuary: ... *He makes me lie down in green pastures... my cup is overflowing...*

THIRTY-NINE

The Government's Joint Task Force, the JTF, whose duty it was to lead the war against terrorism – seeking out terrorist camps and flushing them out – received orders to attack people residing at the Centre for Islamic Knowledge in Kafurzan. They were suspected by the Department of State Security of being members of Jama'atul al-Mujahideen Jihad.

The attack was to take place on Friday afternoon. But while the JTF were busy preparing their operation strategy, the Commanding Officer got a signal. They were to hold off on the attack.

A few hours earlier, a security meeting had been held with the President. Mr Yahaya Ahmed, Director of the Department of State Security, served on the Presidential Security Advisory Committee and argued during the meeting that if the Join Task Force attacked the Centre for Islamic Knowledge with insufficient evidence that it housed terrorists, it would provoke the Northerners and the Muslims. The President had been adamant. He wanted the JTF to storm the place and find out for themselves. But Ahmed held firm that any operation would be a huge blow to the President.

The President was confused. 'Then, Director, why was the JTF ordered to prepare for an attack?'

'If we are investigating a place like this, Your Excellency, we ask the JTF to prepare for an attack then wait for presidential clearance. If you give permission like you did yesterday, they will get the signal to carry on. If you refuse permission, they will hold back. Either way, it is better that they are on alert—'

'All right. All right.' The President knew how long it could take to organize things in Nigeria, so he understood why the Director would want to be prepared. Furthermore, he trusted him. 'I am rushing off for another meeting in fifteen minutes. I want all the documents on the Islamic Centre to be on my desk by the end of the day. Meanwhile put the attack on hold until you find out more. What else can we do?'

The Minister of Defence spoke up. 'Your Excellency, there is only one way to find out. Since there is a mosque inside the Centre, we could send in a spy to worship there and take a look around.'

'Mr Ahmed?'

'Yes. We could send a Muslim in there.'

'Then do it. We cannot attack the Centre based on speculation.' The President scratched his head. 'If we attack every Islamic centre and mosque, the media and international organizations will suck our blood. I have enough headaches already. And this impeachment move from the House. Why is everything happening at once?' He sighed. 'This spy had better move quickly. I am a Muslim, and these men will not shame my religion – if I find a single terrorist in any Islamic centre or mosque I will burn it down! Simple! *Kajiko?*'

Everyone was silent. They understood.

Mr Yahaya Ahmed smiled once they had all been dismissed; his brothers in the Sacred Order would be pleased.

Kwame drove to the Amechi residence to show the pencil he had found to the woman there. Leonard had told him if any building work was being done at the chapel, the Amechis would know of it. When he got to the mansion, he was surprised to see several cars parked there, and young men sitting on benches. Two of them stood when they saw him and approached his car, their hands at the ready on their guns.

Kwame was careful. He stepped slowly out of the car. As soon as his feet touched the red earth, a hulking Alsatian swooped on him. If one of the guards hadn't quickly grabbed the dog's chain it would have sunk its teeth into the detective.

'Who are you?' the guard shouted above the dog's barks.

'I am a detective.'

Other dogs started barking. The guard made Kwame

sit on the bench till Chief Amechi asked for him to be brought round to his gazebo in the garden, where he was sitting on a plastic chair.

'I am told that you came here yesterday asking to see my son,' the Chief said after Kwame sat down. 'What do you want?'

'Sir, I am the detective investigating Adeline Chuba's case.'

'Oh, I see. I was the one that recommended you. I called your mentor in Ghana and put him in touch with the Evangelist.'

Kwame didn't know that.

'Why do you want to see my son?'

'We got information that your son was seen with her twice in town before she disappeared.'

The Chief frowned. 'And?'

Kwame knew to tread carefully. 'Sir, we are trying to tie up every loose end in this case. They are young people and they like to socialize, so I believe that your son could help us with information that may help us find your friend's daughter. Something she may have said to him.'

'Who gave you that information, detective?'

'We've been talking to people, Sir.'

'Well, it is not true. Adeline is known to be a quiet person, a recluse. And my son rarely left the Island. He is an artist, one of the best in the world. He doesn't have time for gallivanting.'

Kwame remembered the clutch pencil.

'He is an artist?'

'Yes, man. That is what I said.'

Kwame brought out the pencil from his pocket. 'I found this, Sir. Do you recognize it?'

'Where did you get this?'

'We found this yesterday at the chapel, lying beneath one of the pews.'

Chief Amechi took it. 'Yes, this belongs to my son. We were looking for it before he left for Port Harcourt. He must have dropped it – he often visits the chapel to see the priest there. Thanks for finding it. I will return it to him.' The Chief placed the pencil beside him and crossed his legs.

Kwame was confused. 'I don't think so, Sir. It is evidence, for now, you see.'

'Why?'

'Sir, we suspect the pencil has been used to commit a crime. It has been modified with a needle instead of a pencil lead. The lab reported that the needle has traces of blood and another substance that appears to be poison on it.' Kwame saw that the Chief's expression had changed. The Chief twisted the pencil. The needle had been removed. 'Sir, I promise to return it when we are through with the investigations.'

'Where is the needle?'

'It's in the lab now.'

'Okay then, give me your business card. If anything comes up I will let you know. Sorry that you cannot speak with Donaldo himself.'

'We may arrange to see him and talk with him at a

281

later time, Sir.'

Kwame wrote down his phone number on a piece of paper and left. The Chief sipped from his drink then lit his cigar. He was deep in thought. *The clutch pencil belongs to Donaldo. It may have been used to murder someone. It's been a while since I last saw it in Donaldo's hands. Apparently he used to bring Adeline to the Island. Kwame said some people saw them together twice in town. The chapel is close to his hut. What if Adeline was killed by Donaldo, or someone else, with the pencil? What if?* He knew that anything was possible.

Chief Donald Amechi stood and paced about. He picked up his phone and made a call. He needed to act fast before someone else found out before him. The Sacred Order of the Universal Forces would demand his son's head if he was the one who had prevented the sacrifice. It had taken a great deal to convince them to choose Adeline. *Why hasn't this occurred to me before?*

That night, Evangelist Chris Chuba and his wife had an argument.

'Listen, woman. You do what I command. Have you forgotten?' he shouted at his wife. The door was closed. She was crying.

'I cannot keep on doing your wish. I don't want to travel to Libya.'

'It's just for a few days.' He was frustrated. The deadline from the Sacred Order was drawing nearer, and he wanted Franca out of the way, even though he knew full well that nowhere would be completely safe.

'We have hundreds of people we could send,' she said.

'You are my wife. And I want to send you.'

'I am not going. It was all this travelling that made us lose Adeline,' she cried, 'my only child! And I could never have had another. I bet you're happy about that, God forbid I should lose my figure!'

'Shut up!' Chuba slapped her. 'It was the will of God that you lost your womb.'

She moaned with pain and held her face where the sting of his slap still tingled her skin.

He turned her around and started to kiss her. She did not object, she was too weak and tired. He pulled down his trousers, unzipped her skirt and entered her.

FORTY

The Sheikh was not the one leading the prayers. His eyes were roving over the worshippers in the mosque in search of the spy whom they had been informed was in their midst.

It was *Subh*, the early morning *Salat*. The Sheikh had watched everyone as they entered the mosque. They came in ones and twos and in groups. Then as the prayers proceeded, a young man strolled in. He was dressed in a very common *quftan*, the cheapest you could find in the market. He was very dark with no tribal marks. He was so tall that the Sheikh would have to look up to his face to talk to him. He had never seen his face before, but his eyes still wandered.

When the prayers were over he asked five of his men to follow the man, and watch his every move. The man did not leave the Centre, like most of the worshippers, but walked round the mosque towards the classrooms. He went to the back of the last classroom, undid the rope of his trousers and urinated, his eyes looking around the whole time. When he finished he walked away.

Just before 8am, a fair-skinned man with a scar on the right side of his forehead was sitting on one of the cushions in Chief Amechi's sitting room. His brown shirt was the same colour as the cushion he sat on. The four ceiling fans whirled noiselessly and the tiled floor seemed to stare up at the fans as if in amazement. The bald headed man was watching the television till Madam Vero took him into the study to meet her boss.

The Chief stood next to the man, who was a forensics expert, as he talked to the old priest in front of his little cottage. The octogenarian vehemently refused to leave his cottage for a few hours.

'Where will I go to?' he asked.

'Go to Mile 50. The Bishop's Court,' the Chief suggested.

'Just because this man here wants to carry out an investigation? For what, even?'

Chief Amechi looked at him sternly, his patience running out. 'Just do what I said, Father, just for today.'

The priest saw the anger in the Chief's face. 'Okay. I'll go, but just today... let me tell you, Donald, I hate staying with the Bishop.'

'Why?'

'He prays all the time. I never have time to read.'

'All right. Leave this morning, Father. You can go anywhere but just leave,' the Chief said. The priest went back into his cottage. He was not happy. He hated anyone ordering him around.

The Chief watched the forensic investigator as he operated the laser detector that he had unpacked from his kit. They moved around the area slowly, the investigator stopping every few steps to examine the debris and search for any trace of evidence – 'blood, saliva, bone fragments, that kind of thing, which the human eye can't see,' he had explained to the Chief.

They searched the whole of Donaldo's hut and the nearby forest where he made his wooden sculptures. They found nothing. They searched the banks of the pond. And the path that led to the chapel. Finally, they reached the chapel itself.

'The pencil was found inside, right?'

'So Mr Kwame said,' the Chief replied.

The investigator manoeuvred the device round the exterior of the chapel and inside it and up to the altar. The fluorescent light highlighted something. He knelt down, focusing in on the area. He noticed that the ground had been disturbed.

'What is it?' the Chief asked, anxious and impatient.

'There's something here.'

'Blood?'

'I cannot be sure. The investigation of a crime scene requires time… and patience,' he added pointedly. 'The ground here has been disturbed. You see how these leaves are scattered? Though the wind has moved them around there is still an unusual concentration in this area, and some of the leaves are mixed with mud, as though the floor was dug up and turned over.'

The investigator stood and removed his jacket.

'Has anyone been buried at the altar recently?' he asked.

'I don't think so... it's only priests who are buried here. Unless the missionaries who used to own this place buried someone here, but that would have been a long time ago.'

'No, this is recent. Very recent. Sir, can you fetch me that shovel we saw near your son's hut?'

The investigator started to dig. The Chief paced up and down the aisle of the chapel, as nervous as a man whose wife was in labour. His hands trembled and he took out a white handkerchief to mop the sweat off his face. After a short while the investigator called him over. Chief Amechi watched as he used the shovel to scrape away the red soil, and it came into view. There before them was the body of a young woman, her long hair in a mess around her.

Chief Amechi's heart was beating so fast he felt he was about to have a heart attack.

'What... do we do? Can you tell how long the body has been here?' he asked, his voice urgent and his eyes red.

'No, Sir, that is not in my expertise, though I do not think it has been too long.' The investigator looked at the Chief, who turned away.

'Never mind, I know someone who can.'

He took out his phone and called the medical examiner.

In the evening, Chief Donald Amechi sat mulling over the the medical examiner's words. *A young woman, aged about 18–20. Dead less than two weeks.*

'I want this to be our little secret,' the Chief said to the investigator and the medical examiner as he handed over two large brown envelopes containing one million naira for each of them. 'You know, a man might be forced to become wicked sometimes, especially when it comes to protecting his family.'

He smiled. It was a warning to them.

The investigator said, 'Chief, every day I deal with different cases. I barely remember one case to the next. If it is not in my files, it does not exist. You do not need to worry.'

'Me too, Chief, I owe you a lot already. No one will hear about this.' The Chief nodded and with that the medical examiner hurried away.

Chief Amechi turned to the investigator. 'No one is to hear that you even came to Ebonyi State.'

'Sir, I have not been to Ebonyi since I was born in downtown Lagos.' Nodding respectfully, the man collected his envelope and walked away.

As soon as the men left, Chief Amechi summoned his son.

FORTY-ONE

Donaldo had just finished a painting he called *Axe of Freedom* when his father called and asked him to return from Port Harcourt the next day. It was painted on thick board, about four metres tall by three metres wide, depicting slaves, about a hundred of them – tiny humans, tied with chains – and soldiers flogging them with whips. Above the slaves was a giant bird holding in its beak an axe, breaking the chains. It was a remarkable painting.

The place where he lived was close to the sea and from his veranda he had a wonderful view of the water. He used the veranda as his studio. It had all he needed for his painting. Different paints, woods from a variety of timbers from across the world, brushes, pencils and every type of art equipment one could think of.

He left the painting and walked to the rear of the veranda to watch the waves. A young girl came out dressed in a silk blouse that emphasized her generous bust and a pair of slacks made from a light material that outlined her full buttocks. Her hair was tied back tight, revealing high cheekbones and an elegant long neck. Her name was Chomy, a painter too who had just graduated from the university. She was working as Donaldo's personal assistant during his stay in Port Harcourt, though she hoped there might have been more between them. Any other man would have found it difficult to control himself alone with such a beautiful woman. But Donaldo was far too troubled to notice her looks.

'Chomy, get me something to drink. Something strong this time, not that light beer you brought before,' he said. He was fast becoming dependent on alcohol, out of despair.

Chomy served him a glass of vodka and looked at him for a while. She liked Donaldo, she liked him a lot, and wondered why he never looked at her as other men did. She was smart enough to recognize her own physical charms, and concluded that Donaldo must be having problems with a girlfriend back home – why else would he not be attracted to her? Finally, she sighed and left him alone to drown his sorrows.

Mr Yahaya Ahmed had informed his brothers that the Government might attack the Centre for Islamic Knowledge. Sheikh Kabiru Ibrahim was alerted. He immediately headed to Katsina. And in less than an hour, all the weapons that had been hidden in the *madrasa* were relocated to a camp in a thick forest where some Fulani herdsmen who were members of JMJ had been encamped for over a year. Over five hundred young men, with more than six hundred cattle, moved into the camp with the weapons. The arms would be returned to the *madrasa* when the time was ripe. They began to watch out for the spy.

As the weapons were being loaded into trucks that night, the terrorists travelled to the outskirts of Katsina and attacked a government research institute. They shot five women and nine men. They then entered a police station and opened fire on those inside. The policemen ran for their lives. The terrorists released the inmates.

As the attacks were going on, Sheikh Seko noticed the stranger again in the Centre. The man, wearing an old *gallabiya*, came into the mosque for the *Ishai Salat* then left. He had been seen earlier that day when he came for the *Subh* and the *Zuhr Salats* in the morning and in the afternoon; he had also gone to the canteen and drunk *kunu* and ate some rice. He chatted with the man who ran the canteen. Then he walked round the Centre visiting the hostels and walking along their verandas.

FORTY-TWO

Sunday, 16th May 2010

Donaldo was collected from the airport in Enugu and driven to Williams Island; throughout the journey he did not utter a word to the driver and the guards.

His face was swollen and lined. His once fine eyes were red and his complexion had darkened. Donaldo knew that he had a serious health problem but would not see a doctor. He had promised Adeline's spirit that he would only see a doctor when he had suffered enough as penance for his sins.

Some metres before the Island gate, the driver pulled up and the guards got out. They accompanied him to the gate from where he could see the outstretched waters. Someone who had not been there in the middle of the rainy season before would doubt that it was in fact Williams Island. For days, it had rained continuously, causing the floods to surround the whole island. The late morning breeze created waves. He could see speedboats already waiting for them.

From his boat he saw Islanders fishing from the banks

and locals who had come in canoes to fish at the tributary that flowed into the bigger mouth of the Ebonyi River, from which the state got its name. On the other side he disembarked and walked down the footpath to a large clearing where his Volkswagen Bug was waiting. He passed it and continued walking. He passed the swampy areas. Saw rice plants and heaps of yams and groundnuts. He passed the golf course, down to the Island restaurant, then past the recreation centre and down to the main road leading to his father's mansion. All the while, thinking, *why has he summoned me?*

A man came out of Murtala Muhammed Airport in Lagos and walked into a waiting Honda Accord. The driver drove off immediately at speed, heading towards the exit.

'*As-Salaamu 'alaykum*, Bala!'

'Thank you, *oga*. '*Alaykum Salam!* How your journey be?'

'Fine, Bala.'

'May Allah be praised. W*elucome, Oga. Welucome!*' the driver responded in his pidgin. As soon as the car left the airport a Hilux gave chase and blocked it, pushing the Honda into the hard shoulder. The Honda hit the kerb, tipped over it and fell into the drainage ditch. Three men, wielding 9mm automatic pistols, got out of the Hilux and shot the driver four times in the chest. They dragged the passenger into another vehicle with tinted windows that had been following behind and sped off.

The Hilux took another route.

That afternoon, the death was announced of a middle-aged driver shot on the airport road, while his boss was kidnapped. A few miles away, Malik Hassan was hanged from a tall tree in a very thick forest. His killers made sure that he was dead before they walked away. It would be better, they had been ordered, if his corpse was left for vultures to feed on.

As soon as Donaldo walked into the mansion, Chief Amechi's phone rang. He saw the number and hurried into his library.

'Hello!' he answered.

'The vultures will dine well today.'

His heart was filled with joy. 'Good. Now proceed as planned. God is your strength.'

Later that afternoon, Chief Amechi sent Madam Vero upstairs to her room and summoned Donaldo to his library. Madam Vero was surprised. What on earth could make the Chief send her upstairs? He had never done that before, not even when people came to discuss business with him. *Something must be wrong*, she thought. But she hurried to her room as she was ordered to do.

Donaldo found his father bent over the table. He could see how neatly dressed the elderly man was. His ashtray was full of cigar butts. Chief Amechi lifted his head and stared at his son for a while, which made Donaldo very uncomfortable. The Chief cleared his throat, so that the gods and his ancestors could pay attention. He sat up and placed his arms on the leather covered table.

'Donaldo, what I want to say might sound ridiculous to your ears. But I want you to tell me the truth. Our people say that *eziokwu bu ndu*, truth is life. You have no other kinsman but me, your father… no matter what, I cannot neglect you nor abandon you.' He paused to light a cigar. 'You must tell me the truth, so that I can protect you if the need arises…'

Donaldo's heart flew into his stomach. *Perhaps they have discovered Adeline.* He began to shiver. And his father noticed it.

'You continued going out with Adeline, even after my warning, didn't you?'

Donaldo did not know what to answer. He was confused and scared.

'Answer me, *nwokem*!' His father's fist hit the table. He jumped. The Chief swept the papers off the table onto the floor.

'She was just my friend.' Tears came to his eyes.

The Chief looked at him hard. 'So, why did you kill her?'

The accusation landed like a bombshell. 'How can you even think that?'

'Are you denying it?'

'You accuse your own son of murder?'

'Listen. You are in deep shit. The sooner you talk

to me the better.' His father stared hard at him. Cigar smoke spiralled into the air. It made Donaldo feel sick. The two men were silent, staring at each other, waiting for the other to make the first move like players in a chess game.

Chief Amechi made the move. 'I found a grave at the chapel.'

Donaldo could not look his father in the face.

'How does that concern me?'

His father continued, 'Adeline's body was in the grave, and your clutch pencil was found nearby. It gave you away Donaldo. The golden pencil I gave you.'

'I didn't kill anybody.' Donaldo's voice was faint. He was sweating profusely.

'When did you last see Adeline, Donaldo?'

Donaldo was surprised his father had not started beating him. Cursing and shouting. Maybe he did not want to raise his voice in case anyone in the house heard.

'I can't remember when.'

The Chief was angry now. 'The girl was your girlfriend, Donaldo. I know she was. You remember the story of Picasso's friend who travelled to Paris with him and later killed himself because of a love affair that went bad... Pray... Pray, Donaldo, that this won't land you in big *wahala*!' The Chief was standing now, facing his son, his cigar burning between his fingers.

'If I knew this was why you summoned me I would not have come.' Donaldo turned his back on his father.

'And if I knew you would be stubborn I would have

allowed the Chubas' detective to carry on with the investigation till he apprehended you. I would have given him leads. But it's not too late. God! I feel like killing you. I cannot have a murderer for a son.' The Chief squared his lips as he said those words. 'You remind me of the witch who gave birth to you.'

Donaldo was enraged. To speak of his mother was to put fuel on a blazing fire. He turned on his father, 'Interesting that you mention my mother, maybe I inherited my killing traits from you.' Donaldo's words made his father recoil in horror. He knew then that it was indeed Donaldo who had killed Adeline.

'I regret the day I held you in my arms as my son. You disgust me. *Inwuranwu*, you are dead!' His father grabbed his collar, and tried to hit him, but Donaldo shook him off and shoved him hard.

'You think I do not know about you? About Christiana.'

The Chief slapped Donaldo so hard that blood flew out of his mouth. 'How dare you! *Anu ofia*, bush animal!' he cursed.

Donaldo wiped his mouth with the back of his left palm.

'The beatings did not start today, so I do not fear them. You know, it's your fault. I hate you just like you hate me. You confined me in a small space. Now, I am a fool. I am anti-social. A dullard. I know nothing. How do you think I'd behave, like a saint? You built the monster in me. You made me like this!'

297

'Shut up, you bloody fool!'

Their eyes were locked, in hatred, anguish and after, despair and blood tie.

'You made me kill Adeline. You, with your twisted ideas about women, about my art and my future. Oh! How I loved her, and you made me kill her. And you know what? I killed Simon too! And I won't stop until I have revenge for me and for Adeline, and for our baby!'

For once Chief Amechi was terrified. He saw madness in his son's eyes. Donaldo ran out and would have collided with Madam Vero, if she had not been fast enough to dodge behind the thick curtain when she heard the doorknob turn.

Madam Vero breathed fast. Tears mixed with fear filled her eyes. She had heard everything.

Sheikh Mohammed Seko assembled over thirty of his fighters. They had been ordered to meet close to the market in Kafurzan, where the spy lived, with their guns and machetes. It was a dark night, the stars and the moon had retreated into the black ocean of cloud.

Some of the men appeared uneasy – even with their lack of education, they knew it was a grave sin to hurt a fellow Muslim. Seko knew he would need to twist those same teachings in order to settle them. He addressed the men before him. 'In *Sahih Bukhari*, Abdullah bin Umar narrated: "A Muslim is a brother of another Muslim. So he should not oppress him. Nor should he hand him over to an oppressor. Whoever fulfilled the needs of his brother, Allah will fulfil his needs; whoever brought his brother out of a discomfort, Allah will bring him out of the discomforts of the Day of Resurrection. And whoever protected a Muslim, Allah will protect him on the Day of the Resurrection." '

Abouzeid and the men nodded.

'For this reason it pains my heart that one of our Muslim brothers who worships with us in the holy place of Allah plots to hand us over to the oppressor. And has failed to protect his brothers! Now it is our duty to protect, we cannot fail.'

The men murmured in agreement. Sheikh Mohammed Seko smiled to himself – it had not taken much after all. His friends in the South and those in the Government were doing their best to protect him. They all wanted the same thing – fame, fortune and power.

The men made their move. The spy was standing inside the house, facing away from the door and saying his prayers, when the men surrounded the dilapidated residence, occupied by market traders. A burly man broke down the door with his military boot. The spy turned swiftly; his hand went to his waist to reach for his gun. A shadow moved to the left. The spy fired his gun, but not before the poisoned dagger had lodged in his neck, paralyzing him.

Abouzeid fell, he was bleeding. The bullet had penetrated his right ribs. In their rage his soldiers hacked the spy's body to pieces. When the police came it had to be packed in plastic bags for removal.

It was 11pm. The Island was as quiet as a graveyard. The mansion was dressed in the same cloak of silence. Donaldo checked his watch. He walked to the wing where his father's room was situated. He pulled at the door handle. It opened.

Donaldo watched as the Chief slept. He knew that under one of the four pillows on the bed was a loaded pistol.

He was confused and for the brief moment that he stood there it was like eternity, waiting for the day Jesus Christ would come. He thought about his future. *If I allow this man to wake in the morning he will ruin my life*.

He shook his head and turned. He was ready to walk away. Then, he remembered Christiana and his only sibling. He stopped. Donaldo could see them drenched in blood. They begged Donaldo to kill his father. He walked back to the bed, and picked up one of the pillows. As the man opened his eyes, he struck, smothering his father's face with the pillow and pushing down with his strong hands.

The Chief threw a punch at his son. It caught Donaldo in the jaw and he was sure that a tooth was dislodged. Donaldo struggled, the pillow shifted and he found himself staring into his father's eyes, just for a second, before he pushed down again with all his might.

Donaldo leaned towards him, avoiding the thrashing hands. 'This is for Christiana – for killing my mother and her baby,' he hissed, 'and for ruining my life.'

Chief Amechi thrashed and flailed, but Donaldo held strong. His father tried to shout but the pillow was suffocating him. After what felt like hours to Donaldo, though he knew it could not have been, his father stopped struggling and slumped on the bed.

Donaldo relaxed, and noticed how hard he was panting. Sweat dripped off him and his hands were trembling. He quickly placed back the pillow and rearranged the bed, before hurrying out of the room.

FORTY-THREE

Monday, 17th May 2010

Donaldo was seated with Madam Vero, eating breakfast. As Donaldo ate some fried yam with fresh pepper sauce and eggs, Madam Vero sat staring at the kitchen door, her right palm holding her chin.

'What is bothering you?'

After a few seconds she said, 'It is very unusual that your father is not down by eight. Let me check on him.'

'Okay.'

She left, and he heard her footsteps up the stairs. When her screams came from the landing, they were so loud that the guards came running in.

Madam Vero was weeping and panting and sweating. The guards held both her and Donaldo, who cried quietly in the corner. Then, one of the guards stepped outside and rang Evangelist Chris Chuba.

When Evangelist Chuba got to the residence and confirmed that his friend was dead, he instantly took Donaldo aside. He gave him his sincere sympathies, but wanted to ensure that the young man would not ask for an autopsy. The Sacred Order of the Universal Forces forbade autopsy on their dead members. Chris Chuba also suspected this was yet another attack againt the Sacred Order, and the last thing they needed was police involvement.

'When do you intend to lay your father to rest?' he asked.

'As soon as possible, Sir.'

'Good. Our Lord in Heaven will have his soul now. Your father was a good man.' He hesitated. 'I hope you do not intend to carry out an autopsy, son?' He looked Donaldo in the eye.

Donaldo was surprised by the statement. 'Why do you ask?'

'Your dad was my friend. The Bible does not support autopsy, son, it is a mutilation of the body and the body houses the soul.'

They could still hear Madam Vero's sobs from her room and the gentle words of the Island women who had come to pay their respects. He saw Father Simeon walk in.

'I don't support autopsy. I am here to guide you as your father's dearest friend—' the Evangelist continued.

'I do not need guidance, Sir. But I do not intend to ask for an autopsy.' *Good riddance*, he thought.

That morning, a doctor was tending to Abouzeid inside the Centre for Islamic Knowledge. The night before, when he was brought back, Shedrack Obong had removed the bullet and given him first aid while they awaited the doctor.

'My Sheikh,' he muttered.

'Brother.' Sheikh Mohammed Seko came to his friend.

'I do not fear death. For I know that if I die I have a place in paradise.'

'*Alhamdulillah!* Thanks to the Almighty for your wisdom. You won't die. Have faith.'

'I need to pray. Give me my prayer beads.'

The Sheikh gave the dying man his *masbaha*. 'Doctor, how is he?'

'I wish I had come sooner, it is a bad wound. I am surprised he has lasted this long. All we can do now is wait, and pray. I have done all I can to stabilize him.' The doctor bandaged his stomach, and set up an IV.

Abouzeid began to say the *Shahadah*. The Sheikh noticed that he could not go past the first few lines. He was saying it repeatedly.

Ash-hadu an laa ilaaha illallah Wa ash-hadu anna Muhammadan rasulullah. Ash-hadu an laa ilaaha illallah Wa ash-hadu anna Muhammadan rasulullah. Ash-hadu an laa ilaaha illallah Wa ash-hadu anna Muhammadan rasulullah…

Sheikh Seko began to say the creed in English.

I bear witness that there is no God but Allah and that Muhammad is His Prophet…

He was clutching his friend's hand tightly. When Abouzeid's mouth stopped moving, his eyes rolled and turned white, staring at the ceiling. The prayer beads fell off the bed onto the floor. The sound startled the Sheikh. He stared at the beads, for he couldn't bear to look at the dead Abouzeid, but Sheikh Seko did not know that an evil person is not worthy to die with the holy beads in his hands, for Islam abhors evil.

Later that morning, Donaldo received some very important visitors in the small sitting room on the upper floor of the mansion. The Governor of Ebonyi State sat on a chair directly opposite the television. Next to him were the Evangelist and three very old men. Two other men in their early thirties sat together on a sofa.

The men patted his back and shook his hand in sympathy.

'We are sorry for the sudden death of your father,' the Governor spoke with a heavy accent. He was a slim man with bushy hair. 'My family send their condolences.'

'Thank you.'

'You may not be aware, for you are still young, but your father was a great man—'

'Yes, I know.'

The others nodded in agreement.

One of the elderly men said, 'We were good friends of your father. These two are from Lagos and I live in Abuja but we had to hurry here because of the friendship we share in our club. So we came by private jet as soon as we heard.'

Donaldo shifted uncomfortably on his seat.

'It is important to us all that we pay our respects to your father – we would like to pray together for him. But sadly, we cannot stay for the funeral, we have responsibilities, you understand?'

Donaldo nodded.

'Good, good. So, with your permission, we would like to be together privately with your father to pray with him – you know his spirit is still here. It is a tradition among us friends, you understand. It won't take long.'

'I see.' Donaldo thought for a while, looking around at the men. He knew they were very powerful and important. Finally he said, 'I agree. You were his friends. Do your will. I am glad you all came from so far to sympathize with me.' He was eager to get everything over with. He didn't care if the men wished to rip out his father's heart.

Officer Leonard and Detective Kwame attended the burial. Kwame saw Donaldo for the first time as Leonard pointed him out, standing beside the woman they had seen at the Amechi residence. They needed to speak with him but Kwame knew it would be callous to broach the issue of Adeline and the pencil when he had just laid his father to rest. They agreed to return the next morning.

Donaldo noticed the two men looking at him. One of

them was clearly from out of town, and he immediately knew that he must be the detective Miss Spencer had mentioned the week before, the same one who had visited Madam Vero and found the pencil. He felt trapped, realizing it was only a matter of time before they would come back to interrogate him.

FORTY-FOUR

Tuesday, 18th May 2010

The Director of the Department of State Security was on the phone with the President. It was the fourth time they had spoken since the previous night. He had been briefing the President on the attacks in the research institute and the police station. The President was very angry.

'This is awful! *Kai!* How can human beings be so cruel? Allah, have mercy.' He paced his office as he spoke. The death of the spy was bad enough, but the treatment of his body beggared belief.

'How do we proceed now, Sir?'

'What was the report from the officer before he died?'

'Your Excellency, he had just been there for a few days, but he worshiped in the mosque, was able to look around the living quarters, the hostels, even some parts of the school. He reported that he was confident the Centre is used for clandestine activities but needed more time to get solid evidence—'

'*Hmmn.* I believe they harbour terrorists in there.

Otherwise, why would he have died the way he did? He was getting close to something.'

'What are your orders, Sir?'

The President was silent. The line crackled. The Director was patient. He knew it was not an easy task running a difficult country like Nigeria. Any action the President took could quickly lead to impeachment.

'Do not attack the place. At least for now. Go back to the drawing board, Director. And this time, come up with a better strategy. Any idea that will not involve the butchering of innocent Nigerians.'

When Kwame arrived at the mansion, Madam Vero informed him that Donaldo had left earlier that morning to catch a flight to Lagos from where he would connect to Port Harcourt.

Kwame was frustrated and confused – why would a man travel so soon after losing his father, his only family member? It seemed cold hearted, though people dealt with grief in strange ways. But in Africa it was like a taboo, Donaldo was supposed to mourn his father by staying in the father's house for at least a week, receiving other mourners – relatives and friends. Kwame took a walk down to the chapel and walked around it, lingering for some time. Then he followed a path facing the exit, where Leonard had stood stoning birds a few days earlier. Kwame came upon a barricaded area. He saw that the rusty gate was locked, so he walked alongside it and found an opening, which he slipped through, and made his way down the path, his clothes wet from the dew on the grass.

When Kwame saw Donaldo's hut, his heartbeat increased. He took his time exploring the place.

As Kwame was leaving, the priest's voice startled him.

'Gentleman, *O gini?* What is it?' The voice was angry and harsh. Kwame turned and saw the old priest in his white cassock.

'Oh! Morning, Father.'

'Who are you?'

'I am a detective and came to look around, Father.'

'Again? Your colleague already came here with Chief Amechi and forced me to leave while he investigated. What more do you need to see?'

Kwame's eyes narrowed, *another investigator with the Chief?* He wondered what to say that would elicit more information.

'Father, perhaps it was one of my boys. I am supposed to be working for the Chief on a particular case but it seems one of my boys has double-crossed me to take over the job.'

'The world has turned upside down. How could your own staff do that? But that is the world for you.' He offered his hand and Kwame took it.

Kwame laughed. 'It is not good, right... double-crossing your own boss?'

'No, it's not good. What is it that you people want here anyway?'

'What did the man who came here look like?'

'I cannot give a full description… they made me leave for a whole day.'

'Why would they make you leave?'

'I don't know… it was a kind of forensic investigation, the Chief told me. They were very serious.'

Kwame drove like a mad man to the road junction close to the police station where Leonard was waiting for him. Together they hurried to meet the Evangelist, telling him they had a significant development in the case of his missing daughter.

The Evangelist was waiting for them when they arrived, pacing to and fro with anticipation. He ushered them into his study and waited for them to begin.

'Sir, I have to warn you that what we are about to suggest may come as a shock, so please, listen patiently,' Kwame began.

The Evangelist nodded, and Kwame continued.

'We found a golden clutch pencil at the chapel on Williams Island. Traces of blood and poison were found on it, and we have reason to believe the pencil belonged to Chief Amechi's son, Donaldo, the artist. We approached the Chief about it but he gave us no information other than to say he would return the pencil to his son. We have not even had the opportunity to speak to the young man.'

'And so? Chief Amechi was my friend. He just died,' he reminded Kwame.

'Sir, something is not right. I just spoke to the priest at

311

the chapel and he informed me that Chief Amechi went to the chapel with a forensic investigator and sent the priest away. Chief Amechi has made no official report of this, and we were not informed.' Kwame looked at Leonard, who nodded in agreement. He knew the next revelation would be even more difficult. 'Furthermore, Sir, we have good reason to believe that Donaldo Amechi was seeing Adeline. Twice they were seen at a café, and we find it difficult to believe that Adeline would have left the house on these two occasions and the night she disappeared without being seen – it seems that your staff are covering up this relationship.'

Kwame held up a placating hand to the Evangelist who was visibly agitated, and continued, 'Sir, I went to the Island and saw Donaldo's hut where he worked on his paintings. Sir, it is possible that he used to take Adeline to this place—'

'What?' The Evangelist was struggling to remain silent.

'Sir. Please listen to him,' Leonard pleaded.

'We have no time to waste. Donaldo Amechi has returned to Port Harcourt, less than twenty-four hours since his father was buried. If he indeed was seeing Adeline at the chapel where we found the pencil, it could mean your daughter is in great danger or worse. This forensic investigator could be the key to solving your daughter's disappearance. But we cannot find him alone.' Kwame knew he had him. The Evangelist was quiet. Without saying anything he picked up his phone and rang the Police Commissioner.

'Commissioner, we required the services of one of your private forensic investigators recently. Sadly, with the passing of the Chief some details have gone missing – are you aware of any recent requests?' He paused to hear what the man was saying. Kwame and Leonard saw his forehead furrow.

'The Chief asked for that – yes, that sounds right. Where is he now? Good... Good. Yes, it is important we speak to him. Come right now and see me.'

Chris Chuba rang off. 'Chief Amechi called the Commissioner some days back requesting the urgent assistance of a forensic investigator. The Commissioner gave him the name of a man in Enugu.'

'Why did the Chief need the investigator?'

'The Commissioner didn't ask that. He is on his way.'

The order to apprehend the forensic investigator from Enugu was given immediately. The Commissioner would never dare refuse the Evangelist anything, especially as his friend Chief Amechi had been instrumental in his becoming commissioner and arranging his transfer to Ebonyi State.

The policemen ordered to pick up the investigator met Kwame and the Evangelist's bodyguards at Ishieke junction. The Evangelist had made one thing very clear: the existence of this investigator was not to be revealed to anyone else – he did not want shame brought upon his friend until they were sure. They should take him to an unknown location.

Reluctantly, Kwame and Leonard had agreed, and they were now being led down a narrow path, far into a bushy area, by the Evangelist's guards. After a while, they brought the investigator out of their car, his head covered with a black hood that smelled of sweat and blood. His mouth was stuffed with his own handkerchief. They had tied his hands and feet.

Kwame was uncomfortable with the treatment. He looked to Leonard who seemed less perturbed. *Maybe this is how things are done here*, he thought. The main thing was to get answers.

One of the bodyguards began to speak to the terrified investigator. 'I don't know who you are and you don't know any of us. I want you to know that you have stepped on the toes of very powerful people. You may have done this unknowingly, while carrying out your job, but you may have injured some people. Now tell me, what job did you do for the late Chief Donald Amechi?'

The forensics expert had heard of the demise of the Chief, and thought nothing of it then, but right there in the bush he wondered if his captors had murdered him. Since the Chief was dead, he needed to tell them the truth, what he had done and what he had seen. So he told them.

When they had cross-examined the investigator and learnt everything they could, Kwame said, 'Let us hurry out of here.'

As soon as the vehicle carrying Kwame drove off,

the second car with the investigator inside veered off in another direction. Kwame would never know that one of the bodyguards pulled out his semi-automatic pistol and shot the hooded man in the head at close range.

Sheikh Mohammed Seko had gone berserk; he had lost almost at the same time his best friend and deputy, and the powerful Chief and Southern ally who had provided him with such a perfect opportunity to gain the wealth and power he so craved. He felt like he was being personally targeted, and he was not going to let anything subvert the plan he had worked so hard on. He knew he had to make a strong statement, one that would show this hidden enemy he could not be stopped.

That evening, a group of armed men led by the Sheikh drove into the Katsina office of the Department of State Security, their Hilux trucks crashing through the two bolted security gates. The attack was so bold and brazen that they took the security operatives unawares. They shot the gateman and two other guards before they were even able to fire their guns.

Other security agents ran for cover, but the terrorists jumped down from their trucks and began a shootout with the agents, surrounding the building. They threw flash grenades through the windows and into the courtyard, then mowed down all the State Security staff as they ran out, dazed and blinded.

Later that night, Shiekh Mohammed Seko sat inside a

makeshift tent in the forest camp. A white blanket with the name *Jama'atul al-Mujahideen Jihad* inscribed boldly on it was used as a backdrop. He made his statement, while one of his soldiers recorded it with a video camera.

In the name of the Almighty, the most beneficent, the most merciful.
We the members of Jama'atul al-Mujahideen Jihad – a group that fights to purge Northern Nigeria of the presence of infidels, and show disaffection for the corruption that has swallowed the Nigerian Government – wish to claim with jubilation responsibility for the five attacks that took place today. These attacks were planned and co-ordinated over several months. We were enraged that after we agreed a truce with the Nigerian Government – after they had paid us millions to stop the war while they worked out negotiations – they attacked innocent Muslims in Yobe and Sokoto. And planned to attack the Centre for Islamic Knowledge in Katsina. We shall continue our attacks until all infidels leave Northern Nigeria. We shall continue our attacks until the Nigerian Government shows genuine commitment to fighting corruption, starting with the Presidency. The Almighty is our strength.

The organization's courier took the message to be uploaded from a secure location and left the camp. Sheikh Seko lay on a mat and smiled to himself.

We know that we are from God, and the whole world lies in the power of the evil one.

I John 5:19
The Holy Bible

FORTY-FIVE

Wednesday, 19th May 2010

The crisis had ripened.

Since Seko's video had gone viral, there was widespread panic in Nigeria and neighbouring countries. Opposition parties were criticizing the President for failing to protect them and they called for him to step down. Human rights organizations and anti-terrorist support groups were making statements. Religious leaders from both Muslim and Christian quarters were condemning the attacks and calling on the President to take action. And in the streets there were protests outside the embassies.

The President responded to force with force. The JRF attacked the Centre for Islamic Knowledge in Kafurzan, searching the entire compound and holding everyone, including the teachers, staff and the *Almajiri*. The children were questioned about their teachers. Everything was turned upside down, but they found no weapons, and no evidence of terrorist activity. Afraid of the uproar that would be caused, they planted heavy weapons in the buildings and arrested men, innocent Muslims, who had come to worship at the mosque, parading them on national television as part of a 'potentially huge clandestine terrorist cell'.

Dr Bode Clark sent out messages to those Senators and members of the House of Representatives – it was time to impeach the President, and no one needed much convincing.

Evangelist Chuba drove with Kwame to the chapel to meet Officer Leonard and some of his police officers there. Chuba sat on the low wall outside the chapel and watched as the old priest fumed. 'You must allow me to take away the Eucharist. You have no respect for Christ, Jesus. You will go to hellfire, all of you.' He had called the Bishop and the Bishop's secretary was on his way.

Two bodyguards with shovels dug up the altar, exactly where the forensics expert had confessed to finding the body. He had confirmed that they had not touched the body, as the Chief had said he would have it removed at a later time, but he had no idea what the Chief had planned to do.

One of the shovels hit something.

'Easy... easy, please,' Leonard ordered. Everyone moved forward. The man with the shovel used it to scrape away some red soil. And then they saw it. Evangelist

Chuba knew it was his daughter, despite her state. He said nothing, but stared in shock as tears rolled down his cheeks. Kwame came forward and touched his shoulder, making the Evangelist snap back to the present moment. He swiftly turned away, leaned over and was sick.

Two medical experts came with the Police Commissioner and collected specimens. The remains were collected into a bodybag and sealed. Kwame showed them Donaldo's hut. They shut the area off, as Chuba's guard led the distraught man away.

Kwame walked to the Chief's mansion and rang the bell. He heard the *flap flap flap* sound of slippers as someone came to answer the door. She wore a yellow blouse made of *Ankara* patterned with tiny stars. Her eyes were red and puffy, and she looked like she had aged since his last visit.

'Hello, I am—'

'I know, I remember you,' Madam Vero interrupted, 'come in.' Then Leonard appeared and both men entered the spacious sitting room together for the first time.

Kwame said, 'I am sorry about your loss.'

'Thank you.'

'We are sorry to come at this difficult time, but we want you to help us, Ma.'

'How?' Madam Vero was burning with fear inside of her.

'We are still investigating Adeline, the Chuba girl,'

Kwame said. He stared into the woman's eyes.

'I told you what I know, which is not much. She was a very sweet but quiet girl.'

'You are very close to Donaldo, right?'

'Like a mother to him, since his poor mother died,' Madam Vero said, looking sad. 'Why do you ask about Donaldo?'

'Was he having a relationship with Adeline Chuba?'

Madam Vero was stunned by the question. She began to rub the back of her hand. 'No, I don't know. I am confused.'

'What are you confused about?' Leonard asked.

'Donaldo is a quiet person. He doesn't cause trouble. He has very few friends, and never had a girlfriend. You have to understand, if he knew anything about Adeline, he would have said so. He is a good boy. Anyway, her father would never allow her a boyfriend. Everyone is saying she was kidnapped, that must be it.' She was rambling now and she knew it, but her nerves had taken over. She kept reliving what she had overheard between Donaldo and his father.

Kwame and Leonard looked at each other. 'You see this pencil.' Kwame produced the golden pencil from his pocket. 'We found it at the altar of the chapel here on the Island. We found poison and blood on it. We suspect it was used to murder someone. Miss Adeline Chuba.' Kwame waited for a response, but she was quiet. 'We found a grave at the altar. Around where we found this pencil. Chief Amechi found the body before he died, he had an investigator dig it up. So, you see, the evidence is overwhelming. If you want to help Donaldo, you must co-operate. Now tell us, why did Donaldo come home before his father died?'

The woman was quiet for a while. Kwame wanted to know if the man had confronted his son after he found the grave. Madam Vero said he'd come back a day before his father died to collect some things. The men looked at each other.

'What happened then?' Kwame asked.

Madam Vero was getting angry. She fidgeted. And her lips trembled. 'Nothing happened.'

Leonard said to her, '*Ge m nti*, listen to me. If you're hiding information from us, and Donaldo is found guilty, you will be charged with obstructing the course of justice and as an accomplice. I am sure you know what that means.'

Madam Vero nodded.

'So tell me what happened the day Donaldo returned. Before the Chief died.'

Madam Vero began to sob.

'Listen, Madam,' Leonard cut in, softening his tone, 'what if another person killed Miss Adeline, then framed your boy. Placed his pencil at the altar. You never can tell. Tell us what happened.'

'Chief summoned Donaldo. I was asked to go upstairs. They wanted to talk in the study… he'd told me.'

'Did he always ask you to go out if they wanted to talk?'

'No. I am like Donaldo's mother. I was never asked to leave if they wanted to talk. Not even when other visitors came. I was surprised... I heard their voices from upstairs. They were shouting. Donaldo never used to shout back at his father. He was afraid of Chief. I came and eavesdropped. Please don't tell Donaldo.'

Kwame nodded. He knew then that the woman loved the young man deep within her.

'Then the next morning Chief was dead. It was strange, I thought. Chief was healthy the previous night. If he was sick that night, he would have called me up—'

'What did you hear that night?' Leonard asked.

'Nothing.'

'You said you eavesdropped,' Kwame pushed.

'Yes.'

'So, what did you hear?'

Madam Vero sighed. 'A long time ago he came back once feeling happy. He told me he'd met a girl. But he never told me who she was.'

'You now think it might be the Chuba girl?'

'His father thought so, and suspected he'd killed her. I heard Chief accuse Donaldo.' She hesitated. 'That was all I heard.'

Kwame suspected she knew more. 'Show us to his room,' hesaid, standing. Madam Vero hesitated. Leonard grabbed her elbow and she came along. She knew it was pointless to demand a search warrant from the Nigerian Police.

They searched the room. They found bottles of paint, chemicals for mixing paint, clothes. They found many artworks, finished and unfinished, drawing sheets, paper of all kinds and colours.

They broke open his locked drawer. And there was Adeline's novel, *Envy* by Sandra Brown – it had her name and signature written on it. There were two sheets of paper inside the novel, letters. Leonard looked at them and recognized the writing from the letter the Evangelist had torn up. The men looked at each other.

'Madam Vero, have you seen what we have found? Donaldo had something going on with Adeline Chuba.' Kwame showed her the book and the letters.

'I never knew,' she responded. 'I swear to God! That girl does not go anywhere without one of her household staff. It would be impossible for her to have a relationship with Donaldo in secret.'

'It means someone in the Chubas' home knew about Adeline and Donaldo,' Leonard said to Kwame. Kwame thought of Miss Spencer.

FORTY-SIX

At the Chubas' residence, everyone was devastated. Even the maids did not bother preparing food, because no one wanted to eat. They sat on stools along the corridor leading to the kitchen. The Evangelist was in the sitting room, talking with the Police Commissioner and some of his friends. Mrs Chuba was in her room weeping. Miss Spencer was finally telling her about Donaldo – most of the stories were lies. She was making them up to clear herself and the other staff.

The men in the sitting room went quiet when Kwame and Leonard came in. They greeted the men, but when they got no response, they sat down.

'How did it go?' the Commissioner asked.

'Sir, the evidence confirms Adeline's relationship with Donaldo,' Officer Leonard said, 'and we believe he murdered her.' Tears formed in the Evangelist's eyes. He thought about his friend, Chief Donald Amechi.

'I still don't believe all that is happening. That Chief Donald's son could murder my daughter—'

'There are indications, Sir, that he killed his father too,' Kwame added. Leonard nodded when the Evangelist looked at him.

'What! How?' the Commissioner asked, astonished.

'We interrogated the madam in charge of the Chief's house... she said that the Chief died the day his son was summoned home,' Leonard explained. 'She said that after the Chief received a visitor, which we believe to be the investigator from Enugu, he summoned his son back home immediately. They sent her upstairs and locked themselves inside the library where they had a long, bitter argument. She heard the Chief accuse his son of killing Adeline, your daughter, Sir.'

The Evangelist's eyes darted round the room. He undid his collar button with shaking hands.

'But why would he kill Adeline?' he asked.

'Because they were lovers, and it seemed his father did not approve of the relationship. He feared it might ruin his son's future.'

'His son's future! His backwards son who can only draw? What about my daughter?' the Evangelist shouted, spittle flying from his lips. 'He defiled her! She was a good girl, a decent girl, his backwards son turned her to evil. And then he stole her from me.' His face was ashen. Guilt, anger and disbelief were running through his veins. 'I want that bastard arrested with immediate effect. He will pay for all his crimes.' He turned and, without saying goodbye, walked towards the door. The Commissioner followed.

At the Commissioner's car, the two men faced each other. They were silent for a while before the Police Chief placed his hand on the Evangelist's shoulder.

'Don't break down, my friend… this is temptation. I will do everything within my powers to bring this boy to book.'

'I have already brought one to book myself.'

'Who?'

'The investigator. I will do it again,' the Evangelist said and leaned forward. 'Watch my back.' He grimaced as he said this. The other man nodded and got into his car.

Just then, Leonard rushed out from the house and waved at the Commissioner to stop. He saluted as the car window wound down.

'Pardon my manners, Sir! But I just got a message. There is another body, Sir!'

Kwame, Leonard, the Commissioner and his aides reached the priest's cottage at the same time as police officers were warding off the Islanders who had gathered there. More police vans began to appear. The Bishop and two other priests arrived at the scene. The Bishop's secretary was being interviewed by Leonard's assistant.

The priests and the officers were allowed to enter the cottage. Inside they saw the body of Father Simeon dangling like a punch bag. His cassock was sparkling white and almost covered his feet, his arms were by his side and there was foam around his mouth. The priests made the sign of the cross and the Bishop said some prayers of forgiveness for the soul of the deceased. He wondered as he said the prayers why the priest would take his own life. *Didn't he know it is a sin? Didn't he know he would go to hell?* But a letter found on the floor answered it all.

I couldn't save Donaldo. I failed Christiana.
I failed God, and I have failed myself.
How will I be able to explain to God that the child under my tutelage buried a dead body in his holy sanctuary?

FORTY-SEVEN

In his new camp, Sheikh Mohammed Seko had just finished the *Magrib Salat* with his men. It was past 7pm. Then he received an unexpected visitor. The visitor wore the *gibba*, *quftan* and the white turban of a Sheikh, while Sheikh Seko was dressed in his *gallabiya*. A transistor radio sat on the mat beside him. The visitor had prayer beads in his hand and his fingers worked on them. He had come with three other people.

'It is an honour that you visit us here!'

'The honour is mine that you do the work of Allah!'

'*As-Salamu 'alaykum*, Sheikh Ibrahim.'

'May the peace remain with you. And guide your path, my son. You make me proud.'

'We have just finished the *Salat*. Please come and sit. They will get you some fresh milk.' The elderly man and his companions followed him to the mat and they all sat down.

'You bring them here, *Ustaz*?' Sheikh Seko asked.

'Are they not friends?'

'They are. I am grateful that people of such high status should seek us in this camp. But here we are trained to trust only our brothers.'

Dr Bode Clark responded, 'And what status is greater than that which you possess, my friend, yet you live here. Because of your love for your religion. We are both your brothers and your friends.'

Sheikh Seko knew in his heart that Dr Clark didn't care if he was fighting because of his love for Islam or not.

'I am saddened by the news of the Chief,' he said.

'We all are. His work will not die. His benevolence lives forever,' Alhaja Amina Zungeru said. She wore a glistening long robe of silk that swept the dust as she walked. There were bangles of gold on her neck and her arms and in her nose she wore a golden ring. When she talked a gold tooth glittered in her mouth. She was an extremely beautiful woman and highly educated.

Sheikh Seko ordered his men to bring some fresh milk. They discussed only mundane issues in the presence of Seko's men. When they finished their milk, which Dr Clark and the other man who was a State Governor found very tasty and rich, Seko told his men to leave, and they entered into the main discussion, their voices low.

'Sheikh, we commiserate with you on the death of your deputy, Abouzeid,' the Governor said. 'May God reward his soul for his efforts on earth.'

'It is the will of Allah,' he said, with a wave of his hand. 'I hear that it is the Chief's son who murdered him?'

'That is likely to be the truth.'

'He has a punishment. And that is death. An eye for an eye!'

The men present knew then that he had loved the Chief deeply.

'Sheikh, we are planning to impeach the President,' Dr Clark told him.

'Why?'

'He is not one of us,' the Governor said.

Alhaja Zungeru added, 'He does not support this cause, even though he is a Muslim.'

Sheikh Seko thought for some time and then said, 'But he is a Northerner. Is it not better to have a son who is troublesome than to have none at all?'

'The paramount thing is the cause. The jihad,' Sheikh Kabiru Ibrahim replied. 'The President is not a true Muslim if he fights against our cause.'

Sheikh Seko looked up to the sky. 'What must we do, then?'

'We go to war!' Dr Clark responded, a little too eagerly.

'*Hmmn*, well said, but this war, will it be in the North or in the South, my friend?'

Dr Clark was silent for a while. He had not expected this question. Why was Sheikh Seko challenging him like this? Perhaps the death of the Chief and his deputy had affected his reasoning.

'Your tone worries me, Sheikh, are you diverting from the cause?'

Sheikh Seko shifted himself, placing his rifle on his lap.

'What is the cause, Dr Clark?'

The men exchanged glances. Sheikh Ibrahim came to their rescue. '*Haba*, Seko. What is wrong with you? We started this. All of us. Have you forgotten Kano? I saw you then, as a young student. I knew that you were destined to fight for Islam. I could not be of much help. But these men. They came and blessed your dreams.'

Sheikh Seko rubbed his palm on his long beard. He said to them with disdain, 'My friends, I am destined to fight for my people. For my religion. For God. You see these men here?' He looked around the camp and they all turned and looked around with him. There were men scattered about carrying Kalashnikovs. 'These men have left their families to fight for the cause. They have no mothers now. Fathers, wives, sons or daughters. They are here not because my friends in the South want a change of government. Or because my friends from the North want to gain power. They are here because they believe in the Holy Book, and because the true religion cannot exist alongside that which is barbaric and evil.' He paused, and drank from his water bottle. 'I was born to do what I am doing now. Abouzeid and I. When I started the *intifada* in Kano, I did it with no funds, no arms. But people listened to my voice. They did my bidding. Allah has used you as a means for us to do greater work. But we abhor your intentions. They are evil in His sight, for He is all seeing and all knowing.'

They stared at him in wonder and fear. Sheikh Ibrahim's mouth was open in surprise. Dr Clark wished that Chief Donald Amechi was still alive. It was Alhaja Amina who dared to speak, 'Sheikh Seko, it seems you are beginning to follow your own sermons. Have you forgotten all our plans, our intentions?'

He turned to her. 'And you, Alhaja. You have wealth and glamour. You wear a gold tooth. But your fellow women groan with hunger. What do you seek in a foreign land?'

Alhaja Amina Zungeru put her hand on her chest. '*Haa*, my Sheikh. *Haba*. Why do you make my heart ache? Have I not been useful? And in my own way do the work of the Almighty? Was I not the one who connected JMJ to the other organizations in Bangladesh, Afghanistan, Pakistan and Somalia? Even in—'

He raised his hand to stop her, then stood, indicating an end to the meeting. They stood too, wearily; their feet felt like they had been wearing heavy boots. It dawned on them then that it was easier to give water to a monkey, but difficult to collect back your cup.

Professor Yerima Musa sat with the President in his private study in the presidential villa. He told him about the terrorism plot – he did not mention the name of the Sacred Order nor the members, but the information he gave the President was overwhelming. He told the President that to survive impeachment he needed to assure the Members of Parliament that he was on top of the security situation.

The President had been shocked, if not completely

surprised. He realized how little he knew of what was happening in his country, and realized then that it was time to use the attack on the Centre for Islamic Knowledge to his advantage. Professor Musa gave him the names of the leader of Jama'atul al-Mujahideen Jihad, Sheikh Mohammed Seko, the man who had built the Centre for Islamic Knowledge, and other leaders. He would address the country first thing in the morning and expose Seko as a traitor to his country and to his religion. All Northern and Muslim members of the House of Representatives would be summoned for an emergency meeting with the President after the broadcast.

Professor Musa was delighted with himself for what he had done. After all, was he not a Muslim? Had he not an obligation to protect his Muslim brother, the President? He had seen what Seko and the other Northern members had not – that in the coming election and in subsequent ones, it would be an uphill task for a Muslim or a Northerner to rule Nigeria again. He knew the Southerners had no interest in allowing Muslim rule in the North; with JMJ they would destroy the Islamic community in Nigeria, they would tarnish the name of the faith.

However, it was not just dissatisfaction with the plot which had prompted him to betray the Brotherhood – he was disappointed that the Sacred Order of the Universal Forces had appointed Dr Bode Clark as the new Sacred Lord and Grandmaster of the Sacred Order in Nigeria after the death of Chief Amechi. Dr Clark might be the richest man in Africa, but he lacked the undaunted temerity and ruthlessness of the Chief. Professor Yerima knew that the impeachment of the President of Nigeria would have been easy if Chief Amechi were still alive, but Dr Clark would not be able to control Seko and his men.

FORTY-EIGHT

Miss Spencer was in the kitchen when the Evangelist came in, dressed in blue trousers and a shirt. He dropped the Bible he was carrying on the kitchen work surface and said, 'I trusted you, Carol. Why did you allow Adeline to go out with that boy?'

Miss Spencer turned, but couldn't look at him so she stared at the floor. 'I am very sorry, Sir. I am so sorry. I loved Adeline like my own child. Perhaps more than I love my own daughter, Mary. Adeline was so happy with him. She made me swear not to tell anyone... to respect her wishes I hid the information from you... from the police. How could I have known?' She raised her face and their eyes met. Everything was in the open now and Miss Spencer had no reason to hide anything from her boss any more.

'They are looking for him in Port Harcourt. He should be arrested today.'

Miss Spencer had mixed feelings. She still couldn't believe that Donaldo had murdered Adeline.

'It still amazes me. My heart is heavy. Adeline was so good to him. She loved him.' She turned and began to cut some vegetables with a knife.

Miss Spencer wondered what the Evangelist was lingering in the kitchen for. She turned round to find the Evangelist close to her, looking into her eyes.

'Carol,' he whispered. 'I need you now.'

Miss Spencer found the Evangelist's hand on her shoulder.

'No. No—'

'But you were once mine—'

'That, Sir, was a long time ago. You have a family now... please leave, Sir.'

'Family? I don't have a family.'

'What do you mean, Sir? You have Madam.'

'I have always loved you, Carol. I want us to rekindle what we had back then in Cameroon, before you came here.'

Miss Spencer shifted away from him. 'Sir, that can't be... what are you saying? We were young then... you were unmarried.'

'Then why did you come to Nigeria in search of me?'

'I loved you then... I couldn't do anything without you. I thought if I found you I could be your wife. But... but when I came back you had a wife and a lovely daughter. I couldn't bring you sadness.'

'I do not have a daughter any more.'

'But you have Madam. You can still make another baby—'

'Carol, she does not have a womb any more.'

'Please, shut up!' Miss Spencer was crying.

'I said, the mother of the brat who posed for portraits – stark naked – has no womb!'

'Please stop!'

The Evangelist suddenly grabbed Miss Spencer. He kissed her hard on the mouth, but she pushed him away.

'You are insane!'

Mrs Chuba burst into the kitchen. 'So you two have been carrying on behind my back!' she screamed.

'No. No, Ma. It was years ago, when he was a student in Yaoundé.' Miss Spencer tried to move towards her madam.

'Liar!' Mrs Chuba yelled, and slapped Miss Spencer across the face.

Evangelist Chuba grabbed his wife away from Miss Spencer, standing between the two women. It was all the confirmation his wife needed.

In a fit of rage Mrs Chuba lunged at her husband and grabbed his tie to strangle him. He fell against the kitchen cabinet and she used her nails to design a tattoo on his face while he struggled to breathe.

'You are a devil! Devil! Devil!' she was screaming. 'You made me have that hysterectomy!'

Miss Spencer ran to the door, whimpering. Her hands were clasped on her head. She marvelled at where the woman got the audacity and strength to fight the Evangelist.

Miss Spencer was in a dilemma, torn between running

out of the kitchen and separating the fighting couple. When she couldn't bear it any longer, she tried to pull her madam off her husband but was thrown back. It was the chance the Evangelist needed to escape, and when his wife tried to grab him again he flung her away. Mrs Chuba fell, hitting her head on the sharp corner of the marble worktop, then flopped down to the floor like a rag doll.

Miss Spencer could not believe her eyes at the scene she had just witnessed. She watched Mrs Chuba as blood began to seep from the wound in her head.

The Evangelist was staring at the dead woman, his eyes bulging wide. Confusion spread across his face, then panic. He began to pace, to flap himself, suddenly hot, his chest constricted. What had he done? How could he ever have killed his wife? He looked at Miss Spencer who stood crying, shocked, looking at the woman lying on the floor. And he knew, just then, that the Sacred Order had made him do it. The sacrifice had been delayed.

'Carol, it wasn't my fault, it was an accident, you saw…'

Miss Spencer looked up at him in terror, as though she had only just registered what had happened. Then in a moment of pure horror she covered her face with her hands and screamed, a guttural, bestial cry, but there was no other person in the large house aside the Evangelist and herself.

Jama'atul al-Mujahideen Jihad had no leader other

than Sheikh Mohammed Seko and some foreign leaders of other organizations that gave them support.

The Sheikh addressed his men. 'We have been very victorious in our jihad. *Alhamdulillah!* It is a sign that the Almighty is our strength. A sign that He is with us. We have lost men in battle, but these men, I tell you, recline today on fine couches in paradise, rejoicing. They are awaiting our arrival soon to join them. Our fight is against the corrupt, evil society. We fight against a government, corrupt and evil, devilish and deceitful. Today, the people of Allah in this country are beggars and live in penury, while a very few in Government live in superfluous wealth and abundance. This is not the kind of society the Almighty envisaged for the people that He loves. And this is what we must fight till the last drop of our blood is spilt. This fight extends not just against the Government but against the constitution of this Government. Against the people who adhere to this constitution, and against the infidels who have rejected the way of Islam!'

After his speech, over three thousand men were given funds for the journey to Southern Nigeria, as sleepers, awaiting orders from their Sheikh. While in the South they were enjoined to work as shoe menders, kiosk traders, nail clippers, *suya* traders, and wanderers with no job who would do whatever came their way, like trench excavators, well diggers and watchmen at offices and homes of wealthy men. They would live in the communities reserved for Muslims, awaiting orders.

Awaiting the day the *intifada* would start.

Sheikh Seko was pleased, but he still had a few more loose ends to tie up. Then nobody would be able to dispute his power and control. He called to one of his men; plans were to be made.

As soon as the Evangelist and Miss Spencer returned from the hospital, after Mrs Chuba's body had been taken to the morgue, he received a call, and while on the phone, he quickly turned on the television.

'The idiot has been arrested. It's all over the news.'

A reporter on CNN was talking about the murder of the world famous Evangelist's daughter, Adeline Chuba, by her lover, a renowned artist who had begun to gain global fame and recognition.

Miss Spencer watched as Donaldo was handcuffed and dragged away by two hefty men, one on either side holding his arms as if he would attempt to run. Miss Spencer gripped the sofa beside her as she saw Donaldo's face on the screen connect with hers. She knew what she had to do.

The Evangelist was relieved to hear the news of the arrest. He sat, his eyes focused sternly on the TV, watching the CNN report, and then his phone rang again.

'Tune your radio or television, Sir,' the caller informed him. 'The President has received a vote of confidence.'

'What?' he screamed at the caller.

He hurriedly switched the channel to AIT and there

it was. The news prompt running on the screen made his head ache.

> The impeachment motion in the Senate against the President of the Federal Republic of Nigeria was today thrown out in what appears to be a monumental victory for the President...
> News reaching us says that the Federal House of Representatives passed a vote of confidence on the President and Commander in Chief of the Armed Forces of the Federal Republic of Nigeria...

FORTY-NINE

The walls of the Sacred Order of the Universal Forces in Nigeria were crashing down with great force. Just as their members were co-ordinating an urgent meeting after the news of the suspended impeachment, they lost the only man who was the remaining link they had left with Jama'atul al-Mujahideen Jihad.

The day the older Sheikh was murdered was his happiest day on earth. That evening, the President of Nigeria made changes and announced Sheikh Kabiru Ibrahim as the Senior Special Advisor to the President on Islamic Affairs – the move was suggested by Professor Yerima Musa to halt the security crisis in the country. When he had found out about his appointment, he had called the new Sacred Lord and received approval, as it was another opportunity for the Brotherhood to have an eye in the presidential villa. Once the announcement was made at 4pm that Friday, Sheikh Ibrahim's sitting room was filled with friends and associates who came to congratulate him. They made merry till evening.

Around 9pm, after he had said his *Ishai Salat*, he sat in his sitting room watching the news, disturbed by the failed impeachment and the news reaching him that Sheikh Seko had announced renewed war against the Government and had deployed his foot soldiers to all the Southern states.

Sheikh Ibrahim now sat alone, deep in thought, as his two wives and children had gone to bed. The door to the sitting room opened and his security man walked in. He had been with him for over five years and ran a small kiosk in front of the gate.

'What is it, Suleman?'

'*Oga*. I get message for you, e from *oga*, Sheikh Seko.'

Sheikh Ibrahim's eyes widened. He hoped Sheikh Seko had come to his senses. He knew the man was ambitious, but he could not understand this sudden change in attitude. He beckoned Suleman to approach. The man came close and kneeled down at the Sheikh's side to whisper into his ear. As Suleman began to relay the message, he drew out his blade from his waist band and, drawing closer, slit the man's throat from ear to ear. Then he used the Sheikh's dressing gown to wipe clean the blade and his hands, and left him slumped there for his children to find the following morning.

The message he whispered was:

Sheikh Seko says: And fight them until there is no *fitnah*…

FIFTY

Donaldo sat in one corner of his cell thinking about his life. His cell was a small square room, with a tiny window high up, close to the ceiling. There was a hole by the corner which he had to use as a toilet. There was no water to flush it down. The cell guard had told him that on Sunday morning someone would come to do that. For the first time he wished for his father's influence – he knew if his father was alive he would not be in such appalling conditions.

He covered his face with his hands and recalled long ago when he used to have beautiful dreams, dreams as lovely as the colours of a rainbow. He used to own the world. He used to think no harm would ever come to him – but his father had ruined his life and stolen his innocence. He knew that it was the Chief who had made him what he had become – a murderer, awaiting conviction.

The cell door opened and a police officer led him into an empty room. Soon after he sat down, a young man walked in. He looked up to behold Ogiji, his friend. Ogiji's face was full of agony. He stood, staring at his friend, the man he revered and worshipped, the man who had made his future bright and took care of his family – he wondered what kind of spirit had eaten up his soul.

'I thought you would look worse than this,' Ogiji said. 'I got a flight home as soon as I heard the news.'

'I haven't showered. I defecate into a hole that is almost full. I sleep on a tattered mattress. How much worse would you have me look?' He tried to laugh. 'Thanks for coming.'

'They have been saying you are sick. Coughing blood. What is it?'

'I don't know. They say it might be serious, but who knows. The doctors are not very concerned with prisoners.'

Ogiji nodded. He fidgeted a little, and then looked directly into Donaldo's eyes. 'Did you kill Adeline?' he asked with a stern face.

Donaldo was silent, then nodded. 'I understand how you must feel—'

'You know nothing about how I feel!' Ogiji erupted. He looked around the room. He had tipped the police officer so that he would leave them alone for as long as they wanted. 'You are a monster. Like your father. I thought you hated him, his wickedness. Now I know you're a witch! Human eater! That is what you are!'

Donaldo's eyes welled with tears. He wiped them away with the back of his hand.

'Donaldo, that girl loved you, man! She gave you all she had. Her lovely heart, oh Donaldo, how she loved you and you killed her. How could you? And the others? How many people did you kill? You are being detained for killing Adeline and your father. How many more, eh?'

Donaldo said nothing.

'You can't talk because you have nothing to tell me.'

'My friend, there is evil in every man's heart.'

Ogiji sighed and rubbed his temples. 'Why did you kill that girl, Donaldo? She will never forgive you.'

'Do you think I need forgiveness? I need death. I am scared but I wish I would die before I am convicted. I long to meet her.'

Ogiji began to walk out of the room. At the door he turned and said to his friend, 'You shouldn't have killed that girl!' The echoes of the words reverberated. He felt like painting echoes. As he was led back into his cell, it came. Total darkness.

Miss Spencer zipped up the last of the four huge suitcases on the floor of her room at Ishieke. Looking into Donaldo's eyes on the TV screen, the way the Evangelist looked at her, she could not bear to stay with the family. Memories were building a skyscraper in her mind, driving her crazy. Since Adeline's disappearance she

348

had cried every night, wishing she had defended the girl more against her father. Sometimes when she turned on the television she would see a telecast of the Evangelist, talking about holiness and purity and generosity. She could no longer stomach the hypocrisy.

When the last of her belongings were packed, she left the house and got into the taxi that would take her to the seaport at Calabar from where she would get to Limbe in Southern Cameroon – home.

FIFTY-ONE

May in London was characterized by showers. Alhaja Amina Zungeru smiled at every passenger she saw as they entered the train, flashing her golden tooth. She made space for the lovely young man who sat beside her – she became shy at how intently he seemed to study her face. She sat quietly, reading Ahdaf Soueif's book, *Map of Love*, till the train stopped at Paddington Station.

Alhaja Amina Zungeru did not alight with the other passengers. Blood dripped from her side to the glistening floor of the train. Ahdaf Soueif's classic novel that she was reading a minute earlier lay on the floor, soaking up some of the blood.

The Evangelist sat inside a large office with Alhaji Damba Tambuwal and Professor Yerima Musa. He realized that Miss Spencer was gone, and he was miserable.

'Alhaji, I am disappointed in a lot of things; it amazes me that the position held by Chief Amechi should be given to Dr Clark.'

'Who should it have gone to?'

The Evangelist hesitated. 'Dr Clark lacks zeal and strength. And I was the closest person to Chief Amechi—'

'Dr Bode Clark is your senior in the Brotherhood. He has influence. Those are the two things that are considered.'

Professor Musa, who had wanted the position just like the Evangelist, spoke up. 'I agree with Evangelist Chuba. Dr Clark lacks military will. But I do not agree that the position should have gone to you, Evangelist.'

Chuba was enraged. 'Things are ruined now. Everything we planned. I have lost more than anyone else. I lost a daughter, I lost my brother. All in two weeks. Now my wife is dead. I am a devastated man.'

'We all have paid a price, Evangelist,' Alhaji Tambuwal reminded him.

'What price did you pay? And this one here – we are aware, Professor, that you betrayed the Brotherhood—'

'Betrayal is not a new thing in the Brotherhood. I was just protecting my people.'

'You deserve to pay for this. Everyone deserves to pay just like I did—'

Professor Musa was angered by the threat. 'Evangelist Chuba, you think you deserve the position as closest to the Chief, your good friend? Perhaps you are not aware that it was your friend, the late Chief, who influenced the decision for the sacrifice of your daughter in the first place.' The Professor's words hit the Evangelist so hard that his mouth fell open, but no words came out of it.

He gawped at the man.

'What?' Alhaji Tambuwal asked.

'Yes. So you see, there is no punishment for betrayal when it is in the interests of all. It takes a strong leader to recognize and appreciate that in this Order.'

The Evangelist rose. 'So I have been made to take the fall for everyone. I conveyed the weapons twice, from Chad and from Mali to Nigeria. Twice. It was a big risk. I did that magnanimously for the Brotherhood… for our cause. Yet I was betrayed. I lost everything, my daughter, my brother at the hands of Malik Hassan. Yet I was betrayed.'

'Calm down, Evangelist,' Alhaji Tambuwal implored.

'Don't tell me to calm down! What happened to JMJ? You people in the North gained power and resources and took it for yourselves while people like us took the fall for you—'

'Evangelist,' Professor Musa said, 'JMJ is on its own now. Sheikh Seko is a man on his own. We have learnt that he wasn't doing this for the sake of Islam in the North. He was fighting for himself – he is an egotist, drunk on power and intoxicated by dreams and visions of greatness. There is no negotiating with him now, we have given him too much power and information. *Kai!*'

Alhaji Tambuwal added, 'He was the one who ordered the murder of Sheikh Ibrahim. We do not know who is next.'

'Spare me that—'

The Professor stood up and walked over to the

Evangelist. 'You claim to be holy now, eh? You claim to be the only good one, eh? *"Professor Yerima Musa betrayed the Brotherhood and saved the President from impeachment. Sheikh Seko abandoned the plot and is killing everyone. The Sacred Order made me sacrifice my family?"* What about you? What about your people?' His voice towered over the Evangelist in his rage. 'You deceived us to establish a terrorist organization in the North. In our own land! You had us use our religion in order to destroy it! Your plots are killing our people, men, women and children. Alhaji Umar Hassan, Alhaji Abu Rabiu Mukhtar, Sheikh Kabiru Ibrahim... name them, we lose our lives and property in thousands and millions... yet you dare open your rotten mouth to talk about your miserable prostitute of a daughter and criminal of a brother.'

The Evangelist grabbed the Professor by the collar and threw him to the floor.

'I will kill you! I swear!' he screamed.

Alhaji Tambuwal separated them.

'To hell with you!' Professor Yerima Musa screamed back.

It was late in the evening in Cameroon.

Miss Spencer hadn't told her daughter why she had returned to Limbe with all her things. Her daughter Mary had thought that it was her usual annual visit but was surprised to see her carrying so much luggage. Mary saw her mother twice a year – when she spent a month in Cameroon and when Mary visited Nigeria to spend two or three weeks at Ishieke.

That night, as millions of people all over the world watched and listened to the telecast of Evangelist Chris Chuba's sermon, Miss Spencer sat transfixed, her eyes capturing and drinking him in with hatred and anguish and guilt, her heart bleeding, her ears soaking in his words.

> I see the illuminations of God. I converse with the
> supreme beings because I am a holy man. Amen!
> I had a happy family, but Satan ruined it. My wife
> could not bear the death of our daughter, and she
> succumbed to heart failure. But I am the prophet and
> messenger of the Almighty. Nothing will daunt me…
> with holiness, purity and prayer we shall win the war
> against sin, against evil and hatred and corruption
> and unrest all over the world. Against terrorism…

As Carol Spencer watched the Evangelist on television, she recalled many years back when the Evangelist was a young student in Yaoundé. They were so much in love. When he graduated he never visited her again until she sold all she had and journeyed to his Sanctuary in Nigeria and found him. He offered her the position she had occupied ever since and made her swear to keep their affair a secret and in return all her siblings in Cameroon and Mary would have the best education.

Miss Spencer's eyes blinked several times, as they

354

filled with tears. She thought of the secrets she kept, all the times she had ignored the Evangelist's abuse of his wife. And now she had failed Adeline. Every time she closed her eyes all she could see was Adeline, her darling Adeline. She felt dizzy and ill. She began to see the television appear in seven places. Her forehead ached so much till she fell to the ground, and passed out. When she came to, she walked out of the front door into the street, tears streaming down her face, the world a blur. Some people shouted as she stepped into the busy road. She closed her eyes and saw Adeline's face before the truck hit her.

FIFTY-TWO

Ogiji and Madam Vero were visiting Donaldo in hospital. It was early but the hospital was surrounded by press; they had been camped outside since Donaldo had been admitted the day before when he had collapsed.

The doctor informed them that Donaldo's kidneys had failed, that he had allowed his kidneys to deteriorate without treatment.

'How bad is it?' Ogiji asked.

'It is very bad. Seems he was taking some self-medication which was making him even more ill. The side effects of the drugs only worsened his condition. We suspect that he had been experiencing some symptoms for some time now and ignored these signs.'

'Will he survive?'

Madam Vero interrupted. 'Of course he will. Doctor?'

'We have to be honest with you: without a transplant very soon, he will not survive. We have a call out but the chances of finding a match in Nigeria in time...'

Madam Vero fell off her chair and sprawled on the

floor, sobbing. Ogiji and the doctor ran to her side and placed her carefully back on the chair. The doctor called a nurse to bring her some water.

'What can we do now?' Ogiji asked him.

'There is very little to do but wait. We are doing the best we can here. I advise you see him, keep his spirits up. My nurse will take you to him when you are ready.'

With that the doctor smiled and left Ogiji and Madam Vero to wait for the nurse. Madam Vero clutched on to Ogiji and wept.

Later that evening, Evangelist Chuba was dressed in jeans and a polo shirt. He wore a fez-cap. He sat in his hotel room, awaiting a phone call. He kept looking at the phone.

A young nurse came out of the nurses' restroom. She met a police detective at the reception being given directions to Donaldo's ward. He said he was assigned to guard Donaldo. She agreed to take the detective to him – the last guard had been called away and no one had been to Donaldo's ward since. She felt sorry for the young man; when she last checked on him, his lips were black like her mother's kitchen pot in the village. His face was swollen and his cheeks looked like a football. His eyes were red and he rarely spoke.

The nurse felt goose bumps on her skin as soon as she entered Donaldo's ward with the detective behind her. She hurried to the bed where his swollen body was.

She was scared to call his name. As she trembled she felt a shadow envelop her. She stared in his eyes. They were wide open. Fiendish.

As the Evangelist sat waiting, his phone rang.

'Sir... The target is already dead.'

Evangelist Chuba was disappointed and furious. 'Are you sure he is dead?'

'Yes, Sir. I'm up there now, he has just been confirmed dead.'

'Jesus Christ! I wanted to bring about the death of that dullard. Those Satans. The jihadists. They got to that idiot before me. May Satan receive his soul in hell!'

As the voice of the muezzin at the National Mosque in Abuja rang out through the air, calling on all Muslim faithful to report for the *Subh Salat*, a student of the University of Abuja sat in a small car, an IED strapped to his body. The car was parked close to the entrance to the hospital's reception area. He brought out his phone from his pocket. He dialled the only number saved in it.

'*As-Salamu 'alaykum*, Sheikh.'

'Brother.'

'Allah has done His work the way He wills—'

'What is it, my friend?'

'He is dead.'

'How? You have not carried out the operation. So what do you mean?'

'There is a lot of commotion here. They found him in

his bed, dead.'

Sheikh Seko hissed. 'It seems those Southern *Shaitans* got to him before us. Now, they take the glory.'

There was silence for a while.

'He killed our friend, his father. His soul will burn in hell. He deserves death.'

Sheikh Seko rang off. The death of the Chief had been a big blow to his plans. He took the murder as a personal attack against him and was determined to seek revenge.

Alhamdulillah! he thought. *The little Shaitan is dead.*

Finally, be strong in the Lord and in the strength of his might. Put on the whole armour of God, that you may be able to stand against the schemes of Satan. For we do not wrestle against flesh and blood, but against the rulers, against the authorities, against the cosmic powers over this present darkness, against the spiritual forces of evil in the heavenly places.

Ephesians 6:10-12
The Holy Bible

And *Shaitan* will say when the matter has been decided: 'Verily, Allah promised you a promise of truth. And I too promised you, but I betrayed you. I had no authority over you except that I called you, and you responded to me. So blame me not, but blame yourselves. I cannot help you, nor can you help me. I deny your former act in associating me as a partner with Allah. Verily, there is a painful torment for the wrongdoers.

Surah 14:22
The Holy Qur'an

Acknowledgement

Many years ago, in 2007, when this story came to me and forced me to tell it, I was lucky to have a friend who listened to it and who, a few years later, would travel down to Enugu to read the first drafts – thanks Amala DonCharles Mmaduka, I am proud that you are now a movie star.

I would like to thank my sister, Adora Udenwe Achi, who read all the drafts in 2009. And to my friends in Enugu who listened to this story for five years and made suggestions – for the laughter and arguments – Michael Iloechuba, Godwin Nwabude, Uchenna Umezurike and Chinedu Achigamonye.

For all the books, over a thousand of them, thanks to my father, Chief Michael Udenwe. For your stories and love, my sweet mother, Felicia Udenwe. For family and comfort, Oketa, Adora, Ujunwa, Ifunanya, Jacinta, Oforbuike, Nduka and Davingson. Chief J.O.J Oketa. Kizito Nwovu. Simeon Opoke. Ifeyinwa Nzeadi Bello – the best aunt in the whole world. Thanks to the greatest of all men Chief Fabian Mmuoneke (Onodugo) for believing in me, and to my beloved godmother, Dr. Franca Ogba, for your motherly love.

My sincere thanks goes to my friend and editor, Jazzmine Breary, for believing in me and then believing in *Satans & Shaitans* more, to Tamsin Shelton for your time and commitment towards making this work better, and to my publisher, Valerie Brandes, and the entire Jacaranda Books family.

To the staff of the National Library Enugu, and the Enugu State Library, thanks for allowing me extensive use of your materials and space. And to those on the same mission as me: Osemome Ndebbio, Diana Eke, and Chioma Iwunze – especially to Osemome for your inputs and Diana for being blunt and caring. And Nwamaka Okpo thank you for being there, always.

My sincere greetings go to my sweetheart, Ainehi Edoro, for believing, and to Jayne Bauling for your love. Karen Jennings, for finding time to read my stories, and to Trisha Nicholson, Andrew Hill and Nora Vasconcelos – for believing that distance is just kilometres and could be breached with commitment and love (for the blog tour that sealed our union).

For teaching me to commit my writings and knowledge to building the African literary tradition, my literary godfather, advisor, brother and confidant, Mukoma Wa Ngugi. Chika Unigwe, for our friendship and for all you have done. Ivor Hartmann, for the skills you shared that helped me to improve my style.

I want to thank Paul Liam for telling people about me always, Chinwoke for the gift, and Kofi Sackey for your poems. To Wale Okediran for believing that we live for the society. Thanks to my staff for your time, Chinedu Nwasum, Emeka Ugwu, Osondu Achi, Davingson Onwuakpa, Ogonna Obaji and Onyeka Ezema –

together we have been both writers and activists. I want to thank you for giving me knowledge and friendship, Dr. Stella Mbeze and Dr. Tim Adibe.

To all my friends who contributed knowledge: Jamiu Akangbe, Osama Mourad, Gihan Abou Zeid and a few that would rather remain anonymous – particularly those in the Department of State Security – for allowing me call you up at nights, and special thanks to Jamiu, for the gift of the Hadith.

Thanks once again, Jazzmine Breary, my editor, publicist and friend – for tolerating my idiosyncrasies, my stubbornness, for prodding me gently throughout the editorial and publication process, for *Satans and Shaitans*.

Ekele nu oh, Obashibu l'ime igwe – for this gift.

Obinna Udenwe is one of the most prolific young short story writers in Southern Nigeria. Born in Abakaliki, Ebonyi State, to a political family in Nigeria's ruling party, Obinna became politically active at a young age, leading Ebonyi State Children's Parliament and training with the British Council. Aged 19, he created the Ugreen Foundation, recognized by Ebonyi State government for its services amongst the youth.

Obinna has appeared in various national and local Nigerian radio, TV and print media, and international blogs, on key issues such as terrorism, youth unemployment, entrepreneurship, children's rights and governance. He won the 2009 National Top 12 Award and the 2012 African International Achievers Award. His stories have appeared in 2013 Stories Naija Anthology, The Short Story is Dead, Long Live the Short Story and Dreams at Dawn. He has also written for several literary magazines, including The Kalahari Review, Tribe-write, Flair Magazine, Brittle Paper, Outside in Literary & Travel Magazine, ANA Review, and more.

Other titles by Jacaranda

ISBN 978-1-909762-18-3   ISBN 978-1-909762-04-6   ISBN 978-1-909762-02-2

ISBN 978-1-909762-03-9   ISBN 978-1-909762-01-5   ISBN 978-1-909762-00-8

www.jacarandabooksartmusic.co.uk